MONDO

& Other Stories

J. M. G. Le Clézio

Translated by Alison Anderson

 & Other Stories

(Mondo et autres histoires)

UNIVERSITY OF NEBRASKA PRESS, LINCOLN AND LONDON

© Éditions Gallimard, Paris, 1978
English translation © 2011
by the Board of Regents of the
University of Nebraska

Library of Congress
Cataloging-in-Publication Data
Le Clézio, J.-M. G.
(Jean-Marie Gustave), 1940–
[Mondo et autres histoires.
English] Mondo and other stories =
Mondo et autres histoires /
J. M. G. Le Clézio; translated [from
the French] by Alison Anderson.
p. cm. ISBN 978-0-8032-2999-0
(cloth: alk. paper)—ISBN 978-0-
8032-3000-2 (pbk.: alk. paper)
I. Anderson, Alison. II. Title.
PQ2672.E25M6613 2011
843'.914—dc22   2010032665

Set in New Caledonia by Bob Reitz.
Designed by Nathan Putens.

"What? You live in Baghdad, and you did not know that this is where Sinbad the Sailor resides, the famous voyager who has sailed all the seas lit by the sun?"

"THE STORY OF SINBAD THE SAILOR"

Contents

Mondo 1

Lullaby 55

The Mountain
of the Living God 89

The Waterwheel 111

Daniel Who Had
Never Seen the Sea 125

Hazaran 145

People of the Sky 167

The Shepherds 187

MONDO

& Other Stories

Mondo

No one really knew where Mondo came from. He just showed up one day, by chance, here in our town, and no one really noticed, and then we got used to him. He was ten years old or so, with a round, tranquil face and fine, slightly slanted black eyes. But it was, above all, his hair that we noticed, ash brown hair that changed color with the light and seemed almost gray at nightfall.

We knew nothing about his family or his home. Maybe he didn't have one. It was always just when you weren't expecting him, when you weren't thinking about him, that he showed up on the street corner, near the beach, or at the marketplace. He walked alone, with a determined air about him, looking all around. He wore the same clothes every day—blue denim pants, tennis shoes, and a green T-shirt that was a bit too big for him.

When he came closer, he looked you right in the eye and smiled, and his narrow eyes were like two bright slits. That was his way of greeting you. When he liked someone, he would stop and ask, quite simply, "Would you like to adopt me?"

And before anyone had time to recover from their surprise, he was already gone.

Why had he come here, to this town? Maybe he got here after a long journey in the hold of a cargo ship, or in the last carriage of a freight train that had rumbled slowly across the land, day after day, night after night. Maybe he just decided to stop here when he saw the sun and the sea, and the white villas and palm gardens. What is certain is that he did come here from very far away, the other side of the mountains, the other side of the sea. Just to look at him you knew he wasn't from here and that he'd seen many countries. He had that dark, shining gaze, that copper-colored skin, and that light, silent way of walking, slightly sideways, dog-like. Above all, there was an elegance and a confidence about him that children don't ordinarily have at that age, and he liked to ask strange questions that were like riddles. And yet, he could neither read nor write.

When he arrived here in our town, it wasn't yet summer. It was already very warm, and every evening there were fires on the hillsides. In the morning the sky was invariably blue, taut and smooth, without a cloud. The wind blew in from the sea, a dry, hot wind that parched the earth and kindled the fires. It was market day. Mondo came to the square and began to walk around among the little blue greengrocers' trucks. He found work right away, because greengrocers always need help unloading their crates.

Mondo would work for one truck and then, when he'd finished, they'd give him a few coins and he'd move on to the next truck. The market folk knew him well. He would come to the marketplace early, to be sure of being hired, and when the little blue trucks began to arrive, the people would see him and call out his name, "Mondo! Hey, Mondo!"

When the market was over, Mondo liked to scavenge. He would weave his way among the stalls and pick up whatever had fallen on the ground—apples, oranges, dates. There were other children looking, too, as well as old people who filled their bags with lettuce leaves and potatoes. The vendors liked Mondo; they never said anything. Sometimes the fat fruit vendor called Rosa would give him apples or bananas from her display. It was very noisy in the market, and wasps buzzed above the dates and the raisins.

Mondo would stay at the marketplace until the blue trucks had left. He waited for the man with the spraying truck, who was his friend. He was a tall, thin man dressed in a navy blue overall. Mondo liked to watch him as he worked with his spray nozzle, but he never spoke to him. The sprinkler man would aim the jet at the refuse on the ground and make it scurry ahead of him like little animals, and a cloud of droplets rose in the air. It made a noise like a storm, like thunder, as water surged across the pavement, and you could see faint rainbows above the parked cars. That's why Mondo was the sprinkler man's friend. He liked to see the droplets of spray rise up and fall again like rain on the surface

4

of the cars and the windshields. The sprinkler man liked Mondo, too, but didn't speak to him. Besides, they wouldn't have been able to say much to each other because of the noise of the hose. Mondo looked at the long black tube that wriggled like a snake. He would have liked to try spraying, too, but he didn't dare ask the sprinkler man to lend him the hose. And maybe he wouldn't have been strong enough to stay on his feet, because the jet was very powerful.

Mondo stood on the square until the sprinkler man had finished spraying. Fine drops fell on his face, dampened his hair, and it was like a cool mist that was good for him. When the sprinkler man had finished, he would disassemble his hose and go off somewhere else. And then there were always people who came along and looked at the wet pavement and said, "Has it been raining?"

After that, Mondo would go down to the sea, to gaze at the burning hills, or he would go looking for his other friends.

In those days, he didn't really live anywhere. He had his hiding places where he slept, down near the beach or even farther along, among the white rocks on the way out of town. They were good hiding places, where no one could find him. The police and the people from the social services didn't like children living like that, free, eating any old thing and sleeping any old place. But Mondo was clever, he knew when they were looking for him, and he kept out of sight.

When there was no danger, he would walk around in the town all day, watching what was going on. He liked to walk around without any purpose, heading down this street, then that one, taking shortcuts, stopping for a while in a garden, then heading off again. When he saw someone he liked, he would go up to them and say quite calmly, "Hello. Wouldn't you like to adopt me?"

There were people who would have liked to adopt him, because Mondo looked like a nice boy, with his round face and his shining eyes. But it was hard. People couldn't adopt him just like that, right away. They began to ask him questions—how old was he, what was his name, where did he live, where were his parents—and Mondo didn't like questions like that. He replied, "I don't know, I don't know."

And ran away.

Mondo had a lot of friends, just from walking around in the streets. But he didn't talk to everyone. They weren't friends to talk to or to play with. They were friends to greet in passing, quickly, with a wink or a wave from the distance, from the other side of the street. There were friends, too, who were about food, like the baker lady who gave him a piece of bread every day. She had an old, pink face, very even and smooth like an Italian statue. She was always dressed in black, and she wore her white hair braided in a chignon. Her name was Italian, actually; she was called Ida, and Mondo liked going into her shop. Sometimes he would work for her, taking bread to the merchants in the neighborhood. When he came back she would cut a thick slice from a round loaf and hand it to him wrapped in waxed paper. Mondo had never asked her to adopt him, maybe because he really liked her a lot and he felt intimidated.

Mondo would walk slowly down to the sea, eating his slice of bread. He'd break it into little pieces, to make it last, and he would walk and eat without hurrying. He seemed to live mostly on bread in those days. But he still saved a few crumbs to toss to his friends the seagulls.

There were a lot of streets, and squares, and a public garden before you could smell the sea. Then all of a sudden it was there, on the wind, with the monotonous sound of the waves.

At the far end of the garden there was a newspaper stand. Mondo stopped and bought a comic. He hesitated between a few Akim stories, and finally he chose a Kit Carson story. Mondo chose Kit Carson because of a picture that showed him wearing his famous fringed jacket. Then he looked for a bench where he could sit and read the comic. It wasn't easy, because there had to be someone on the bench who could read the words to the Kit Carson story. Just before noon was the best time, because then there were nearly always a few retired people from the Post Office who sat smoking their cigarettes and who were bored. When Mondo found one of them, he sat down next to him on the bench and looked at the pictures and listened to the story.

An Indian stood before Kit Carson with his arms crossed and said,

"Ten moons have passed, and my people have had enough. Let us dig up the hatchet of the Ancients!"

Kit Carson raised his hand.

"Don't listen to your anger, Crazy Horse. Soon we will see that justice is done."

"It is too late," said Crazy Horse. "See!"

He pointed to the warriors gathered at the foot of the hill.

"My people have waited too long. The war will begin, and you all will die, and you too will die, Kit Carson!"

The warriors obeyed Crazy Horse's command, but Kit Carson knocked them over with his fist and escaped on his horse. He turned around one last time and shouted to Crazy Horse, "I will return, and we will render justice!"

Once Mondo had heard the Kit Carson story, he took his comic and thanked the retired man.

"Good-bye!" said the man.

"Good-bye!" said Mondo.

Mondo walked quickly down to the pier that went out into the sea. He looked at the sea for a moment, squinting so that he wouldn't be dazzled by the sun's reflection on the water. The sky was a deep, cloudless blue, and the short waves sparkled.

Mondo went down the little stairway that led to the breakwater. He was very fond of this place. The stone dike was very long, with huge rectangular blocks of cement on either side. At the end of the dike was the lighthouse. Seabirds dipped and glided on the wind, turning slowly and giving their child-like cries. They flew above Mondo, brushing his head, calling to him. Mondo threw crumbs of bread as high as he could, and the seabirds caught them on the wing.

Mondo loved to walk here, on the breakwater. He would jump from one cement block to the next, watching the sea. He could feel the wind against his right cheek, tugging his hair to one side. The sun was very warm, despite the wind. The waves crashed against the base of the cement blocks, hurling the spindrift into the light.

From time to time Mondo stopped to look at the shore. It was already far behind him, a brown strip strewn with little white boxes. Above the houses the hills were gray and green. The smoke from the fires rose here and there, making a strange smudge against the sky. But you couldn't see any flames.

"I have to go have a look over there," said Mondo.

He thought about the huge red flames that were devouring the bushes and forests of cork oak. He thought too about the firefighters' trucks that were stopped along the roads, because he really liked the red trucks.

To the west there was something like a fire on the sea, but it was only the reflection of the sun. Mondo stood there motionless, and he could feel the little flames of the sun's rays dancing on his eyelids, then he went on his way, jumping along the breakwater.

Mondo knew every single one of the cement blocks; they looked like huge animals sleeping half immersed in the water with their broad backs in the sunlight. They had funny little symbols etched in their backs, brown and red spots, shells that were embedded in the cement. At the base of the breakwater, just where the sea was pounding, there was a green carpet of wrack, and there were colonies of mollusks with white shells. There was one block in particular that Mondo knew well, almost at the end of the dike. That was where he always went to sit, his favorite block. There was a slight incline but not too steep, and the cement was worn down and very smooth. Mondo would settle there, sitting cross-legged, and he would talk to his block, very quietly, to say hello. Sometimes he would even tell it stories, to entertain it, because it must surely get bored there, stuck there all the time, not able to leave. So he'd talk about voyages, and ships and the sea, of course, and about the huge marine mammals that drift slowly from one pole to the other. The breakwater didn't say anything, didn't move, but it liked the stories Mondo told. That must be why it was so smooth.

Mondo sat for a long time on his breakwater, gazing at the sparks on the sea and listening to the sound of the waves. When the sun was hotter, toward the end of the afternoon, he curled up with his cheek against the warm cement, and he dozed for a while.

It was on one of those afternoons that he made the acquaintance of Giordan the Fisherman. Through the cement Mondo heard the footsteps of someone walking on the breakwater. He'd sat up, ready to run and hide, but then he saw the man, who was in his fifties, carrying a long fishing rod on his shoulder, and he wasn't afraid of him. The man came as far as the neighboring slab and gave him a friendly little wave.

"What are you doing here?"

He sat down on the breakwater and pulled from his oilskin bag all sorts of hooks and line. Once he'd started fishing, Mondo came next to him on the breakwater and watched the fisherman preparing his hooks. The fisherman showed him how to bait, then how to cast, slowly to begin with, then faster and faster as the line paid out. He lent his rod to Mondo, so he'd learn to turn the reel with a continuous movement, swaying the rod gently from left to right.

Mondo liked Giordan the Fisherman, because he never asked him anything. His face was reddened by the sun, with deep creases and two intensely green little eyes that surprised you.

He would sit fishing for a long time on the breakwater, until the sun was very close to the horizon. Giordan didn't say much, no doubt so as not to frighten the fish, but he laughed every time he'd pull one in. He removed the hook from the fish's jaw with neat, precise movements and put his catch into the oilskin bag. From time to time Mondo would go and fetch gray crabs for him, for bait. He'd go down to the base of the breakwater and peer in between the clumps of seaweed. When the waves drew back, the little gray crabs came out, and Mondo would catch them with his hand. Giordan crushed them on the slab of cement and cut them up with a rusty little penknife.

One day, not far out to sea, they saw a big black cargo ship sail noiselessly past.

"What's it called?" asked Mondo.

Giordan the Fisherman raised his hand to his forehead and squinted.

"*Eritrea*," he said, then added with surprise, "your eyesight isn't so great."

"That's not it," said Mondo. "I don't know how to read."

"Really?" said Giordan.

They stared for a long time at the cargo steaming by.

"What does it mean, the ship's name?" asked Mondo.

"Eritrea? It's the name of a country, on the coast of Africa, on the Red Sea."

"It's a nice name," said Mondo. "It must be a nice country."

Mondo thought for a moment.

"And the sea there is called the Red Sea?"

Giordan the Fisherman laughed: "Did you think the sea there is really red?"

"I don't know," said Mondo.

"When the sun sets, the sea turns red, it's true. But they call it that because of the people who used to live there."

Mondo watched as the cargo ship headed off into the distance.

"It must be bound there now, to Africa."

"It's far away," said Giordan the Fisherman. "It's very hot there. There's a lot of sunshine, and the coast is like the desert."

"Are there palm trees?"

"Yes, and very long sandy beaches. During the day, the sea is very blue, and there are lots of little fishing boats with sails like wings, and they sail up and down the coast, from village to village."

"So you can stay there sitting on the beach and watch the ships go by? You can stay there sitting in the shade and tell stories and watch the ships on the sea?"

"The men work. They repair their nets and nail plates of zinc to the hulls of the boats they've dragged up onto the sand. The children go and look for dry twigs and light fires on the beach to heat up the pitch they use to fill in the cracks in the boats."

Giordan the Fisherman wasn't looking at his line now. He was looking off into the distance, toward the horizon, as if he were really trying to see all of that.

"Are there sharks in the Red Sea?"

"Yes, there are always one or two following the boats, but the people are used to them, so they don't pay them any mind."

"Aren't they mean?"

"Sharks are like foxes, you know. They're always looking for the garbage that falls into the water, something to pilfer. But they're not mean, no."

"It must be big, the Red Sea."

"Yes, it's very big . . . There are a lot of towns along the coast, ports with funny names . . . Ballul, Barasali, Debba . . . Massawa is a big town, all white. The boats are far offshore, sailing down the coast for days and nights, sailing north as far as Ras Kasar, or they go out to the islands, to Dahlak Kebir, to the Nora archipelago, sometimes even as far as the Farasan islands on the other side of the sea."

Mondo liked islands a lot.

"Oh, yes, there are plenty of islands, islands with red rocks and sand beaches, and on the islands there are palm trees!

"During the rainy season there are storms, and the wind blows so hard that it uproots the palm trees and blows the roofs off the houses."

"Are there shipwrecks?"

"No, the people stay home, they stay sheltered, nobody goes out to sea.

"But it doesn't last long.

"On a little island, there's a fisherman with all his family. They live in a house made of palm leaves, by the beach. The fisherman's oldest son is already grown; he must be about your age. He goes out on the boat with his father and casts the nets onto the sea. When he pulls them in, they're filled with fish. He likes going out with his father on the boat, he's strong, and he already knows how to handle the sail to catch the wind. When the weather's fine and the sea is calm, the fisherman takes his whole family along, and they go to see relatives and friends on the neighboring islands, and in the evening they come back.

"The boat moves all by itself, without a sound, and the Red Sea is all red because the sun is setting."

While they were talking, the *Eritrea* had made a huge turn on the sea. The pilot boat was on its way back to shore, pitching in the wake of the ship, and the cargo gave a short blow of its horn to say good-bye.

"When will you be going there?" asked Mondo.

"To Africa and the Red Sea?" Giordan the Fisherman laughed. "I can't go there. I have to stay here, on the dike."

"Why?"

He sought for a reply.

"Because . . . Because I'm a sailor who has no ship."

Then he began staring at his fishing rod again.

When the sun was very close to the horizon, Giordan the Fisherman placed his rod down on the cement slab and pulled a sandwich from his jacket pocket. He gave half to Mondo and together they sat eating and looking at the reflections of the sun on the sea.

Mondo left before nightfall, to find a hiding place to sleep.

"Good-bye!" said Mondo.

"Good-bye!" said Giordan. When Mondo was a short ways away, he shouted, "Come back to see me! I'll teach you to read. It's not hard."

He stayed there fishing until it was totally dark and the lighthouse had begun to flash its regular signals, every four seconds.

THAT WAS ALL WELL AND GOOD, BUT YOU HAD TO WATCH OUT for the Dogcatcher. Every morning, as the sun was rising, the little gray truck with its wire mesh windows drove slowly through the city streets without making a sound, right next to the curb. Lurking through the streets that were still sleepy with morning mist, looking for dogs and lost children.

Mondo had noticed it one day when he had just left his hiding place by the seaside and was walking through a garden. The little truck stopped only a few yards away, and he had just had time to hunch down behind a bush. He saw the back door open, and two men wearing gray overalls climbed out. They were carrying two big canvas sacks and some ropes. They began to search along the paths in the garden, and Mondo heard what they were saying when they went right by his bush.

"He went that way."

"Did you see him?"

"Yes, he can't be far."

The two men in gray moved off, each one in a different direction, and Mondo stayed motionless behind his bush, scarcely breathing. A moment later there was a sort of strange hoarse cry, then it was stifled, then silence. When the two men came back, Mondo saw they were carrying something in one of the sacks. They loaded the sack in the back of the truck, and Mondo heard shrill cries that were painful to his ears. It was a dog that they'd tied up in the sack. The gray truck drove off again, not in a hurry, disappearing behind the trees in the garden. Someone who was walking by told Mondo that this was the Dogcatcher that took away the dogs that had no home; he'd looked closely at Mondo and added, to frighten him, that the truck sometimes took away children who were wandering around when they should be in school. Since that day Mondo kept a look out, all the time, on either side and even behind him, to be sure to see the gray truck coming.

When it was time for the children to get out of school or when they were on holidays, Mondo knew he had nothing to fear. It was when there weren't many people in the streets, early in the morning or at nightfall, that he had to be careful. Maybe that was why he had a sort of sideways trot, like a dog.

It was around then that he made the acquaintance of the Gypsy, the Cossack, and their old friend Dadi. Those were names they'd been given, here in our town, because no one knew their real names. The Gypsy wasn't a gypsy, but they called him that because of his swarthy skin, his deep black hair, and his eagle profile; but surely he'd also earned his name because he lived in an old black Hotchkiss that was parked on the esplanade, and he made his living doing magic tricks. As for the Cossack, he was a strange sort, with Mongol features, and he always wore a big fur cap that made him look like a bear. He played the accordion outside the sidewalk cafés, mainly at night, because during the day he was completely drunk.

But the one Mondo liked best was old Dadi. One day as he was walking along the beach, he'd seen him sitting on the ground on a sheet of newspaper. The old man was warming himself in the sun, paying no mind to the people passing by. Mondo had been intrigued by a little yellow cardboard suitcase punched with holes that old Dadi had placed next to him on the ground on another sheet of newspaper. Dadi looked gentle and quiet, and Mondo wasn't at all afraid of him. He drew closer to look at the yellow suitcase, and he asked Dadi, "What's inside your suitcase?"

The man had opened his eyes just a touch. Without saying a thing, he put the suitcase on his lap and raised the lid slightly. He smiled with a mysterious air as he put his hand underneath the lid, and then he brought out a pair of doves.

"They're beautiful," said Mondo. "What do you call them?"

Dadi smoothed the birds' feathers, then raised them next to his cheeks.

"That one's Pilou, and this one is Zoé."

He held the doves in his hands, gently caressing them close to his face. He looked off in the distance, with his clear, moist eyes that didn't see very well.

Mondo gently stroked the doves' heads. The sunlight dazzled them, and they wanted to go back into their suitcase. Dadi spoke to them in a soft voice to calm them, then he put them back in under the lid.

"They are beautiful," said Mondo again. And he left, while the old man closed his eyes and went back to dozing on his newspaper.

When night fell, Mondo went to see Dadi on the esplanade. He worked with the Gypsy and the Cossack for their public performances; in other words he would sit off to one side with his yellow suitcase while the Gypsy played the banjo and the Cossack called out in his deep loud voice to attract the passers-by. The Gypsy played quickly, watching his fingers as they moved, singing to himself. His dark face shone in the light of the streetlamps.

Mondo stood in the front row among the spectators and called out a greeting to Dadi. Now the Gypsy began the performance. Standing before the spectators, he pulled handkerchiefs of many colors from his closed fist, incredibly quickly. The light handkerchiefs drifted to the ground, and it was Mondo's job to pick them up, one after the other. Then the Gypsy pulled all sorts of strange objects from his hand—keys, rings, pencils, pictures, ping-pong balls, and even cigarettes, already lit, that he handed out to people. He did it so quickly that you didn't have time to see his hands moving. People laughed and applauded, and coins began to fall on the ground.

"Lad, help us pick up the coins," said the Cossack.

The Gypsy's hands picked up an egg, wrapped it in a red handkerchief, then paused for a second.

"Careful . . . now!"

He clapped his hands together. When he unfolded the handkerchief, the egg had vanished. People were applauding louder than ever, and Mondo picked up some more coins and placed them in a tin box.

When there were no more coins, Mondo sat down on his heels and watched the Gypsy's hands again. They were moving quickly, as if they were independent of his body. The Gypsy pulled other eggs from his closed fist, then he made them disappear between his hands, just like that. Each time an egg was about to disappear, he would look at Mondo and wink.

"Hup! Hup!"

But the finest thing the Gypsy knew how to do was when he would take the two white eggs that had appeared in his hands, and you couldn't understand how it had happened; he would wrap them up in two large red and yellow handkerchiefs, then he lifted his arms in the air and stayed for a moment like that without moving. All the spectators were watching, holding their breath.

"Careful . . . now!"

The Gypsy lowered his arms and shook out the handkerchiefs, and two white doves flew out of them and circled above his head before going to settle on old Dadi's shoulders.

People exclaimed, "Oh!" and applauded very loudly and coins rained down onto the ground.

When the performance was over, the Gypsy went to buy sandwiches and beer, and everyone went to sit on the running board of the old black Hotchkiss.

"You were a real help to me," said the Gypsy to Mondo.

The Cossack was drinking beer, and he exclaimed, very loudly, "Is he your son, Gypsy?"

"No, he's my friend Mondo."

"Well, here's to your health, my friend Mondo!"

He was already a bit drunk.

"Can you play any music?"

"No, sir," said Mondo.

The Cossack burst out laughing.

"No, sir! No, sir!" He said it over and over, with a shout, but Mondo didn't understand what was so funny.

Then the Cossack picked up his little accordion and began to play. It wasn't really music that he produced; it was more like a sequence of strange, monotonous sounds that rose and fell, sometimes quickly, sometimes slowly. The Cossack tapped his foot against the ground as he played, and he sang in his deep voice, repeating the same syllables over and over.

"Ay, ay, yaya, yaya, ayaya, yaya, ayaya, yaya, ay, ay!" He sang and played the accordion, swaying to and fro, and Mondo thought he looked just like a big bear.

The people passing by would pause a moment to look at him, laugh a little, then be on their way.

Later, when darkness had fallen for good, the Cossack stopped playing and sat on the running board of the Hotchkiss next to the Gypsy. They lit their cigarettes of strong-smelling dark tobacco and they talked, drinking some more cans of beer. They talked about faraway things that Mondo didn't really understand, memories of war and travel. Sometimes old Dadi would talk, too, and Mondo listened to his words, because he would talk mainly about birds and doves and carrier pigeons. In his quiet, somewhat breathless voice, Dadi would tell them stories about these birds that flew a long way, over the countryside, the earth sliding beneath them with its meandering rivers, and little trees growing along the roads that were like black ribbons, and the houses with their red or gray roofs, and the farms surrounded by fields of every color, prairies, hills, mountains that were like piles of pebbles. And the little man would tell them too how the birds always came back to their home, reading the countryside like a map, or navigating with the stars like sailors and aviators. The birds' houses were like towers, but they had no doors—only narrow windows just below the roof. When it was hot, you could hear their cooing rising from the towers, and you knew that the birds had come home.

Mondo listened to Dadi's voice and saw the glow of their cigarettes in the night. All around the esplanade cars went by, making a sound as gentle as water, and one by one the lights in the houses went out. It was very late, and Mondo could sense his vision blurring because he was about to fall asleep. So the Gypsy sent him to sleep on the back seat of the Hotchkiss, and that was where he spent the night. Old Dadi went home, but the Gypsy and the Cossack didn't sleep. They went on sitting on the running board of the car until morning, just like that, drinking, smoking, and talking.

HERE'S WHAT MONDO LIKED TO DO: SIT ON THE BEACH WITH his arms around his knees and watch the sun rise. At 4:50 the sky was pure and gray, only a few clouds of vapor above the sea. The sun didn't come out right away, but Mondo sensed its arrival, on the far side of the horizon, where it rose slowly like the initial blaze of a flame. First there was a pale aureole spreading its stain through the air, and deep within you could feel that strange vibration that caused the horizon to tremble, as if through an effort. At that moment the disc appeared above the water, casting a ray of light straight into your eyes, and the sea and the earth seemed to be the same color. An instant later the first colors came, and the first shadows. But the city streetlamps were still lit with their pale, tired light, because no one was really quite sure that the day had begun.

Mondo watched as the sun climbed above the sea. He hummed to himself, swaying his head and his torso, repeating the Cossack's chant:

"Ayaya, yaya, yayaya, yaya . . ."

There was no one on the beach, only a few seagulls drifting on the sea. The water was transparent, gray, blue and pink, and the pebbles were very white.

Mondo thought about daybreak beneath the sea, too, for the fish and the crabs. Perhaps at the bottom of the sea everything was turning pink and clear, like on the surface of the earth? The fish were waking up and moving slowly below their sky that was like a mirror, they were happy in the middle of a thousand dancing suns, and the seahorses rose along the tendrils of seaweed, the better to see the new light. Even the shellfish were opening their valves, just enough to let the daylight in. Mondo thought about them a lot and watched the slow waves that fell on the pebbles on the beach, making sparks.

When the sun was a little higher, Mondo stood up, because he was getting cold. He took off his clothes. The seawater was softer and warmer than the air, and Mondo dove in up to his neck. He lowered his head, opened his eyes in the water to see the bottom. He heard the fragile swish of the waves unfurling, and it created a music unknown on earth.

Mondo stayed for a long time in the water, until his fingers turned white and his legs began to tremble. Then he went and sat down again on the beach, his back against the supporting wall of the road, and he waited with his eyes closed for the heat of the sun to envelop his body.

Above the city the hills seemed closer. The lovely light shone on the trees and the white façades of the villas, and Mondo said again, "I have to go and see that."

Then he got dressed and left the beach.

It was a holiday, and there was no need to be afraid of the Dog-catcher. On holidays, dogs and children could wander freely through the streets.

The problem was that everything was closed. The vendors didn't come to sell their vegetables, the bakeries had their steel shutters pulled down. Mondo was hungry. Earlier, walking by an ice-cream shop that was called La Boule de Neige, he'd bought a vanilla ice-cream cone and ate it as he walked through the streets.

Now the sidewalks were well lit by the sun. But people weren't coming out. They must be tired. From time to time people passed by, and Mondo would greet them, but they looked at him with surprise because his hair and eyelashes were white with salt and his face was dark brown with the sun. Maybe they thought he was a beggar.

Mondo looked into the window displays while he licked his ice cream. At the back of a shop window where the light was on he could see a big bed made of red wood, with flowered sheets and pillowcases, as if someone were about to lie down there and go to sleep. A bit farther along there was a window full of snow-white kitchen stoves and a rotis-serie where a cardboard chicken was slowly turning. It was all strange. Under a shop door Mondo found an illustrated magazine, and he sat down on a bench to read it.

The magazine told a story with color photographs that showed a beautiful blond woman cooking and playing with her children. It was a long story, and Mondo read it out loud, lifting the pictures up to his eyes so the colors ran together.

"The boy is called Jacques and the girl is Camille. Their mom is in the kitchen and she's making all kinds of nice things to eat—bread, roast chicken, cakes. She asked them, What yummy food would you like today? Make a big strawberry pie, please, asked Jacques. But their mom told them there were no strawberries, only apples. So Camille and Jacques peeled the apples and cut them into little pieces, and their mom made the pie. She put the pie into the oven. It smells good all through the house. When the pie is cooked, their mom puts it on the table and cuts it up into slices. Jacques and Camille eat the lovely pie and drink hot chocolate. Then they say, We've never eaten such a delicious pie!"

When Mondo had finished reading the story, he hid the illustrated magazine in a bush in the garden to read again later. He would have liked to buy another illustrated magazine, with a story about Akim in the jungle, for example, but the newsagent's was closed.

In the middle of the garden there was a retired postal worker sleeping on a bench. Next to him on the bench were an unfolded newspaper and a hat.

When the sun had climbed into the sky, the light was softer. Cars appeared in the streets, blowing their horns. At the other end of the garden, near the gate, a little boy was playing with a red tricycle. Mondo stopped next to him.

"Is it yours?" he asked.

"Yes," said the little boy.

"Will you lend it to me?"

The little boy clung to the handlebars with all his might.

"No! No! Go away!"

"Does your bicycle have a name?"

The little boy lowered his head without replying at first, then he said, very quickly, "Mini."

"It's very nice," said Mondo.

He looked at the tricycle for a moment—its red frame, black saddle, handlebars, and chrome fenders. He rang the bell once or twice, but the little boy pushed him away and rode off, pedaling.

There weren't a lot of people at the marketplace. People headed to mass in little groups or strolled toward the sea. It was on holidays that Mondo would so much have liked to meet someone to whom he could ask, "Would you like to adopt me?"

But maybe on days like that no one would have heard him.

Mondo went into apartment buildings, at random. He stopped to look at the empty letter boxes and the fire warnings. He pushed the button on the timed overhead light and listened to it ticking until the light went off again. At the end of the hallway were the first steps of the stairways, the waxed wooden banister, and a large, tarnished mirror surrounded by plaster statues. Mondo would have liked to take a ride in the elevator, but he didn't dare, because children weren't allowed to play in the elevator.

A young woman came into the building. She was beautiful, with wavy chestnut hair and a light dress that rustled as she moved. She smelled good.

Mondo came out of the corner by the door, and she was startled.

"What do you want?"

"May I go up in the elevator with you?"

The young woman smiled sweetly.

"Of course you can! Come!"

The elevator shifted a little beneath his feet, like a boat.

"Where are you going?" she asked.

"All the way to the top."

"Seventh floor? Me too."

The elevator rose slowly. Through the windowpanes Mondo looked at the ceilings as they receded. The doors vibrated, and at each floor they heard a strange clicking sound. They could also hear the cables thrumming inside the elevator shaft.

"Do you live here?" Curious, the woman looked at Mondo.

"No, Madame."

"Are you coming to see friends?"

"No, Madame, I'm just walking around."

"Oh?"

The young woman was still looking at Mondo, her big eyes calm and gentle, slightly moist. She had opened her handbag and now she gave Mondo a candy wrapped in a transparent paper.

Mondo watched as each floor went by, very slowly.

"We're high up, like in an airplane," said Mondo.

"Have you been in a plane before?"

"Oh no, Madame, not yet. It must be really nice."

The young woman gave a little laugh.

"It goes faster than the elevator, you know!"

"It goes higher, too!"

"Yes, much higher!"

The elevator had arrived, with a groan and a shudder. The young woman got out.

"Are you coming out?"

"No," said Mondo, "I'll go straight back down."

"Oh? Suit yourself. To go back down, push that button, next to last. Be careful, don't touch the red button. That's the alarm."

Before she closed the door behind him, she was still smiling.

"Bon voyage!"

"Good-bye!" said Mondo.

When he left the building, Mondo saw that the sun was high in the sky, almost at its zenith. The days went by quickly, from morning to evening. If you didn't pay attention, they went by even more quickly. That was why people were always in such a hurry. They were hurrying to do everything they had to do before the sun set again.

At noon, people walked with great strides through the city streets. They came out of their houses, climbed into their cars, slammed the doors. Mondo would have liked to say, "Wait! Wait for me!" But no one paid any attention to him.

Mondo felt his heart racing, pounding too, so he stopped in out-of-the-way corners. He stood still, his arms crossed, and watched the crowd as it moved along the street. They no longer looked tired, the way they had in the morning. They walked quickly, making noise with their feet, and they spoke and laughed very loudly.

In their midst an old woman was slowly making her way along the pavement, hunched over, seeing no one. Her shopping bag was filled with food, and it was so heavy that it banged against the ground at every step. Mondo went up to her and helped to carry her bag. He could hear the old woman breathing, puffing a little just behind him.

The old woman stopped outside the door to a gray building, and Mondo went up the stairs with her. He thought that this old woman might be his grandmother or his aunt, but he didn't speak to her, because she was a bit deaf. She opened her door on the fifth floor and went into the kitchen to slice a piece of stale gingerbread. She gave it to Mondo, and he saw that her hand was trembling a lot. Her voice trembled too when she said, "God bless you."

A bit farther along down the street, Mondo felt as if he were becoming very small. He hugged the wall of the building, and the people around him became tall as trees, with faraway faces, like the balconies on the buildings. Mondo wove his way among all these giants with their long strides. He avoided the women who were tall as church spires, with their enormous polka dot dresses, and the men as broad as cliff faces, wearing blue suits and white shirts. Perhaps it was the daylight that caused it, a light that makes things bigger and shortens shadows. Mondo slipped through their midst, and only those who looked down could see him. He wasn't frightened, except from time to time when he had to cross the street. But he was looking for someone, all over town, in the gardens, on the beach. He wasn't quite sure whom he was looking for, nor why, but someone, just like that—simply someone to whom he could say, very quickly, and then read the answer in their eyes:

"Would you like to adopt me?"

IT WAS AT AROUND THAT TIME THAT MONDO MET THI CHIN, when the days were fine and the nights were long and warm. Mondo had left his evening hiding place at the base of the breakwater. A warm wind was blowing off the land, the dry wind that makes your hair electric and causes the forests of cork oak to burn. On the hills above the city Mondo saw large white clouds of smoke spreading across the sky.

For a moment Mondo looked at the hills lit by the sun, and then he took the path leading that way. It was a winding path, and here and there it became a set of stairs with large steps made of cinder blocks. On either side of the path were gutters filled with dead leaves and bits of paper.

Mondo liked to climb the stairs. They zigzagged across the hill, unhurriedly, as if they weren't actually leading anywhere. All along the path there were high stone walls topped with shards of bottle glass, so you didn't really know where you were. Mondo climbed the steps slowly, looking to see if he could find anything interesting in the gutters. Sometimes he found a coin, or a rusty nail, or a picture, or a strange fruit.

The higher you climbed, the flatter the city became, with all the rectangles of the buildings and the straight lines of streets with their streams of red and blue cars. The sea, too, became flat at the foot of the hill, shining like a sheet of metal. Mondo turned back from time to time to look at it all through the branches of the trees, above the walls of the villas.

There was no one along the steps, except once, a big tabby cat lurking in the gutter, eating scraps of meat left in a rusty can. The cat had crouched down and put its ears back, staring at Mondo with its round pupils, its yellow eyes.

Mondo went by without saying a thing. He could sense the black pupils still looking at him until he went round the bend.

Mondo climbed the steps without a sound. He walked as quietly as he could, avoiding the twigs and shoots; he glided silently, like a shadow.

The stairway didn't make much sense. Sometimes it was steep, with high, narrow little steps that left you breathless. Sometimes it was lazy, winding slowly between the villas and the vacant lots. Sometimes it even seemed to want to go downhill again.

Mondo wasn't in a hurry. He made his way, zigzagging too, from one wall to the other. He stopped to look in the gutters or to tear leaves from the trees. He took a leaf from a pepper plant and crushed it between his fingers to smell the scent that stung his nose and eyes. He picked honeysuckle flowers and sucked the sugary little drop that formed a pearl at the base of the calyx. Or he made music with a blade of grass pressed against his lips.

Mondo liked walking up there, all alone, across the hill. As he climbed, the sunlight became more and more yellow, and soft, as if it were flowing from the leaves of the plants and the stones of the old walls. During the day the light had soaked into the earth, and now it was coming back out, spreading its heat, swelling its clouds.

There was no one on the hillside. No doubt because it was late afternoon, and also because the neighborhood was somewhat abandoned. The villas were buried in the trees; they weren't sad, but they looked as if they were sleeping, with their rusty gates and their peeling shutters that didn't close properly.

Mondo listened to the sounds of the birds in the trees, the faint snapping of the branches in the wind. Above all there was the sound of a cricket, a strident clicking that moved constantly and seemed to be following Mondo. Now and again the sound grew fainter, then returned, so close that Mondo turned around to try to see the insect. But the noise went off again and resurfaced ahead of him, or above him, at the top of the wall. Mondo called to it in turn, blowing into his blade of grass. But the cricket didn't show itself; it preferred to remain hidden.

At the very top of the hill, because of the heat, the clouds appeared.

They drifted slowly northward, and when they crossed the sun Mondo. could feel their shadow on his face. The colors changed and shifted; the yellow light flared then went out.

Mondo had wanted to go to the top of the hill for a long time. He'd often gazed that way from his hiding places by the sea, gazed at the hill with all its trees, and at the beautiful light shining on the façades of the villas, radiating into the sky like a halo. That was why he had wanted to climb up the hill—because the pathway of stairs seemed to lead up to the sky and the light. It really was a beautiful hill, just above the sea, close to the clouds, and Mondo had looked at it for a long time, in the morning when it was still gray and far away, and in the evening, and even at night when it sparkled with all the electric lights. Now he was happy to be climbing up the hill.

There were piles of dead leaves along the walls where salamanders fled from sight. Mondo tried to sneak up on them, drawing closer without making a sound; but they heard him all the same and ran to hide in the crevices.

Mondo tried to call to the salamanders, whistling through his teeth. He would have liked to have a salamander. He thought he could tame it and put it in the pocket of his trousers and take it for a walk. He would catch flies to feed it, and when he sat in the sun on the beach or on the rocks along the breakwater, the salamander would come out of his pocket and scurry up onto his shoulder. It would stay there without moving, making its throat quiver, because that's the way salamanders purr.

Then Mondo arrived outside the House of the Golden Light. That's what Mondo had called it the first time he went there, and ever since, the name had stuck. It was a beautiful old house, of the Italian type, covered with a yellowish-orange plaster, with high windows and dilapidated shutters and a Virginia creeper invading the porch. Around the house there was a garden; it wasn't very big, but it was so overwhelmed with brambles and weeds that you couldn't see where it ended. Mondo had pushed open the iron gate and walked without making a sound along the gravel lane that led to the house. The yellow house was simple—there were no stucco embellishments or mascarons—but Mondo thought he had never seen such a beautiful house.

In the untidy garden, in front of the house, there were two fine palm trees that rose above the roof, and when the wind was blowing a little, their palms rubbed against the gutters and the tiles. Around the palm trees the bushes were thick and dark, interwoven with long violet brambles that crawled along the ground like snakes.

What was most beautiful of all was the light that enveloped the house. It was for the light that Mondo had given the house its name, right from the start, the House of the Golden Light. The light of the sun at the end of the afternoon was of a very gentle and serene color, a color as warm as the leaves in autumn or the sand, bathing you, intoxicating you. As he walked slowly along the gravel path, Mondo felt the light caressing his face. He felt like sleeping, and his heart was beating very slowly. He was scarcely breathing.

The song of the cricket reverberated loudly once again, as if it were coming from the bushes in the garden. Mondo stopped to listen, then he walked slowly toward the house, ready to run away in case a dog came out. But there was no one. The plants in the garden around him were motionless, their leaves heavy with the heat.

Mondo went into the undergrowth. On all fours he slipped beneath the branches of the shrubbery, carefully pushing the brambles aside. He settled into a hiding place, under cover of the bushes, and from there he gazed at the yellow house.

The light was declining almost imperceptibly along the façade. There wasn't a sound, except the voice of the cricket and the shrill buzz of the mosquitoes dancing around Mondo's hair. He sat on the ground under the leaves of a laurel bush and stared at the door to the house, at the steps of the half-moon stairway that led to the porch. Grass was growing in the joints of the steps. After a while, Mondo curled up on the ground, his head against his elbow.

IT FELT GOOD TO SLEEP LIKE THAT, AT THE FOOT OF THE strong-smelling tree, not very far from the House of the Golden Light, surrounded by warmth and peace, by the strident call of the cricket endlessly coming and going. When you were asleep, Mondo, you weren't there. You were off elsewhere, far from your body. You had left your sleeping body on the ground, a few feet from the gravel path, and you were walking elsewhere. That was the strange thing. Your body stayed on the ground, quietly breathing; the wind carried the shadow of the clouds over your face, your closed eyes. Tiger mosquitoes danced around your cheeks and black ants explored your clothes and hands. The evening breeze ruffled your hair. But you weren't there. You were elsewhere, vanished into the warm light of the house, into the scent of the bay leaves, into the dampness that rose from the clumps of earth. Spiders trembled on their webs, for it was time for them to wake. The old black and yellow salamanders slipped from their crevices onto the wall of the house, and they stayed there watching you, suspended from their little feet, with their toes widespread. The entire world was looking at you, because you had your eyes closed. And somewhere at the far end of the garden, between a thick clump of brambles and a holly bush, near an old dried-out cypress tree, a pilot-insect was making its saw-like sound, relentlessly, to speak to you, to call to you. But you didn't hear it, you were gone, you were far away.

"WHO ARE YOU?" ASKED THE SHRILL VOICE.

Now there was a woman next to Mondo, but she was so small that for a moment Mondo thought she was a child. Her black hair was cut in a bowl round her face, and she wore a long blue-gray apron.

She was smiling.

"Who are you?"

Mondo was standing, and he was hardly any shorter than her. He yawned.

"Were you asleep?"

"Excuse me," said Mondo. "I came into your garden. I was kind of tired so I slept. I'll leave now."

"Why do you want to leave right away? Don't you like the garden?"

"I do, it's very beautiful," said Mondo. He searched the little woman's face for a sign of anger. But she continued to smile. Her slanted eyes had a curious expression, like a cat's. Around her eyes and her mouth there were deep wrinkles, and Mondo thought that the woman must be old.

"Come and see the house, too," she said.

She went up the little half-moon staircase and opened the door.

"Come on!"

Mondo went in behind her. They were in a large room, nearly empty, lit on all four sides by high windows. At the center of the room were a wooden table and chairs, and on the table was a lacquer tray with a black tea pot and bowls. Mondo stood motionless on the threshold, looking at the room and the windows. The windows were made of little panes of frosted glass, and the light coming in was even warmer and more golden. Mondo had never seen such beautiful light.

The little woman stood by the table and poured tea into the bowls.

"Do you like tea?"

"Yes," said Mondo.

"Then come and sit over here."

Mondo sat slowly on the edge of the chair and drank. The liquid was also the color of gold. It burned his lips and throat.

"It's hot," he said.

The little woman took a sip, without making a sound.

"You haven't told me who you are," she said. Her voice was like gentle music.

"I'm Mondo," said Mondo.

The little woman looked at him, smiling. She seemed even smaller on her chair.

"And my name is Thi Chin."

"Are you Chinese?" asked Mondo. The little woman shook her head.

"I'm Vietnamese, not Chinese."

"Is it far away, your country?"

"Yes, it's very, very far away."

Mondo drank the tea and his fatigue vanished.

"And you? Where do you come from? You're not from here, are you?"

Mondo didn't really know what to say.

"No, I'm not from here," he said. Lowering his head, he spread the locks of his hair. The little woman never stopped smiling, but her narrow eyes had suddenly become somewhat anxious.

"Stay a little while longer," she said. "You don't want to leave right away?"

"I shouldn't have come into your garden," said Mondo. "But the gate was open, and I was kind of tired."

"You were right to come in," said Thi Chin simply. "You see, I had left the gate open for you."

"So you knew I was going to come?" said Mondo. The notion reassured him.

Thi Chin nodded and handed Mondo a tin box full of macaroons.

"Are you hungry?"

"Yes," said Mondo. He nibbled on a macaroon and looked at the tall windows that let in the light.

"It's beautiful," he said. "What is it that makes all the gold?"

"It's the light of the sun," said Thi Chin.

"So are you rich?"

Thi Chin laughed.

"This gold doesn't belong to anyone."

They looked at the beautiful light, as if they were in a dream.

"It's like that in my country," said Thi Chin in a low voice. "When the sun goes down, the sky turns all yellow, like this, with very light little black clouds, like birds' feathers."

The golden light filled the entire room, and Mondo felt calmer and stronger, the way he had after drinking the hot tea.

"Do you like my house?" asked Thi Chin.

"Yes," said Mondo. His eyes reflected the color of the sun.

"Then it's your house, too, whenever you like."

That was how Mondo became acquainted with Thi Chin and the House of the Golden Light. He stayed in the big room for a long time, looking at the windows. The light lingered until the sun disappeared completely behind the hills. Even then, the walls of the room were so drenched with light that it was as if it would never fade. Then shadow came, and everything turned gray—the walls, the windows, Mondo's hair. And it turned cold, too. The little woman got up to switch on a lamp, then she took Mondo into the garden to look at the night. Above the trees, the stars shone and there was a thin crescent moon.

That night, Mondo slept on the cushions at the far end of the big room. He slept there the following nights, too, because he liked this house. Sometimes, when the night was warm, he slept in the garden, beneath the bay tree, or on the steps of the porch, outside the door. Thi Chin did not speak much, and perhaps that was why he liked her. From the time she had first asked him his name and where he was from, she had not asked him anything else. She simply took him by the hand and showed him things that were fun, in the garden or in the house. She showed him pebbles with odd shapes or patterns, or fine-veined leaves on a tree, or the red seeds on the palm trees, or the little white and yellow flowers that grew among the stones. In her palm she would show him black beetles or caterpillars, and in exchange Mondo gave her shells or seagull feathers that he found on the shore.

Thi Chin gave him rice to eat, and a bowl of half-cooked red and green vegetables, always with hot tea in little white bowls. Sometimes when the night was very dark, Thi Chin took down a picture book and told him an ancient story. It was a long story that took place in an unknown country where there were monuments with pointed roofs, and dragons and animals that knew how to speak, like people. The story was so beautiful that Mondo couldn't hear it to the end. He fell asleep, and the little woman went away without making a sound, after she had switched off the light. She slept on the second floor, in a narrow room. In the morning, when she woke up, Mondo was already gone.

THERE WERE FIRES ON MOST OF THE HILLS, BECAUSE SUMMER was coming. During the day you could see tall columns of white smoke streaking the sky, and at night there was a disquieting red glow, like the embers of a cigarette. Mondo often looked in the direction of the fires when he was on the beach, or when he was going up the stairway toward Thi Chin's house. One afternoon he even came back earlier than usual to clear the weeds that grew around the house, and when Thi Chin asked him what he was doing, he said, "It's so the fires won't come here."

Now that he slept nearly every night in the House of the Golden Light, or in the garden, he was less frightened of the Dogcatcher's gray truck. He no longer went to his hiding places among the rocks near the breakwater. As soon as the sun had risen, he went off to swim in the sea. He loved the transparent morning sea, the strange sound of the waves when you had your head beneath the water, and the cry of the seagulls in the sky. Then he went over to the market to unload a few crates and to scavenge some fruit and vegetables. He would take them back to Thi Chin for the evening meal.

After midday, he went to talk a while with the Gypsy, who sat day-dreaming on the running board of his car. They didn't say much, but the Gypsy seemed happy to see him. Then the Cossack would come, with a bottle of alcohol. He was always a bit drunk, and he would shout in his deep loud voice, "Hey! Mondo, my friend!"

There was a woman who came some of the time, too, a fat woman with a red face and very pale eyes, who could read fortunes in the palms of the people passing by; but Mondo left when she arrived, because he didn't like her.

He went off to look for old Dadi. It wasn't easy to find him, because the old man often changed his spot. He was sitting on the sheets of his newspaper, and next to him was his little yellow suitcase with the holes in it, and the people passing by thought he was a beggar. As a rule, Mondo found him on the square outside a church, and he would sit down beside him. Mondo liked it when Dadi talked, because he knew a lot of stories about carrier pigeons and doves. He talked about their country, a country where there were a lot of trees, and tranquil rivers, and green fields, and a gentle sky. Next to the houses there were pointed towers covered with red and green tiles where the doves and pigeons lived. Old Dadi spoke in his slow voice, and it was like the flight of birds in the sky, hesitant, turning round and round above the villages. But he didn't talk about that with anyone else.

When Mondo was sitting on the square outside a church with old Dadi, people were a little taken aback. They stopped to look at the little boy and the old man with his doves, and they gave more coins because they were moved. But Mondo did not sit there begging for long, because there was always a woman or two who didn't like what she saw and who began asking questions. And he had to watch out for the Dogcatcher. If the gray truck had gone by at that particular moment, surely the men in uniform would have jumped out of their truck and taken him away. They might even have taken old Dadi and his doves away.

One day, there was a very strong wind, and the Gypsy said to Mondo, "Let's go see the battle of the kites."

It was only on Sundays when it was very windy that the kite battles were held. They got to the beach early, and the children were already there with their kites. There were kites of every sort and color, kites shaped like lozenges, or square, monoplanes and biplanes, kites painted with little animal heads. But the most beautiful kite belonged to a man in his fifties who stood at the far end of the beach. His kite was like a great yellow and black butterfly, with immense wings. When he launched it, everyone stood still to watch. The great yellow and black butterfly glided for a moment a few yards above the sea, then the man pulled on the string and arched his back. The wind filled the wings and the kite began to climb, very high in the sky above the sea. The canvas wings snapped in the wind. On the beach the man was hardly moving. He unwound the reel of twine, and his gaze never left the yellow and black butterfly soaring above the sea. From time to time the man pulled on the twine, rolled it around the spool, and the kite climbed ever higher into the sky. Now it was higher than all the others, gliding above the beach with its wings widespread. It stayed up there, hovering effortlessly in the raging wind, so far from the earth that you could no longer see the string that held it.

When Mondo and the Gypsy came over, the man handed the spool and the twine to Mondo.

"Keep a good hold of it!" he said.

He went to sit on the beach and lit a cigarette.

Mondo tried to resist the wind.

"If it pulls too hard, let go a little, then you tighten it up again afterward."

Taking turns, Mondo, the Gypsy, and the man held the kite, until all the others, tired out, fell into the sea. All the spectators were craning their necks, watching the huge yellow and black butterfly as it continued to glide. It really was the champion of all the kites; no others had been able to climb so high and fly for so long.

Then, very slowly, the man made the big butterfly come down, foot by foot. The kite swayed in the wind, and you could hear its sail snapping and the high-pitched whistling of the twine. This was the most dangerous moment, because the twine could break under the tension, and the man moved slowly forward as he wound the twine. When the kite was close to the shore, the man stepped off to one side, giving one tug, then letting go of the twine, and the kite landed on the pebbles, very slowly, like an airplane.

Afterward, as they were very tired, they sat for a while on the beach. The Gypsy bought some hot dogs and they ate them, looking at the sea. The man told Mondo about the kite battles on the beaches in Turkey, where they fixed razor blades to the tails of the kites. When they were very high in the sky, they would hurl the kites against each other, trying to make them fall. The razor blades cut the sails. Once, a very long time ago, he had even managed to cut the twine of a kite, and it disappeared into the distance, borne away on the wind like a dead leaf. When it was very windy, the children came out in the hundreds to fly their kites, and the blue sky was covered with spots of many colors.

"It must have been beautiful," said Mondo.

"Yes, it was. But people don't know how to do it anymore," said the man. He got up and wrapped the big yellow and black butterfly in a plastic sheet.

"Next time, I'll teach you how to make a real kite," said the man. "In September, that's the good season, and you can fly your kite like a bird, almost without touching it."

Mondo thought he'd make his kite all white, like a seagull.

THERE WAS ANOTHER PERSON MONDO LIKED TO GO AND SEE, from time to time. There was a boat called *Oxyton*. The first time he encountered it was in the afternoon, at around two, when the sun was beating down on the water in the harbor. The boat was moored alongside the pier, among all the other boats, and she was bobbing on the water. It wasn't a big boat at all, like all those other ones with prows like shark's noses and their huge white sails. No, *Oxyton* was just a boat with a big belly and a short mast to the fore, but Mondo thought she was a likeable sort of boat. He asked someone who was working in the harbor what the boat was called, and he liked the name, too.

So he often came to see her, when he was in the neighborhood. He would stop on the edge of the pier and say the name out loud, in a sing-song sort of way, "*Oxyton! Oxyton!*"

The boat tugged at her moorings, came to bump against the pier, drifted away again. Her hull was blue and red, with a white trim. Mondo sat on the pier, next to the mooring ring, and looked at *Oxyton* while he ate his orange. He also looked at the reflection of the sun in the water, the soft waves that rocked the hull. *Oxyton* looked like she was bored, because no one ever took her out. So Mondo jumped on board. He sat on the wooden seat, at the helm, and waited, feeling the motion of the waves. The boat bobbed gently, turned a bit, moved away, made her moorings creak. Mondo would have liked to set off with her on the sea, aimlessly. As he sailed by the breakwater, he would tell Giordan the Fisherman to hop on board, and they would go off together to the Red Sea.

Mondo sat for a long time in the aft of the boat, watching the sun's reflections and the schools of tiny fishes that moved about, quivering. Sometimes he hummed a song for the boat, a song he'd invented for himself:

"*Oxyton, Oxyton, Oxyton*,
Let's go sailing,
Let's go fishing
Let's go fishing
For sardines and shrimp and tuna!"

Then Mondo walked along the piers for a while, over by the cargo ships, because there was a derrick over there that was his friend, too.

There were so many things to see, everywhere, in the street and on the beach and on the vacant lots. Mondo didn't especially like the places where there were a lot of people. He preferred the open spaces, where you could see into the distance—esplanades, and jetties that went right out into the sea, and straight avenues where the huge tank trucks passed. It was in places like that where he could find people to talk to, and to whom he could say, "Would you like to adopt me?"

They were a dreaming sort of people, who walked with their hands behind their backs, thinking about other things. Among them there were astronomers, and history teachers, and musicians, and customs officers. And sometimes there was a Sunday painter, painting the boats and the trees and the sunsets, sitting on a folding stool. The painter turned around and said, "Do you like it?"

Mondo nodded. He pointed to a man and his dog who were walking along the pier in the distance.

"And what about them? Will you draw them too?"

"If you like," said the painter. With his finest brush he added a tiny black figure to the canvas that looked something like an insect.

Mondo thought for a moment and said, "Do you know how to draw the sky?"

The painter stopped painting and looked at him with astonishment. "The sky?"

"Yes, the sky, with clouds and the sun. That would be nice."

The painter had never thought about this. He looked at the sky above him and laughed.

"You're right. The next painting I do will be nothing but sky."

"With the clouds and the sun?"

"Yes, with all the clouds, and the sun lighting everything."

"It will be beautiful," said Mondo approvingly. "I wish I could see it right away."

The painter looked up at the sky.

"I'll start tomorrow morning. I hope the weather will be fine."

"Yes, it will be fine, and the sky will be even more beautiful than today," said Mondo, because he had a certain gift for predicting the weather.

And then there was the chair-bottomer. Mondo often went to see the chair-bottomer in the afternoon. He worked in the courtyard of an old building, with his grandson called Pipo sitting next to him bundled in a big jacket. Mondo liked to watch the chair-bottomer at work, because he might be old but he knew how to move his fingers very quickly to interweave and tie the blades of straw. His grandson sat motionless next to him, with that jacket that covered him like an overcoat, and Mondo played with him a little bit. He brought him things he'd found while he was out walking—strange pebbles from the beach, or clumps of seaweed, or mussel shells, or handfuls of lovely green and blue shards of bottle polished by the sea. Pipo took the pebbles and looked at them for a long time, then put them into the pockets of his jacket. He did not know how to speak, but Mondo liked him because he sat there by his grandfather without moving, bundled in the gray jacket that went down to his feet and covered his hands the way Chinese people's clothes do. Mondo liked people who knew how to sit in the sun without moving or speaking, people who had daydreams in their eyes.

Mondo knew a lot of people here, in the town, but he didn't really have that many friends. The people he liked to meet were the ones who had a lovely, shining gaze in their eyes and who would smile when they saw you as if they were glad to meet you. So Mondo would stop and talk to them for a while, and he'd ask them a few questions—about the sea, or the sky, or the birds—and when the people went away again they were completely changed. Mondo didn't ask them things that were very difficult, but they were things that people had forgotten, things they hadn't thought about in years, such as why bottles are green or why there are shooting stars. It was as if the people had been waiting for a long time for a word, just a few words, like that, there on the street, and Mondo knew just the words to say.

And there were the questions, too. Most people don't know how to ask the right questions. Mondo knew how to ask questions, just at the right time, when you weren't expecting it. People paused for a few seconds, they stopped thinking about themselves and their own business, they thought, and their eyes seemed to blur, because they remembered asking those questions themselves, long ago.

There was one person Mondo really liked to meet. He was a young man, fairly tall and strong, with a very red face and blue eyes. He wore a dark blue uniform and carried a big leather satchel filled with letters. Mondo often met him in the morning, along the stairway that led up the hillside. The first time that Mondo asked him, "Do you have a letter for me?" the tall man laughed. But Mondo ran into him every day, and every day he went up to him and asked him the same question: "And today? Do you have a letter for me?"

So the man opened his satchel and searched inside.

"Let's see now . . . What's your name again?"

"Mondo," said Mondo.

"Mondo . . . Mondo . . . No, no letters for you today."

But sometimes, all the same, he took a small printed newspaper out of his satchel, or an advertising flier, and he handed them to Mondo.

"Look, this arrived for you today."

He winked at Mondo and went on his way.

One day Mondo felt very much like writing letters, and he decided to find someone who would teach him how to read and write. He walked through the city streets and over by the public gardens, but it was very hot and the retired postal workers weren't there. He looked elsewhere, and he ended up by the seaside. The sun was blazing down, and the pebbles on the beach sparkled with salt dust. Mondo looked at the children playing by the water's edge. They wore swimsuits of strange colors, tomato red and apple green, and maybe that was why they were shouting so loudly as they played. But Mondo did not feel like going over to them.

Near the wooden building on the private beach, Mondo saw an old man who was leveling the sand with a long rake. He was really very old indeed, wearing faded, stained blue shorts. His body was the color of burnt toast, and his skin was all wizened and wrinkled like an old elephant's. The man pulled the long rake slowly over the pebbles all along the beach, up and down, paying no mind to the children or the swimmers. The sun glistened on his back and legs, and sweat trickled down his face. From time to time he would stop and pull a handkerchief from the pocket of his shorts and wipe his face and hands.

Mondo sat against the wall beside the old man. He waited a long time, until the man had finished raking his patch of beach. When he came to sit down by the wall, he glanced at Mondo. His eyes were very light, a pale gray color that made them seem like two holes in the brown skin of his face. He looked a bit like an Indian.

He looked at Mondo as if he had understood his question. All he said was, "Hi, there!"

"I'd like you to teach me to read and write, please," said Mondo.

The old man did not move, but he didn't seem surprised.

"Don't you go to school?"

"No, sir," said Mondo.

The old man sat on the beach, his back to the wall, his face toward the sun. He looked straight ahead, and his expression was very calm and gentle, despite his hook nose and the wrinkles that crisscrossed his cheeks. When he looked at Mondo it was as if he could see through him, because his irises were so light. Then a gleam of amusement entered his gaze, and he said, "I'll teach you how to read and write, if that's what you want." His voice was like his eyes, very calm and faraway, as if he were afraid of making too much noise when he spoke.

"You really don't know anything at all?"

"No, sir," said Mondo.

From his beach bag the man took an old penknife with a red handle and began to etch the signs of letters onto nice flat pebbles. At the same time, he spoke to Mondo about everything there was in the letters, about everything you could see in them when you looked and when you listened. He spoke about *A*, which is like a big fly with its wings pulled back; about *B*, which is funny, with its two tummies; or *C* and *D*, which are like the moon, a crescent moon or a half-full one; and then there was *O*, which was the full moon in the black sky. *H* is high, a ladder to climb up trees or to reach the roofs of houses; *E* and *F* look like a rake and a shovel; and *G* is like a fat man sitting in an armchair. *I* dances on tiptoes, with a little head popping up each time it bounces, whereas *J* likes to swing. *K* is broken like an old man, *R* takes big strides like a soldier, and *Y* stands tall, its arms in the air, and it shouts: help! *L* is a tree on the river's edge, *M* is a mountain, *N* is for names, and people waving with their hands, *P* is asleep on one paw, and *Q* is sitting on its tail; *S* is always a snake, *Z* is always a bolt of lightning, *T* is beautiful, like the mast on a ship, *U* is like a vase, *V* and *W* are birds, birds in flight; and *X* is a cross, to help you remember.

With the tip of his penknife the old man traced the marks on the pebbles and placed them in front of Mondo.

"What is your name?"

"Mondo," said Mondo.

The old man picked up a few pebbles and added another one.

"Look. That's your name, there."

"It's beautiful!" said Mondo. "There's a mountain, then the moon, and someone greeting the crescent moon, and then the moon again. Why are there so many moons?"

"It's in your name, that's all," said the old man. "That's how you're called."

He picked up the pebbles.

"And you, sir? What is in your name?"

The old man showed him the pebbles, one after the other, and Mondo picked them up and set them down in a row in front of him.

"There's a mountain."

"Yes, the one where I was born."

"There's a fly."

"Perhaps I was a fly, a long time ago, before I became a man."

"And there's a man walking, a soldier."

"I have been a soldier."

"There's a crescent moon."

"That is the moon that was there when I was born."

"A rake!"

"Here it is!"

The old man pointed to the rake that was lying on the beach.

"There's a tree by the river."

"Yes, perhaps that's how I'll come back after I die—a motionless tree next to a lovely river."

"It's good to know how to read," said Mondo. "I'd like to know all the letters."

"You're going to write, too," said the old man. He handed him his penknife, and Mondo sat for a long time etching the drawings of the letters onto the pebbles on the beach. Then he set them to one side, to see what names they made. There were always a lot of *O*'s and *I*'s because those were the ones he liked best. He liked the *T*'s as well, and Z, and the birds, *V* and *W*. The old man read,

OVO OWO OTTO IZTI

and they both had a good laugh.

The old man also knew a lot of other rather strange things, and he would talk about them in his soft voice while he gazed out to sea. He talked about a foreign country very far away, on the other side of the sea, a very big country where the people were beautiful and gentle and where there were no wars, and where no one was afraid of dying.

In this country there was a river as wide as the sea, and people went to swim there every evening as the sun went down. And while he was talking about that country the old man's voice became even softer and slower, and his pale eyes seemed to be looking even farther away, as if he were already there, on the banks of that river.

"Can I come with you?" asked Mondo.

The old man placed his hand on Mondo's shoulder.

"Yes, I'll take you with me."

"When will you be leaving?"

"I don't know. When I have enough money. In a year, maybe. But I'll take you with me."

Later, the old man picked up his rake and went back to work a bit farther down the beach. Mondo put the pebbles with his name on them into his pocket, and he waved to his friend and went away.

Now there were a lot of signs, everywhere, written on the walls, the doors, or the iron shutters. Mondo saw them as he walked through the streets of the town, and he recognized a few of them along the way. In the cement, on the sidewalk, were letters carved like this:

D
E
N A D I N E
E

but it wasn't easy for Mondo to understand.

When night fell, Mondo went back to the House of the Golden Light. He ate the rice and the vegetables in the big room, with Thi Chin, then he went out into the garden. He waited for the little woman to come and join him, and they walked together very slowly along the gravel path until they were completely surrounded by the trees and bushes. Thi Chin took Mondo's hand and squeezed it so hard that it hurt. But it was good all the same to walk like that in the dark, without lights, feeling your way with your toes so you wouldn't fall, guided solely by the sound of the gravel crunching beneath your feet. Mondo listened to the hidden cricket's strident song, and he smelled the odors of the bushes that spread their leaves in the night. It made your head spin a little, and that was why the little woman squeezed his hand so hard, so that she wouldn't feel dizzy.

"At night everything smells good," said Mondo.

"That's because you can't see," said Thi Chin. "You can smell better and hear better when you can't see."

She paused on the path.

"Look, we're going to see the stars, now."

The cricket's shrill chirring sounded very near now, as if it were coming to them right out of the sky. The stars appeared, one after the other, faintly throbbing in the moist night. Mondo looked at them, holding his breath, his head thrown back.

"They're beautiful. Are they saying something, Thi Chin?"

"Yes, they're saying a lot of things, but we can't understand what they're saying."

"Even if we knew how to read, we wouldn't be able to understand?"

"No, we wouldn't, Mondo. Humans can't understand what the stars are saying."

"Maybe they're telling us what's going to happen later, in a very long time."

"Yes, or maybe they're telling each other stories."

Thi Chin also looked at the stars without moving, holding Mondo's hand very tight.

"Maybe they're saying what road we have to follow, the countries where we have to go."

Mondo thought for a moment.

"They're shining very brightly now. Maybe they're souls."

Thi Chin would have liked to see Mondo's face, but everything was dark. Then all of a sudden she began to tremble, as if she were afraid. She squeezed Mondo's hand against her chest and placed her cheek against his shoulder. Her voice was very strange and sad, as if something were hurting her.

"Mondo, Mondo . . ."

She said his name over and over in her muffled voice, and her body trembled.

"What's wrong, Thi Chin?" asked Mondo. He tried to calm her, talking to her. "I'm here, I'm not going anywhere, I don't want to leave."

He could not see Thi Chin's face, but he sensed that she was crying, and that was why her body was trembling. Thi Chin moved to one side, so that Mondo would not feel her tears flowing.

"Forgive me, I'm stupid," she said, but her voice couldn't speak.

"Don't be sad," said Mondo. He led her to the other end of the garden. "Come, let's go see the lights of the city in the sky."

They went to the place where they could see the vast pink glow in the shape of a mushroom above the trees. There was even an airplane flying by, its lights twinkling, and that made them laugh.

Then they sat down on the gravel path, still holding hands. The little woman had forgotten her sadness, and she was talking again, in a low voice, not thinking about what she was saying. Mondo talked, too, and the cricket made its shrill sound from its hiding place among the leaves. Mondo and Thi Chin sat like that for a very long time, until their eyelids grew very heavy. Then they fell asleep on the ground, and the garden moved gently, gently, like the deck of a ship.

THE LAST TIME WAS AT THE BEGINNING OF SUMMER. MONDO had left at sunrise, without making a sound. He went down the path of stairs across the hill, without hurrying. The trees and the grasses were covered with dew, and there was a sort of mist above the sea. In the large leaves of morning glory along the old walls a drop of water hung and shone like a diamond. Mondo came near with his mouth open, flipped the leaf, and drank the cool drop. They were little tiny drops, but they spread through his mouth and his body and eased his thirst. On either side of the path the dry stone walls were already warm. The salamanders came out of their crevices to look at the light of day.

Mondo went down the hill to the sea and sat in his place on the deserted beach. There was no one else there, only the seagulls. They floated on the water along the shore, or waddled over the pebbles. They opened their beaks, just enough to cry. They flew off, made a circle, then landed a bit farther along. The seagulls always had strange cries in the morning, as if they were calling to each other before a departure.

When the sun was a little higher in the pink sky, the streetlamps were extinguished and you could hear the city begin to rumble. It was a faraway noise, which came from the streets between the tall buildings, a dull sound that vibrated through the pebbles on the beach. Mopeds sped along the avenues with their bumblebee sound, carrying men and women wearing parkas, their heads hidden in woolen hoods.

Mondo didn't move, and he waited for the sun to warm up the air. He listened to the sound of the waves against the pebbles. He liked that hour of the day, because there was no one at all by the sea, just himself and the seagulls. So then he could think about all those people in the city, all the people he would meet. He thought about them while he looked at the sea and the sky, and it was as if the people were both very far away and very near, sitting around him. It was as if all he had to do was look at them to make them exist, and then look away and they were gone.

On the deserted beach Mondo spoke to people. He spoke to them in his own way, wordlessly, sending waves; the waves reached the people, wherever they were, mingling with the sound of the sea and the light, and the people received the waves without knowing where they came from. Mondo thought about the Gypsy, and the Cossack, and the chair-bottomer, and Rosa, and Ida the baker, and the kite champion, or the old man who had taught him to read, and all of them heard him. They heard him like a whistling in their ears or like the drone of an airplane, and they shook their heads a little because they could not understand what it was. But Mondo was happy to be able to speak to them that way and to send them the waves from the sea and the sun and the sky.

Then Mondo walked along the shore to the wooden hut on the private beach. At the foot of the retaining wall he hunted for the pebbles on which the old man had carved his drawings of letters. Mondo had not been back there for several days, and the salt and the light had already half erased the drawings. With a sharp flint Mondo retraced the signs, and he set the pebbles on the edge of the wall, to write his name, like this:

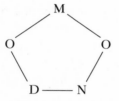

so that the old man would see his name, when he came, and he would know that Mondo had been there.

That day was not like other days, because someone was missing in the town. Mondo went looking for the old beggar with the doves, and his heart was beating faster, because he already knew that he would not find him. He looked for him everywhere—in the streets and alleyways, at the marketplace, outside the churches. Mondo really wanted to see him. But during the night the gray truck had gone by, and the men in uniform had taken old Dadi away.

Mondo kept looking everywhere for Dadi, without resting. His heart was pounding harder and harder as he ran from one hiding place to the next. He looked everywhere the old beggar used to go, in all the spots behind the heavy doors, or in the stairways, near the fountains, in the public gardens, in the entrances to the old buildings. Sometimes he saw a section of newspaper on the pavement, and he stopped to look all around, as if old Dadi were going to come back and sit there on the ground.

In the end, it was the Cossack who told Mondo what had happened. Mondo ran into him in the street, near the market. He was making his way with some difficulty, holding to the wall, because he was completely drunk. People stopped to look at him, laughing. He'd even lost his little black accordion; someone had stolen it from him while he was sleeping off his wine. When Mondo asked him where old Dadi and his doves were, he looked at Mondo for a moment, his eyes vacant, not understanding. Then he simply grunted, "Dunno . . . they took him away, last night . . ."

"Where did they take him?"

"Dunno . . . hospital, could be."

The Cossack was making a great effort to continue on his way.

"Wait! And the doves? Did they take them away, too?"

The Cossack didn't understand.

"The white birds!"

"Oh, yeah, I don't know . . ." The Cossack shrugged. "Don't know what they did with his pigeons . . . maybe they're going to eat them."

And he went on his way, staggering along the wall.

All of a sudden Mondo felt very weary. He wanted to go back and sit by the sea, on the beach, and sleep. But it was too far, and he didn't have the strength. Maybe he'd been eating badly for too long, or maybe it was fear. It was as if all the sounds were echoing in his head, and the earth was moving under his feet.

Mondo looked for a place in the street, on the sidewalk, and he sat there, his back against the wall. Now he waited. A bit farther along, there was a furniture store with a big window that reflected the light. Mondo sat there without moving; he didn't even see the legs of the people walking right in front of him, and who stopped sometimes. He didn't listen to the voices speaking around him. He felt a sort of drowsiness stealing over his entire body, rising like a chill, numbing his lips and preventing his eyes from moving.

His heart wasn't beating very hard anymore; now it was far away and not strong at all, moving slowly in his chest, as if it were on the verge of stopping.

Mondo thought about all his good hiding places, all the ones he knew—by the seaside, in the white rocks, between the breakwaters, or in the garden at the House of the Golden Light. And he thought about the boat, the *Oxyton*, which would tug at its moorings to get away, because it wanted to sail to the Red Sea. But at the same time, it was as if he could not leave this place, on the sidewalk, against this patch of wall; as if his legs could walk no farther.

When the people spoke to him, Mondo did not look up. He remained motionless on the sidewalk, his forehead resting on his forearms. Now there were people's legs that had stopped right in front of him, and they made a semicircle all around him, like the time the Gypsy had given his performance. Mondo thought that they'd do better to go away, to keep walking wherever they were headed. He looked at all those feet stopped there in front of him—the men's big black leather shoes or the women's high-heeled sandals. He heard the voices speaking above him, but he couldn't understand what they were saying.

"Telephone," said the voices. Telephone who? Mondo thought he had become a dog, an old dog with a musky coat sleeping curled up in a ball on the pavement. No one could see him, no one would pay attention to an old yellow dog. He felt the chill spreading through his body, slowly, into his limbs, into his belly, right up to his head.

So the Dogcatcher's gray van was here. In his sleepy state, Mondo had heard it pull up; he had heard the brakes screech and the doors open. But he didn't care. The people's legs had drawn back a little, and Mondo had seen some navy blue pants and black shoes with thick soles coming closer to him.

"Are you sick?"

Mondo heard the voices of the men in uniform. They echoed as if they were thousands of miles away.

"What's your name? Where do you live?"

"You're coming with us now, okay?"

Mondo thought about the hills that were burning all around the town. It was as if he were sitting by the side of the road, and he could see the fields burning, the huge red flames, and he could smell the odor of resin and white smoke rising into the sky; he could even see the red firemen's trucks where they had stopped by the undergrowth, and the long hoses they were unwinding.

"Can you walk?"

The men lifted Mondo from under his shoulders, a light burden, and carried him to the van with its open doors. Mondo felt his legs banging against the ground, against the rungs of the footladder, but it was as if they were not his at all, some puppet's legs made of wood and screws. Then the doors closed with a bang, and the van began to make its way through the town. It was the last time.

TWO DAYS LATER, THE LITTLE VIETNAMESE WOMAN WENT INTO the police chief's office. She was pale, and her eyes were tired, because she hadn't slept. She had waited for Mondo for two nights, and during the day she'd searched for him all over the town. The police chief looked at her without curiosity.

"Are you a relative?"

"No, no," said Thi Chin. She struggled for words. "I'm a—a friend."

She seemed smaller than ever, almost a child despite the wrinkles on her face.

"Do you know where he is?"

The police chief looked at her, in no hurry to reply.

"He's over at the social services."

The little woman repeated, as if she hadn't understood, "The social services . . ."

Then, almost a shout: "It can't be!"

"Why can't it be?" asked the police chief.

"But why? What has he done?"

"He told us he didn't have any family, so that's where he was taken."

"It can't be!" said Thi Chin again. "You don't realize . . ."

The police chief gave her a hard look.

"You are the one who does not realize, Madame," he said. "A child without a family or a home, who was hanging around in the streets with the bums and the beggars, maybe worse! Living like a savage, eating any old thing, sleeping any old place! Besides, his case had already been pointed out to us. There had been some complaints, and we'd been looking for him for a while already, but he was a clever kid, he knew how to hide. It was time for all of that to come to an end."

The little woman was staring straight ahead, and her body was trembling. The police chief took a slightly gentler tone.

"And you—did you look after him, Madame?"

Thi Chin nodded.

"Listen, if you want to take responsibility for the child . . . If you want to become his guardian, it's surely a possibility."

"But he has to get out of—"

"But for the time being he has to stay at the social services until he—until his condition improves. If you want to take charge of him, you'll have to file a request, prepare a case, and it won't happen overnight."

Thi Chin was hunting for the words in her head and couldn't say a thing.

"For the time being, let the administration take care of things. This kid—what's his name, already?"

"Mondo," said Thi Chin. "I—"

"The child is under observation. He has to be treated. They'll look after him at the social services and put together a file. You know that at his age he doesn't know how to read and write, and he's never been to school?"

Thi Chin was trying to speak, but she was too choked up.

"Will I be able to see him?" she managed to say, finally.

"Yes, of course." The chief of police rose to his feet. "In a few days, when he's in better shape, you'll go to see him and you'll get permission from the director."

"But today!" said Thi Chin. She was shouting again, and her voice grew hoarse. "It's today, it's today that I have to see him!"

"No, that's out of the question. You cannot see him for four or five days."

"Please, I beg you! It's very important for him, now!"

The chief of police led Thi Chin to the door.

"Not for four or five days."

Just as he was about to open the door, he paused.

"Give me your name and your address, so we can reach you."

He wrote it down in an old notebook.

"Good. Call me in two days so we can start the file." But the next day, the chief of police came to Thi Chin's house. He opened the gate and walked along the gravel path to the front door.

When Thi Chin opened, he walked right in, almost forcing his way, and he looked into the big living room.

"Your Mondo," he began.

"What has happened to him?" asked Thi Chin. She was even paler than the other day, and she looked up at the police chief with fear in her eyes.

"He's gone."

"Gone?"

"Yes, gone, vanished. Into thin air!"

Over Thi Chin's head, the policeman observed the interior of the house.

"You haven't seen him, by any chance? He didn't come this way?"

"No!" shouted Thi Chin.

"He set fire to his mattress at the infirmary and got away during the panic. I thought you might have seen him go by?"

"No! No!" shouted Thi Chin again. Now her narrow eyes were shining with anger. The chief of police stepped back.

"Listen, I came right away to warn you. We have to find this boy, before he does any more foolish things."

The chief of police headed down the semicircular stairs from the porch.

"If he comes back here, let me know!"

He was already on the gravel path, on his way out, by the gate.

"I told you the other day. He's a savage."

Standing on the threshold, Thi Chin did not move. Her eyes filled with tears and her throat was so dry that she could not breathe.

"You don't understand a thing, not a thing!" She spoke in a low voice, to herself, while the police chief pushed the gate shut and hurried down the steps along the path to his black car.

Then Thi Chin sat down on the white steps. For a long time she did not move, did not look at the golden light that was filling the big empty living room, did not listen to the shrill chirring of the hidden cricket. She was crying, unaware, and her tears fell onto her blue apron. She knew that the child with the ash-colored hair would not come back the next day or any of the days after that. Summer was about to begin, but the weather seemed cold. All of us here, in this town, felt it. People continued to come and go, selling and buying, and cars continued to drive through the streets and along the avenues, making a lot of noise with their engines and their horns. From time to time, in the blue sky, a plane flew overhead, leaving a long white vapor trail. Beggars continued to beg, at the foot of a wall, or at the door to the town hall, or outside the churches. But it wasn't the same. It was as if there were an invisible cloud covering the earth, preventing the light from shining full and whole.

Things weren't the same anymore. Moreover, not long afterward, the Gypsy was arrested by the police, on a day when people realized that his prestidigitation extended to the pockets of passers-by, too. The Cossack was a drunkard who wasn't even a Cossack, since he was born in the Auvergne. Giordan the Fisherman broke his fishing lines on the breakwater, and he would never go to Eritrea, nor anywhere else for that matter. Old Dadi finally left the hospital, but he never found his doves, and in their place he bought a cat. The Sunday painter did not manage to paint the sky, and he started drawing seascapes and still lifes again, and the little boy in the public garden got his beautiful red tricycle stolen. As for the old man with a face like an Indian, he went on raking his patch of beach and didn't leave for the banks of the Ganges. At the end of its mooring line, fastened to the rusty ring on the pier, the *Oxyton* stayed all alone, rocking on the harbor waters amidst the diesel slick, and no one came to sit in the stern to sing her a song.

Years, months, days went by, without Mondo now, because it was a time that was both too long and too short, and many people here, in our town, were waiting for someone, but they didn't dare say who. Often, without realizing, we looked for him in the crowd, along the street, outside the door. We looked at the white pebbles on the beach and the sea that is like a wall. And then we forgot, a bit.

One day, long afterward, the little Vietnamese woman was walking in her garden at the top of the hill. She sat under the bay laurel bush where there were a lot of tiger mosquitoes dancing in the air, and she picked up a strange pebble polished by seawater. She saw something had been carved along the edge of the pebble, half erased by the dust. Carefully, her heartbeat quickening, she wiped the dust off with a corner of her apron, and she saw three words written in clumsy capital letters:

ALWAYS   VERY MUCH

Lullaby

THE DAY THAT LULLABY DECIDED SHE WOULDN'T GO TO SCHOOL anymore, it was still very early in the morning, toward the middle of October. She got out of her bed, crossed the room in her bare feet, and peeked outside through the slats of the blinds. There was a lot of sunshine, and if you leaned forward a bit, you could see a patch of blue sky. Down on the sidewalk three or four pigeons were hopping along, their feathers ruffled by the wind. The sea beyond the roofs of the parked cars was dark blue, and a white sailboat was painfully working its way forward. Lullaby looked at it all and felt relieved that she had decided not to go to school anymore.

She went back to the middle of her room and sat at her table, and without switching on the light she began to write a letter.

Hi my dear Ppa.
The weather is fine today, the sky the way I like it, very very blue.
I wish you were here to see the sky. The sea is also very very blue.
Soon it will be winter. Another very long year is starting. I hope you
can come soon because I don't know if the sky and the sea will wait
much longer for you. This morning when I woke up (it was over an
hour ago) I thought I was in Istanbul again. I would like to close my
eyes and when I open them again it would be like in Istanbul. Do
you remember? You bought two bouquets of flowers, one for me
and one for sister Laurence. Big white flowers that smelled strong
(is that why they're called aroma lilies?). They smelled so strong that
we had to put them in the bathroom. You told us you could drink
water from them, so I went to the bathroom and I drank for a long
time, and my flowers were all ruined. Do you remember?

Lullaby stopped writing. She chewed on the end of her blue ballpoint pen for a moment, staring at the stationery. But she wasn't reading. She was just looking at the whiteness of the paper, and she thought maybe something would appear, like birds in the sky, or a little white boat going slowly by.

She looked at the alarm clock on the table: 8:10. It was a little travel clock, in a black lizard-skin case, and you only had to wind it every eight days.

Lullaby wrote on the sheet of paper.

Dear Ppa, I'd like you to come and get the alarm clock. You gave it to me before I left Tehran and mommy and sister Laurence said it was very nice. I think it's very nice, too, but I think I won't need it any more now. That's why I'd like you to come and get it. You can use it again. It works fine. It doesn't make any noise during the night.

She placed the letter in an air-mail envelope. Before closing the envelope, she hunted for something else to slip inside. But there was nothing on the table but papers and books and toast crumbs. So she wrote the address on the envelope.

Mr. Paul Ferlande
P.R.O.C.O.M.
84, avenue Ferdowski
Tehran
Iran

She placed the envelope on the edge of the table and went quickly to the bathroom to brush her teeth and wash her face. She felt like taking a cold shower, but she was afraid the noise would wake her mother. Still barefoot, she went back to her room. She quickly got dressed, in a green sweater and brown velvet pants and a dark brown jacket. Then she pulled on her socks and her ankle boots with the crepe soles. She combed her blond hair without even looking at herself in the mirror, and into her bag she crammed everything she saw around her on the table and on the chair: lipstick, paper handkerchiefs, ballpoint pen, keys, tube of aspirin. She didn't know exactly what she might need, so she hastily grabbed things from her room, any old how: a red scarf rolled up in a ball, an old leatherette photo album, a penknife, a little porcelain dog. She opened a shoebox in the cupboard and took out a packet of letters. In another box she found a big drawing that she folded and put in her bag with the letters. In the pocket of her raincoat she found a few banknotes and a handful of coins that she dropped into her bag, too. Just as she was about to go out, she went back to the table and took the letter she had just written. She opened the left-hand drawer and rummaged among the objects and papers until she found a little harmonica engraved with the words

ECHO Super Vamper GERMANY MADE IN

and, etched with the tip of a knife,

david

She looked at the harmonica for a second, then she dropped it into the bag, placed the strap over her right shoulder, and went out.

Outside, the sun was hot, the sky and the sea were dazzling. Lullaby looked for the pigeons, but they had disappeared. In the distance, near the horizon, the white sailboat was moving slowly, leaning against the sea.

Lullaby felt her heart pounding. It seemed to be thudding noisily in her breast. Why was it in such a state? Perhaps it was all the light in the sky, making it drunk. Lullaby stopped against the railing, squeezing her arms tight against her chest. She even hissed, between her teeth, somewhat angrily, "What a pain, stupid thing!"

Then she set off again, trying not to pay any attention to her heartbeat.

People were on their way to work. They sped along in their cars, down the avenue, toward the center of town. Mopeds chased each other in a din of whirring metal. In their new cars, windows closed, people looked like they were in a hurry. When they went by, they turned around slightly to look at Lullaby. There were even men who gave little toots with their car horns, but Lullaby didn't look at them.

She too was walking quickly down the avenue, noiselessly, on her crepe-soled shoes. She was headed the opposite way, toward the hills and the rocks. She had to squint to look at the sea because she'd forgotten to take her dark glasses. The white sailboat seemed to be following her own route, with its big triangular sail ballooning in the wind. As she walked, Lullaby looked at the blue sea and sky, the white sail, and the rocks on the headland, and she was very happy she'd decided not to go to school anymore. Everything was so beautiful; it was as if school had never existed.

The wind blew her hair, tangling it, a cold wind that stung her eyes and reddened the skin on her cheeks and hands. Lullaby thought it was good to be walking like this in the sun and the wind, without a clue where she was headed.

When she had left the town behind, she came to the smugglers' path. The path started in the middle of a grove of umbrella pines and made its way along the coast, to the rocks. The sea here was even more beautiful, intense, bathed with light.

Lullaby went along the smugglers' path and saw that the sea had risen. The short waves crashed against the rocks, creating an undertow that swept deep then surged back again. The young girl stopped among the rocks to listen to the sea. She knew the sound well, the water slapping and breaking, then merging and exploding into the air; it was something she liked, but today it was as if she were hearing it for the first time. There was nothing else there but white rocks, the sea, the wind, the sun. It was like being on a boat, far out to sea, where the tuna and dolphins live.

Lullaby wasn't even thinking about school anymore. The sea is like that: it erases things from the earth because it is the most important thing in the world. The vast blue, the vast light, the wind, the sound of the waves, violent or gentle, and the sea resembled a huge beast swaying its head and whipping the air with its tail.

Lullaby felt good. She sat on a flat rock by the edge of the smugglers' path and looked around her. She saw the sharp horizon, the black line separating sea from sky. She didn't think about streets any more, or houses, or cars, or motorcycles.

She stayed for a long time on her rock. Then she continued along the path. There were no more houses; the last villas were behind her. Lullaby turned around to look at them, and she thought they looked odd, with their shutters closed against white façades, as if they were asleep. There were no more gardens here. On the rocky ground there were strange, heavy plants, round tufts pricked with quills, yellow prickly pears covered with scars, aloe plants, thorns, creepers. No one lived here. Only lizards, running between the slabs of stone, and two or three wasps flying above the honey-scented grasses.

The sun was burning strong in the sky. The white rocks sparkled, and the foam was dazzling as snow. You could be happy here, as if you were at the ends of the earth. You no longer expected a thing, you didn't need a soul. Lullaby watched as the headland grew, the cliff sheered off into the sea. The smugglers' path led to a German bunker, and you had to go down through a narrow underground passageway. The cold air in the tunnel made the girl shiver. The air was damp and dark like the interior of a cave. The walls of the fortress smelled of mold and urine. On the other side of the tunnel you came out onto a cement platform surrounded by a low wall. Small tufts of grass grew in the cracks in the ground.

Lullaby closed her eyes, dazzled by the light. She was directly facing the sea and the wind.

All of a sudden, on the wall of the platform, she saw the first signs. Written in chalk, in large irregular letters that said:

"FIND ME"

Lullaby looked around her for a moment, then she said, in a subdued voice, "Yes, but who are you?"

A large white tern flew over the platform, shrieking.

Lullaby shrugged her shoulders and continued on her way. It was more difficult from here on, because the smugglers' path had been destroyed. It might have been during the last war, by those who had built the bunker. You had to climb and jump from one rock to the next, using your hands to keep from slipping. The coast was steeper and steeper, and far below her Lullaby could see the deep emerald-colored water pounding against the rocks.

Fortunately, she was good at walking in the rocks; in fact it was what she did best. You have to reckon very quickly with your eyes to see where the good footholds are, the rocks that will act as stairs or springboards; you have to gauge which way will lead you up. You have to avoid the dead ends, the crumbling stones, the crevices, the thorny bushes.

It could be a problem for math class. "A rock with an angle of 45 degrees and another rock at a distance of 2.5 meters from a clump of broom, where will the tangent lie?" The white rocks were like desks, and Lullaby imagined Mademoiselle Lorti's strict face looking down imposingly on a large rock in the shape of a trapezoid, her back turned to the sea. But maybe it wasn't really a problem for math class. Here, above all, you had to work out the center of gravity. "Trace a line perpendicular to the horizontal to indicate clearly the direction," said Monsieur Filippi. He was standing balanced on a leaning rock, smiling indulgently. His white hair was a crown in the sunlight, and behind his bottle-bottom glasses his blue eyes shone strangely.

Lullaby was pleased to discover that her body could find the solution to the problems so easily. She leaned forward, backward, balanced on one leg, then jumped, supple, and her feet landed exactly where she intended.

"This is very, very good, Mademoiselle," said Monsieur Filippi's voice in her ear. "Physics is a science of nature, never forget that. Continue like that, you're on the right path."

"Yes, but to go where?" murmured Lullaby.

In fact, she didn't really know where it would take her. To catch her breath, she stopped again and looked at the sea, but there, too, there was a problem, because she had to calculate the angle of refraction of sunlight on the surface of the water.

"I'll never manage," she thought.

"Come now, apply Descartes's laws," said Monsieur Filippi's voice in her ear.

Lullaby made an effort to remember.

"The refracted ray . . ."

". . . always remains in the plane of incidence," said Lullaby.

Filippi: "Right. The second law?"

"When the angle of incidence is increased, the angle of refraction increases and the ratio of the sines of these angles is constant."

"Constant," said the voice. "Therefore?"

"Sin i/Sin r = constant."

"Index of water/air?"

"1.33."

"Foucault's law?"

"The index of one medium in relation to another is equal to the relation of the speed of the first medium to the second."

"Which gives us?"

"$N_{2/1} = v_1/v_2$."

But the sun's rays constantly rose from the sea, and they went so quickly from the state of refraction to the state of total reflection that Lullaby did not manage to do the calculations. She thought at some point she would write to Monsieur Filippi to ask him.

It was really hot. The young girl looked for a place where she could swim. A bit farther along she found a tiny inlet where there was a ruined jetty. Lullaby went down to the water's edge and took off her clothes.

The water was very transparent, cold. Lullaby jumped in without hesitating, and she felt the water tightening the pores of her skin. She swam for a long time underwater, her eyes open. Then she sat on the cement jetty to dry off. Now the sun was at its zenith, and the light no longer reverberated. It shone very bright within the droplets clinging to the skin on her stomach and the fine hair on her thighs.

The icy water had done her good. It had cleansed the ideas in her head, and the young girl no longer thought about tangents or absolute indexes of bodies. She felt like writing another letter to her father. She looked for the pad of air-mail paper in her bag and began to write with her ballpoint pen, starting right at the bottom of the page. Her wet hands left traces on the paper.

LLBY
sends kisses
come quick see me where I am!

Then in the middle of the sheet she wrote:

Maybe I've done something silly. Don't be mad at me. I really felt like I was in a prison. You have no idea. Well, maybe you do, but you had the courage to stay, and I don't. Imagine all those walls everywhere, so many walls that you couldn't even count them, with barbed wire, and fences, and bars on the windows! Imagine the yard with all those trees I hate, chestnut trees and linden trees and plane trees. The plane trees are especially horrible, they lose their skin, they look like they're sick!

A bit higher up she wrote:

You know, there are so many things I would like. So many, many, many things I would like, I don't know if I could begin to tell you. Things that are really missing here, things I loved to see in the old days. Green grass, flowers, birds, rivers. If you were here, you could talk to me about them and I'd see them appear all around me, but at the lycée there's no one who knows how to talk about things like that. The girls are so stupid you could cry! The boys are idiots. All they care about is their motorbikes and leather jackets!

Then she went right up to the top of the page.

Hello, dear Ppa. I'm writing to you from a little tiny beach, it's so tiny I think it really is a beach for one person, with a ruined jetty where I'm sitting (I just had a nice swim). The sea would like to eat the little beach, it's lapping with its tongue all the way across the sand, and there's no way to keep dry! There will be a lot of spots of seawater on my letter, I hope you'll like that. I'm all alone here, but I'm having a good time. I'm not going to school at all anymore, I've decided, it's over. I'll never go back, even if they have to put me in jail. Anyway it couldn't be any worse.

There was not much space left on the sheet of paper. So Lullaby had fun filling in the spaces, one after the other, writing words and phrases at random:

"The sea is blue."

"Sun."

"Send white orchids."

"Too bad the wooden cabin isn't here."

"Write to me."

"There's a boat sailing by, where's it going?"

"I would like to be on a high mountaintop."

"Tell me what the light is like where you are."

"Tell me about the coral fishermen."

"How is Sloughi?"

She filled the last remaining blank spaces with words:

"Seaweed"

"Mirror"

"Far"

"Fireflies"

"Rally"

"Swing"

"Coriander"

"Star"

Then she folded the paper and put it into an envelope, with the leaf from an herb that smelled like honey.

When she climbed back up through the rocks, for the second time she saw strange signs written in chalk on the rocks. There were arrows, too, to show which way to go. On a big flat rock, she read:

"DON'T GIVE UP!"

And a bit farther along:

"IT MAY COME TO AN ABRUPT END"

Lullaby looked around her yet again, but there was no one in the rocks, as far as she could see. So she continued on her way. She climbed, went back down, jumped over the cracks, and in the end she came to the tip of the headland, where there was a broad flat space of stone, and the Greek house.

Lullaby stopped, full of wonder. She had never seen such a beautiful house. It was built in the middle of the rocks and the succulents, facing the sea, a little square house, simple, with a veranda held up by six columns, and it looked like a miniature temple. It was dazzling white, silent, tucked in against the steep cliff that sheltered it from the wind and from view.

Lullaby went slowly up to the house, her heart pounding. There was no one around, and it must have been abandoned years ago, because the grass and the creepers had invaded the veranda, and morning glories were curling around the columns.

When Lullaby was quite close to the house, she saw there was a word carved above the door, in the plaster of the peristyle:

ΧΑΡΙΣΜΑ

Lullaby read the name out loud, and she thought that she had never seen such a beautiful name for a house.

A rusty wire fence surrounded the house. Lullaby went along the fence to find a way in. She found a spot where there was a gap between the ground and the fence, and that was where she went through, on all fours. She wasn't afraid—everything was silent. Lullaby walked through the garden to the steps to the veranda and stopped outside the front door. After a moment's hesitation, she went through the door. The interior of the house was dark, and she had to wait for her eyes to adjust. Then she saw a single room with damaged walls, and the floor was littered with debris, old rags, and newspapers. It was cold inside the house. The windows had probably not been opened for years. Lullaby tried to open the shutters, but they were stuck. When her eyes had adjusted to the semidarkness, Lullaby saw she was not the only one who had come in here. The walls were covered with graffiti and obscene drawings. It made her angry, as if the house were hers. She tried to wipe off the graffiti with a rag. Then she went back out on the veranda, and she pulled the door so hard behind her that the handle broke off and she nearly fell over.

But outside, the house was lovely. Lullaby sat on the veranda, her back against a column, and she looked at the sea below her. It felt good, like this, with nothing but the sound of the water and the wind blowing between the white columns. When you looked through the tall columns, the sky and the sea seemed endless. You were no longer on earth, here; you had no more roots. Lullaby breathed slowly, her back very straight and her neck pressed against the warm column, and every time the air came into her lungs it was as if she were rising ever higher into the pure sky, above the disc of the sea. The horizon was a thin thread that curved like an arc, the light sent out its rectilinear rays, and you were in a different world, on the edge of a prism.

Lullaby heard a voice on the wind, speaking close to her ears. It wasn't Monsieur Filippi's voice now but a very ancient voice that had traveled through the sky and the sea. The gentle, somewhat grave voice echoed around her in the warm light, repeating the name she used to use, the name her father had given her one day as she was drifting off to sleep.

"Ariel . . . Ariel . . ."

Very softly at first, then louder and louder, Lullaby sang the air she had not forgotten after so many years:

"Where the bee sucks, there suck I;
In the cowslip's bell I lie:
There I couch when the owls do cry
On the bat's back I do fly
After summer merrily:
Merrily, merrily shall I live now,
Under the blossom that hangs on the bough."

Her clear voice rang into the open air, carried her above the sea. She saw everything, beyond the misty coastline, beyond the towns, the mountains. She saw the wide route of the sea, where the rows of waves advanced; she saw everything all the way to the far shore, the long strip of dark gray land where cedar forests grew, and even farther, like a mirage, the snowy summit of Kuhha-Ye Alborz.

Lullaby stayed sitting against the column for a long time, looking at the sea and singing Ariel's song to herself, and other songs her father had made up. She stayed until the sun was very near the thread of the horizon and the sea had turned violet. Then she left the Greek house and set off along the smugglers' path again in the direction of the town. When she came alongside the bunker, she noticed a little boy who was on his way home from fishing. He turned around to wait for her.

"Good evening!" said Lullaby.

"Hi!" said the little boy.

He had a serious face, and his blue eyes were hidden by glasses. He was carrying a long fishing rod and a creel, and he'd slung his shoes around his neck to walk.

They went together along the path, chatting. When they got to the end of the path, there were still a few minutes of daylight left, and they sat on the rocks to look at the sea. The little boy put his shoes on. He told Lullaby the story of his glasses. He said that one day, a few years ago, he had wanted to watch an eclipse of the sun, and since that time the sun had left its mark in his eyes.

In the meantime, night was falling. They saw the lamp at the lighthouse come on, then the streetlamps and the beacons for airplanes. The water had turned black. Then the little boy with the glasses got up. He picked up his fishing rod and his satchel, and he waved to Lullaby before he went away.

When he was already some distance away, Lullaby called, "Make a drawing for me, tomorrow!"

The little boy nodded.

2

Lullaby had been going over to the Greek house for several days now. She liked the moment when, after jumping over all the rocks, out of breath from running and climbing everywhere, a bit drunk on the wind and the light, she saw the mysterious white silhouette etched against the wall of the cliff, like a boat at its mooring. The weather was beautiful at that time, the sky and the sea were blue, and the horizon was so pure that you could see the crests of the waves. When Lullaby arrived outside the house she would stop; her heart beat faster and stronger, and she felt a strange warmth in the veins of her body, because there was surely a secret here, in this place.

The wind dropped all of a sudden, and she felt all the sunlight gently enfolding her, electrifying her hair and her skin. She breathed more deeply, the way you do before a long swim underwater.

She walked slowly around the wire fence to the opening. She went up to the house, looking at the six regular columns, white with light. She read the magical word written in the plaster of the peristyle out loud, and perhaps it was because of the word that there was so much peace and light in that place:

"Kharisma . . ."

The word radiated throughout her body, as if it were also written inside her and was waiting for her. Lullaby sat on the ground by the veranda, her back against the last column on the right, and she looked at the sea.

The sun was burning her face. The beams of light emerged from inside her, from her fingers, her eyes, her mouth, her hair, and went to sparkle against the rocks and the waves.

There was the silence, above all, a silence so great, so strong, that Lullaby felt as if she would die. Very quickly the life drained out of her and went elsewhere, into the sky and the sea. It was hard to understand, but Lullaby was certain that this must be what death felt like. Her body stayed where it was, sitting with her back against the white column, all wrapped in heat and light. But all movement vanished, dissolved before her. She could not hold it back. She felt everything that was leaving her, escaping from her so quickly, like the flight of starlings, like whirlwinds of dust. She felt it in any movement of her arms and legs, all the inner trembling, shivers, and starts. It left so quickly, shooting out into space toward the light and the sea. But it was a pleasant feeling and Lullaby did not resist. She did not close her eyes. Her pupils dilated; she looked straight ahead, unblinking, always at the same spot on the thin thread of the horizon, where there was the fold between the sky and the sea.

Her breathing slowed still more, and in her chest her heart beat more and more slowly. There was almost no more movement, almost no more life in her, only her gaze expanding, mingling with space like a ray of light. Lullaby felt her body opening very gently, like a door, and she waited to join the sea. She knew she would see it soon, so she didn't think about anything—there was nothing else she wanted. Her body would stay far behind; it would be like the white columns and the walls covered with plaster, motionless, silent. That was the secret of the house. To arrive at the highest point of the sea, right at the summit of the great blue wall, at the place where at last you can see what is on the far side. Lullaby's gaze expanded, glided on the air, the light, above the water.

Her body was not getting cold, like the dead in their death chambers. The light continued to enter, to the depth of her organs, to the core of her bones, and she was living at the temperature of the air, the way lizards do.

Lullaby was like a cloud, a vapor; she mingled with whatever surrounded her. She was like the scent of pine trees warmed by the sun on the hills, like the scent of the grass that smelled of honey. She was the spindrift of the waves where a quicksilver rainbow shines. She was the wind, the cold breath that comes from the sea, the warm breath from the fermented earth beneath the bushes. She was salt, the salt that shines like frost on the old stones, or the salt of the sea, the heavy acrid salt of underwater ravines. There was no longer just one Lullaby sitting on the veranda of an old ruined pseudo-Greek villa. There were as many Lullabies as there were glints of light on the waves.

Lullaby saw with all her eyes, wherever she looked. She saw things she could never have imagined before. Tiny things—insects' hiding places, worms' galleries. She saw the leaves of the succulents, the roots. She saw very big things—the underbellies of the clouds, the stars behind the screen of the sky, the polar icecaps, the immense valleys and infinite peaks at the depths of the sea. She saw it all in the same instant, and each gaze lasted months, years. But she saw without understanding, because it was the discrete movements of her body, traveling through the space ahead of her.

It was as if she could at last, after death, examine the laws that form the world. They were strange laws, laws that were nothing like the ones written in books that you learn by heart at school. There was the law of the horizon that attracts the body, a very long and thin law, one single hard line uniting the two mobile spheres of sky and sea. There, everything was born, multiplied, forming flights of numbers and signs that obscured the sun and grew more and more distant, fading toward the unknown. There was the law of the sea, without beginning or end, where the rays of light were shattered. There was the law of the sky, the law of the wind, the law of the sun, but you could not understand those laws, because their signs did not belong to mankind.

Later, when Lullaby awoke, she tried to remember what she had seen. She would have liked to write it all down for Monsieur Filippi, because perhaps he would have understood what all those signs and numbers meant. But she could only recall snatches of sentences, which she repeated out loud several times over:

"Where we drink the sea . . ."

"The fulcrum of the horizon . . ."

"The wheels (or the ways) of the sea . . ."

She shrugged her shoulders, because it didn't really make much sense.

Then Lullaby got up from where she was sitting, went out of the garden of the Greek house, and down to the sea. The wind had returned all at once, furiously tossing her hair and her clothes, as if to put everything back where it belonged.

Lullaby liked that wind. She wanted to give it things, because the wind needs to eat often—leaves, dust and dirt, gentlemen's hats, or the little drops it scoops up from the sea and the clouds.

Lullaby sat down in a hollow between two rocks, so close to the water that the waves came to lap against her feet. The sun beat down on the sea, dazzling her, reverberating on the crests of the waves.

There was absolutely no one else there, only the sun and the wind and the sea, and Lullaby reached into her bag for the packet of letters. She pulled them out one by one, moving the rubber band to one side, and she read a few words, a few expressions, at random. Sometimes she did not understand, and she would read out loud to make it more true.

". . . The red cloths floating like flags . . ."

"The yellow narcissi on my desk, right by the window, do you see them, Ariel?"

"I hear your voice, you're speaking in the air . . ."

". . . Ariel, air of Ariel . . ."

"It's for you, so that you'll always remember."

Lullaby tossed the sheets of paper into the wind. They blew away, quickly, with a tearing sound; they flew for a moment above the sea, reeling like butterflies in the gusts. They were bluish sheets of air-mail paper, then they disappeared all at once into the sea. It felt good to be tossing these sheets of paper into the wind, scattering their words, and Lullaby watched with joy as the wind swallowed them.

She felt like building a fire. She looked among the rocks for a place where the wind would not blow too hard. A bit farther along she came to the little inlet with the ruined pier, and that was where she set up camp.

It was a fine spot to make a fire. The white rocks surrounded the pier, and the gusts of wind could not reach her there. At the base of the rock, there was a hollow that was dry and warm, and right away the flames rose—light, pale, with a gentle crackling. Lullaby kept feeding new sheets of paper to the fire. They flared up at once, because they were very dry and thin, and they burned up in an instant.

It was good to see the blue pages twisting in the flames and the words escaping as if backward, who knows where. Lullaby thought that her father would have liked to have been there to see his letters burning, because he did not write words that were meant to keep. He had told her so, one day, on the beach, and he had put a letter in an old blue bottle and tossed it far out to sea. He had written words that were meant only for her, so that she would read them and hear the sound of his voice, and now the words could go back to the place whence they had come, just like that, quickly, in light and smoke, in the air, and become invisible. Maybe someone, on the far side of the sea, would see the little column of smoke and the flame shining like a mirror, and he would understand.

Lullaby fed the fire with little pieces of wood, twigs, dried seaweed, to make the flames last. There were all sorts of smells that escaped into the air: the light and somewhat sweet smell of the air-mail paper, the strong smell of charcoal and wood, the heavy smoke of the seaweed.

Lullaby watched the words as they hurried away, so quickly that they pierced thought like lightning. From time to time she recognized them as they burned, or they became distorted and strange, twisted by the fire, and she laughed:

"raaaiiin!"

"navre!"

"eeelan!"

"etetetete!"

"Awiel, iel, eeel . . ."

Suddenly she felt a presence behind her, and she turned around. It was the little boy with the glasses; he was staring at her, standing on a rock up above. He had his fishing rod in his hand and his shoes tied around his shoulders, as always.

"Why are you burning those papers?" he asked.

Lullaby gave him a smile.

"Because it's fun," she said. "Look!"

She set fire to a big blue page with the drawing of a tree.

"They really burn," said the little boy.

"You see, they really wanted to burn," explained Lullaby. "They've been waiting for a long time. They were as dry as dead leaves, that's why they burn so well."

The little boy with the glasses put down his fishing rod and went to collect twigs for the fire. They amused themselves for a good while, burning everything they could. Lullaby's hands were black with smoke, and her eyes stung. Both of them were very tired and breathless from having tended the fire. Now the fire too seemed a bit tired. Its flames were smaller, and the twigs and the paper went out, one after the other.

"The fire is going to go out," said the little boy, wiping his glasses.

"That's because there are no more letters. It's what he wanted."

The little boy pulled a piece of paper folded in four from his pocket.

"What's that?" asked Lullaby. She took the sheet and opened it. It was a drawing of a woman with a black face. Lullaby recognized her green cardigan.

"Is this my drawing?"

"I made it for you," said the little boy. "But we can burn it."

But Lullaby folded the drawing and watched as the fire went out.

"You don't want to burn it now?" asked the little boy.

"No, not today," said Lullaby.

After the fire, it was the smoke that died. The wind blew over the ashes.

"I'll burn it when I have begun to love it very much," said Lullaby.

They stayed sitting on the pier for a long time, looking at the sea, hardly speaking. The wind blew over the sea, raising drops of spray that stung their faces. It was like sitting in the bow of a boat, out at sea. All you could hear was the sound of the waves and the endless whistling of the wind.

When the sun had reached its zenith, the little boy with the glasses picked up his fishing rod and his shoes.

"I'm going," he said.

"Don't you want to stay?"

"I can't, I have to go home."

Lullaby stood up, too.

"Are you going to stay here?" asked the little boy.

"No, I'm going to have a look over there, farther along."

She pointed to the rocks at the end of the headland.

"Over there, there's another house, but it's much bigger. It looks like a theatre," explained the little boy. "You have to climb up the rocks and then you can get in from below."

"Have you already been there?"

"Yes, many times. It's beautiful, but it's hard to get there."

The little boy with the glasses put his shoes around his neck and hurried away.

"Good-bye!" said Lullaby.

"Bye!" said the little boy.

Lullaby walked toward the end of the headland. She was practically running, jumping from one rock to the next. There were no more paths over here. You had to climb the rocks, clinging to the roots of the heather and the grasses. It was a faraway place, lost in the middle of the white rocks, suspended between sky and sea. Despite the chill wind, Lullaby could feel the sun burning. Under her clothes she was sweating. Her bag bothered her, and she decided to hide it somewhere and pick it up again later. She stuffed it into a hollow spot in the ground, at the foot of a big aloe. She covered the hiding place by pushing two or three stones over it.

Above her now was the strange cement house the little boy had talked about. To get there, you had to climb up a mass of scree-covered slope. The white ruin shone in the sunlight. Lullaby hesitated for a moment, because everything was so strange and silent in this place. Above the sea, clinging to a rocky wall, the long cement walls had no windows.

A seabird drew circles above the ruins, and Lullaby suddenly wanted very much to be up there. She began to climb up the scree-covered slope. The sharp-edged stones scraped her hands and knees, and little landslides followed in her wake. When she had made it to the top of the slope, she turned around to look at the sea, and she had to close her eyes to keep from feeling dizzy. Below her, as far as you could see, there was nothing else: the sea. Immense, blue, filling the space all the way to the expanded horizon, and it was like a never-ending roof, a giant dome made of dark metal, where all the ridges of the waves were moving. In places the sun flared on the sea, and Lullaby could see the marks and the dark streaks of the currents, forests of seaweed, traces of spume. The wind swept the sea incessantly, flattening its surface.

Lullaby opened her eyes and looked at everything, clinging to the rocks with her nails. The sea was so beautiful; she felt as if it were going through her head and her body at great speed, as if it were hurrying thousands of thoughts at once.

Slowly, very carefully, Lullaby approached the ruins. It was just as the little boy with the glasses had said—a sort of theater, made of great walls of reinforced cement. Vegetation grew between the high walls, brambles and creepers that completely covered the ground. Above the walls, the concrete tile roof had caved in here and there. The wind from the sea was sucked in through the gaping holes on either side of the building, with violent gusts that rattled the iron struts of the roof's framework. The struts banged together, making a strange noise, and Lullaby stayed there motionless, listening. It was like the cries of the terns, like the murmur of the waves, a strange, unreal music without any rhythm, a noise that made you shiver. Lullaby walked on. Along the outside wall there was a narrow path that cut through the under-growth and led to a half-demolished staircase. Lullaby went up the stairs and came to a platform beneath the roof, and through a breach you could look out over the sea. That was where Lullaby sat down, facing the horizon, in the sun, and she looked at the sea again. Then she closed her eyes.

Suddenly she was startled because she sensed that someone was coming. There was no sound other than the wind rattling the iron struts of the roof, and yet she sensed danger. On the far side of the ruins, on the path through the brambles, someone was coming. A shaggy-haired man, wearing blue canvas trousers and a jacket, his face blackened by the sun. He walked without making a sound, stopping from time to time as if he were looking for something. Lullaby stayed motionless against the wall, her heart pounding, and she hoped he hadn't seen her. Without really understanding why, she knew that the man was looking for her, and she held her breath so he wouldn't hear her. But when the man was halfway along the path, he calmly lifted his gaze and stared at the young girl. His green eyes shone strangely in his dark face. Without hurrying, he began walking toward the stairway. It was too late to go back down; in a single bound Lullaby was through the breach and out onto the roof. The wind was blowing so hard that she nearly fell. As quickly as she could she began to run toward the other end of the roof, and she heard the sound of her feet echoing in the huge ruined theater. Her heart was beating wildly in her chest. When she reached the end of the roof, she stopped: just ahead a deep gap separated her from the wall of the cliff. She listened all around. There was still nothing but the sound of the wind in the iron struts on the roof, but she knew that the stranger was not far away; he was running on the path through the brambles to make his way around the ruins and cut her off. So Lullaby jumped. As she fell onto the slope of the cliff, her left ankle twisted beneath her, and she felt a sharp pain; she only cried out, "Oh!"

Suddenly the man was there before her, and she could not understand where he had come from. His hands had been scratched by the brambles and he was out of breath. He stood before her, not moving, his green eyes hard, like little chips of glass. Was he the one who had written the messages in chalk on the rocks, all along the path? Or had he gone into the lovely Greek house and dirtied the walls with all those obscene messages? He was so close to Lullaby that she could smell him, a faint acrid smell of sweat impregnating his clothes and his hair. Suddenly, he took a step forward, his mouth open, his eyes narrowed. Despite the pain in her ankle, Lullaby leapt forward and began to scramble down the slope amid an avalanche of pebbles. When she got to the bottom of the cliff, she stopped and turned around. In front of the white walls of the ruin, the man was standing, his arms outspread, as if to keep his balance.

The sun beat down on the sea, and thanks to the cold wind, Lullaby could feel her strength returning. She also felt disgust and anger gradually replacing her fear. Now she understood that nothing could ever happen to her, ever. It was the wind, the sea, the sun. She remembered what her father had told her one day, about the wind, the sea, the sun, a long sentence that spoke of freedom, and space, something like that. Lullaby stopped on a rock that was the shape of a ship's prow, above the sea, and she threw her head back, the better to feel the heat of the light on her forehead and her eyelids. It was her father who had taught her how to do this, to regain her strength; he called it "drinking the sun."

Lullaby looked at the swell of the sea beneath her as it pounded against the base of the rock, swirling, tossing up clouds of fleeting bubbles. She plunged head first into the wave. The cold water enveloped her, pressing on her eardrums and nostrils, and her eyes were dazzled with light. When she came back up to the surface, she shook her hair and let out a cry. Far behind her, like an immense gray cargo ship, the earth seemed to vibrate with its load of stones and plants. At the top of the hill, the ruined white house was like a footbridge open onto the sky.

Lullaby let herself be carried for a moment in the slow movement of the waves, and her clothes clung to her skin like seaweed. Then she began to swim, a very slow crawl, out to sea, until she rounded the headland and could see far in the distance, scarcely visible through the haze cloud of heat, the pale line of the town's buildings.

3

IT COULD NOT LAST FOREVER. LULLABY KNEW THAT PERFECTLY
well. First of all there were all those people at school and in the street.
They said things, they talked too much. There were even girls who
stopped Lullaby to tell her she was going too far, that the headmistress
and everybody knew perfectly well that she wasn't sick. And then
there were the letters asking for an explanation. Lullaby had opened
the letters, and she had replied signing her mother's name; she had
even phoned the vice-principal's office one day, imitating her mother's
voice to explain that her daughter was sick, very sick, and couldn't
return to class.

But it couldn't last, thought Lullaby. And then there was Monsieur
Filippi, who had written a letter, not a very long one, a strange letter asking her to come back. Lullaby had put the letter in her jacket
pocket, and she always had it on her. She would have liked to reply
to Monsieur Filippi, to explain to him, but she was afraid that the
headmistress might read the letter and find out that Lullaby was not
sick but spending her time walking around.

In the morning, the weather was extraordinary when Lullaby left
the apartment. Her mother was still asleep, because of the pills she
took every night, since her accident. Lullaby went out into the street,
and she was dazzled by the light.

The sky was almost white, the sea was sparkling. As on every other
day, Lullaby took the smugglers' path. The white rocks were like ice-
bergs standing on the water. Leaning forward into the wind, Lullaby
walked for a long time along the coast. But she didn't dare go to the
cement platform on the far side of the bunker anymore. She would
have liked to see the beautiful Greek house with the six columns again,
to sit there and let herself be carried to the heart of the sea. But she
was afraid of meeting the hairy man who wrote on the walls and on the
rocks. So she sat on a rock by the edge of the path and tried to imagine

the house. It was very small, huddling against the cliff, its shutters and doors closed. Maybe no one would go there anymore now. Above the columns, on the triangular capital, the name of the house was lit by the sun and still said:

ΧΑΡΙΣΜΑ

Because it was the most beautiful word in the world.

Leaning against the rock, Lullaby looked one more time, for a very long time, at the sea, as if she might never see it again. All the way to the horizon, the waves were moving in close ranks. The light sparkled on their crests, like crushed glass. The salt wind blew. The sea roared across the surface of the rocks, the branches of the bushes whistled. Lullaby succumbed once again to the strange intoxication of the sea and the empty sky. Then, at around noon, she turned her back to the sea and ran toward the road that led to the center of town.

In the streets, the wind was not the same. It whirled around, coming in gusts that banged the shutters and raised clouds of dust. People didn't like the wind. They hurried down the streets to find shelter behind walls.

The wind and the dry air charged everything with electricity. The men seemed to skip nervously, calling out, bumping into each other, and sometimes on the black asphalt two cars would collide in a great noise of crashing metal and jammed car horns.

Lullaby walked through the streets, taking long strides, her eyes half closed because of the dust. When she came to the center of town, her head was spinning as if she had vertigo. The crowd came and went, whirling like dead leaves. Groups of men and women formed, split apart, formed again farther along, like iron filings in a magnetic field. Where were they going? What did they want? It had been so long since Lullaby last saw so many faces, eyes, hands that she could not understand. The slow procession of the crowd along the sidewalks carried her along, pushed her forward, and she could not understand where she was going. People walked by, very close to her, and she could sense their breath, their hands brushing. A man leaned toward her face and murmured something, but it was as if he were speaking an unknown language.

Without even realizing, Lullaby went into a department store, full of light and noise. It was as if the wind were also blowing inside the store, along the aisles, in the stairways, causing huge signs to whirl. Doorknobs emitted electric shocks; the neon lights glowed like pale lightning.

Almost running, Lullaby looked for the way out of the store. When she went through the door, she bumped into someone and murmured, "Excuse me, Madame," but it was only a huge plastic mannequin, wearing a green loden cape. The mannequin's widespread arms were vibrating slightly, and its pointed face, the color of wax, looked like that of her headmistress. The mannequin's black wig had slid to one side when Lullaby bumped into it, and now it had dropped onto one eye with its eyelashes that were like an insect's legs, and Lullaby began to laugh and shiver at the same time.

She felt very tired now, empty. Perhaps it was because she hadn't eaten since the day before, so she went into a café. She sat at the back of the room, where the light was dimmer. The waiter stood before her.

"I'd like an omelet," said Lullaby.

The waiter looked at her for a moment, as if he did not understand. Then he shouted to the counter, "An omelet for the young lady!"

He continued to look at her.

Lullaby took a sheet of paper from her jacket pocket, and she tried to write. She wanted to write a long letter, but she did not know who to send it to. She wanted to write to her father, to sister Laurence, to Monsieur Filippi, and to the little boy with glasses, to thank him for his drawing. But she couldn't manage it. So she crumpled the sheet of paper and took another. She began:

To the headmistress:
Please excuse my daughter, she cannot start class just yet, because her health requires—

She paused again. Requires what? She couldn't seem to get her thoughts around anything.

"One omelet for the young lady," said the waiter. He put the plate on the table and gave Lullaby a strange look.

Lullaby crumpled the second sheet of paper and began to eat her omelet, without lifting her head. The hot food did her good, and before long she was able to get up and walk again.

When she came to the entrance to the lycée, she hesitated for a moment.

She went in. The sound of children's voices suddenly surrounded her. She immediately recognized every chestnut tree, every plane tree. Their thin branches were shaken by the gusts of wind, and their leaves whirled around the schoolyard. She also recognized every brick, every blue plastic bench, every one of the frosted windows. To avoid the running children, she went to sit on a bench at the far side of the schoolyard. She waited. Nobody seemed to notice her.

Then the noise faded. Groups of pupils returned to their classrooms, doors closed one after the other. Soon there was nothing left but the trees shaken by the wind, and the dust and the dead leaves dancing around the schoolyard.

Lullaby was cold. She got up and went to look for Monsieur Filippi. She opened the door to the prefabricated building, where the laboratories were located. Every time she opened a door, a voice stopped in mid-sentence, leaving words suspended in the air, then continued again as soon as she closed the door.

Lullaby crossed the schoolyard again and knocked on the supervisor's glass door.

"I would like to see Monsieur Filippi," she said.

The man looked at her, astonished.

"He isn't here yet," he said. He thought for a moment. "But I think the headmistress is looking for you. Come with me."

Docile, Lullaby followed the supervisor. He stopped outside a varnished door and knocked. Then he opened the door and motioned to Lullaby to go in.

From behind her desk, the headmistress gave Lullaby a piercing gaze.

"Come in and sit down. What do you have to say for yourself?"

Lullaby sat on the chair and looked at the polished desk. The silence was so threatening that she felt she had to speak.

"I would like to see Monsieur Filippi," she said. "He wrote me a letter."

The headmistress interrupted her. Her voice was cold and hard, like her gaze.

"I know. He wrote to you. So did I. That is not the issue—you are. Where were you? You must have some interesting things to tell us. Well, I am all ears, Mademoiselle."

Lullaby avoided her gaze.

"My mother . . . ," she began.

The headmistress almost shouted.

"Your mother will be informed about all of this later, and your father too, naturally."

She waved a sheet of paper; Lullaby immediately recognized it.

"And what about this letter—it's a fake!"

Lullaby did not deny it. She was not even surprised.

"I'm all ears," said the headmistress again. She seemed to be beside herself in the face of Lullaby's indifference. It may also have been the fault of the wind, which had made everything electric.

"Where have you been, all this time?"

Lullaby spoke. She spoke slowly, groping for her words, because she wasn't really used to speaking now, and while she was speaking, in the place of the headmistress she could see the house with white columns, the rocks, and the beautiful Greek name shining in the sun. She tried to convey it all to the headmistress—the blue sea sparkling with diamond brilliance, the deep murmur of the waves, the horizon like a black thread, the salt wind where terns were gliding. The headmistress listened, and for a moment her face wore an expression of intense astonishment. She looked exactly like the mannequin with its crooked black wig, and Lullaby had to make an effort not to smile. When she stopped speaking, there were a few seconds of silence. Then the headmistress's face changed again, as if she were searching for her voice. Lullaby was astonished when she heard it. It was no longer the same voice; it had become much deeper and softer.

"Listen, my child," said the headmistress.

She placed her elbows on her waxed desk, looking at Lullaby. In her right hand she held a black pen that was ringed with a gold thread.

"My child, I am ready to forget all that. You will be able to return to class like before. But you have to tell me . . ."

She hesitated.

"You understand, I want what's good for you. You have to tell me the whole truth."

Lullaby did not reply. She did not understand what the headmistress wanted.

"You can speak to me without fear. This will stay between us."

As Lullaby still did not reply, the headmistress said, very quickly, in a quiet voice, "You have a boyfriend, don't you?"

Lullaby tried to protest, but the headmistress would not let her speak.

"It's pointless to deny it. Some—some of your classmates saw you with a boy."

"But it's not true!" said Lullaby. She did not shout, but the headmistress acted as if she had and said very loudly, "I want to know his name!"

"I don't have a boyfriend," said Lullaby. Suddenly she understood why the headmistress's face had changed: it was because she was lying. And then she felt her own face become like a stone, cold and smooth, and she looked the headmistress straight in the eye, because she no longer feared her.

The headmistress seemed upset and had to look away. And then she said, in a very gentle, almost tender voice, "You have to tell me the truth, my child. It's for your own good."

Then once again her voice was hard, mean.

"I want to know the boy's name!"

Lullaby felt the anger rising in her. Cold and heavy, like stone, and it settled into her lungs, into her throat; her heart began to beat very fast, the way it had when she had read the obscene sentences on the walls of the Greek house.

"I don't know any boy, it's not true, it's not true!" she cried, and she wanted to get up, to leave. But the headmistress's gesture held her back.

"Stay, stay, don't go!" Again she lowered her voice, somewhat broken now. "I'm not saying that for you—it's for your good, my child, it's just to help you, you've got to understand—I mean—"

She put down the little black pen with the gold nib and nervously joined her thin hands. Lullaby sat back down and did not move. She was hardly breathing, and her face had gone completely white, like a stone mask. She felt weak, perhaps because she had eaten and slept so little, all these days, by the sea.

"It is my duty to protect you from life's dangers," said the headmistress. "You cannot know, you are too young. Monsieur Filippi has spoken very highly of you; you are a good pupil to have in class, and I wouldn't want—it would be so stupid for an accident to go and spoil all that . . ."

Lullaby heard her voice as if from very far away, from behind a wall, distorted by the wind. She wanted to speak, but she could hardly move her lips.

"You have been through a difficult period, since—since what happened to your mother, her time in the hospital. You see, I know about all that, and it helps me to understand you, but you have to help me too. You have to make an effort . . ."

"I would like to see . . . Monsieur Filippi . . . ," said Lullaby, finally.

"You will see him later, you will see him," said the headmistress. "But you really have to tell me the truth about where you were."

"I told you, I was gazing at the sea. I hid in the rocks and I gazed at the sea."

"Who were you with?"

"I was alone, I told you, alone."

"That's not true!"

The headmistress shouted, then immediately pulled herself together.

"If you don't want to tell me who you were with, I shall be obliged to write to your parents. Your father . . ."

Lullaby's heart began to beat very fast.

"If you do that, I'll never come back!" She could feel the force of her words, and she slowly repeated it, without looking away.

"If you write to my father, I will never come back here. I'll never go to any school."

The headmistress was silent for a long time, and the silence filled the big room like a cold wind. Then the headmistress stood up. She looked carefully at the young girl.

"Don't get yourself into a state," she said at last. "You're so pale, you must be tired. We'll talk about all this some other time."

She looked at her watch.

"Monsieur Filippi's class is about to start in a few minutes. You can go."

Lullaby stood up slowly. She walked toward the big door. She turned around one more time before going out.

"Thank you," she said.

The schoolyard was full of pupils. The wind shook the branches of the plane trees and the chestnut trees, and the children's voices made a dizzying roar. Lullaby slowly crossed the schoolyard, avoiding the pupils and children running. A few girls waved to her, from a distance, but did not dare come any closer, and Lullaby responded with a faint smile. When she was outside the prefabricated building, she saw Monsieur Filippi, next to the pillar. He was still wearing his blue-gray suit, smoking a cigarette and staring straight ahead. Lullaby stopped. The teacher saw her and came over, making joyful signs with his hands.

"Well? Well?" he said. That was all he could find to say.

"I wanted to ask you . . . ," Lullaby began.

"What?"

"About the sea, the light. I had lots of questions to ask you."

But suddenly Lullaby realized that she had forgotten her questions. Monsieur Filippi gave her an amused look.

"Were you traveling?" he asked.

"Yes . . . ," said Lullaby.

"And . . . was it nice?"

"Oh yes! It was very nice."

The bell rang out, above the schoolyard, along the corridors.

"Well I'm glad . . . ," said Monsieur Filippi. He crushed his cigarette beneath his heel.

"You'll have to tell me about all that later on," he said. Behind his glasses there still shone an amused glow in his blue eyes.

"You're not going off traveling again now are you?"

"No," said Lullaby.

"Right, time to go," said Monsieur Filippi. Again he said, "Well I'm glad." He turned to the young girl before going into the prefabricated building.

"And you can ask me whatever you like, later on, after class. I'm actually rather fond of the sea, myself."

The Mountain of
the Living God

MOUNT REYÐARBARMUR WAS TO THE RIGHT OF THE DIRT PATH. In the light of June 21 it was very high and wide, dominating the land of steppes and the great cold lake, and Jon saw nothing else. And yet, it was not the only mountain. A bit farther there was the massif of Kalfstindar, and then there were the long valleys that had dug their way down to the sea and, to the north, the dark mass of the guardians of the glaciers. But Reyðarbarmur was more beautiful than all the others; it seemed higher, purer, because of the gentle line that rose uninterrupted from its base to its summit. It touched the sky, and the scrolls of clouds passed over like the vapors from a volcano.

Jon was walking toward Reyðarbarmur now. He had left his new bicycle against a mound by the side of the path, and he was walking across the field of heather and lichen. He did not really know why he was heading toward Reyðarbarmur. He had always known this mountain, had seen it every morning since childhood, and yet, today, it was as if Reyðarbarmur had appeared before him for the first time. It looked just as high to him when he set off on foot for school, along the paved road. There was not a single place in the valley where you could not see the mountain. It was like a dark castle reaching a pinnacle above the expanses of moss and lichen, above the sheep pasture and the villages, looking down over all the land.

Jon had left his bicycle against the damp mound. Today was the first day he'd gone out on his bicycle, and he was out of breath from struggling against the wind, all along the slope that led to the foot of the mountain, and his cheeks and ears were burning.

Perhaps it was the light that had made him want to go to Reyðarbarmur. During the winter months, when the clouds stole along the ground, trailing their fine stones of hail, the mountain seemed very far away, inaccessible. Sometimes it was surrounded by lightning, all blue in the dark sky, and the people in the valley were afraid. But Jon was not afraid of the mountain. He looked at it, and it was rather as if the mountain were also looking at him, from the depths of the clouds, above the vast gray steppe.

It may have been the light of the month of June that had led him to the mountain today. The light was beautiful and soft, despite the chill wind. While he was walking across the damp moss, Jon saw insects moving in the light, young mosquitoes and midges that hovered above the plants. Wild bees circled among the white flowers, and in the sky slender birds suspended above the pools of water flapped their wings very quickly, then disappeared suddenly in the wind. They were the only living creatures.

Jon stopped to listen to the sound of the wind. It made a strange and beautiful music in the hollows of the earth and the branches of the bushes. There were also the cries of the birds hidden in the moss; their high-pitched cheeping grew louder on the wind, then was stifled.

The mountain was clear and bright in the beautiful light of June. The closer Jon came, the better he could see that the mountain was not as regular as it seemed from a distance; it rose in a single mass from the basalt plain, like a large ruined house. Some of the rockfaces reached very high, others broke off halfway up, and black crevices split its walls as if cracked by some great blow. At the foot of the mountain flowed a stream.

Jon had never seen a stream like this one. It was limpid, the color of the sky, gliding slowly as it wound its way through the green moss. Jon went closer, slowly, feeling the soil with the tips of his toes, so as not to sink into a bog. He knelt by the edge of the stream.

The blue water flowed melodically, very smooth and pure like glass. The bottom was covered with tiny pebbles, and Jon plunged his arm into the water to take one. The water was icy and deeper than he thought, and he had to reach in all the way up to his armpit. His fingers closed around a pebble that was white, almost transparent, in the shape of a heart.

Suddenly, once again, Jon felt as if someone was watching him. He stood up straight, shivering, the sleeve of his jacket soaked in icy water.

He turned and looked all around him. But as far as he could see there was only the valley, sloping gently beneath him, and the vast plain of moss and lichen where the wind blew. Now there were not even any birds.

At the very bottom of the slope Jon could see the red spot of his new bicycle leaning against the mossy mound, and this reassured him.

It wasn't exactly something gazing at him, that feeling when he was leaning over the water of the stream. It was also something like a voice that might have said his name, very quietly, inside his ear—a light, soft voice that didn't sound like anything he knew. Or it was a wave that had enveloped him, like light, and made him quiver, like a cloud parting and revealing the sun.

Jon walked along the stream for a while, looking for a place to ford it. He found one higher up as he came around a bend, and he crossed over. The water cascaded over the flat pebbles of the ford, and clumps of green moss that had come loose from the banks slipped noiselessly downstream. Before continuing on his way, Jon knelt again by the edge of the stream and drank several gulps of the fine icy water.

The clouds parted, closed again; the light was constantly changing. It was a strange light, because it seemed to owe nothing to the sun; it floated in the air, around the walls of the mountain. It was a very slow light, and Jon understood that it would last for months, without growing any weaker, day after day, without yielding to the dark. It was born now, it had come from the earth, it was illuminated in the sky among the clouds, as if it would live forever. Jon felt the light enter him through the skin on his body, on his face. It burned and penetrated his pores like a hot liquid; it soaked his clothes and his hair. Suddenly he wanted to be naked. He found a spot where the field of moss made a bowl sheltered from the wind, and he quickly removed all his clothes. Then he rolled on the damp ground, rubbing his arms and legs in the moss. The spongy earth squelched beneath the weight of his body and covered him with cold droplets. Jon remained motionless, lying on his back, his arms widespread as he looked at the sky and listened to the wind. At that moment, above Reyðarbarmur, the clouds parted and the sun burned Jon's face and chest and belly.

He got dressed and headed once again toward the wall of the mountain. His face was hot and his ears were ringing, as if he had been drinking beer. The soft moss made his steps spring, and it was hard to walk straight. When the field of moss came to an end, Jon began to climb the foothills. The terrain became chaotic, made of blocks of dark basalt and paths of pumice that crunched and crumbled beneath his soles.

Ahead of him the face of the mountain rose so high that he could not see the summit. There was no way he could climb from here. Heading north, Jon went around the great wall, looking for a way through. Suddenly he found it. He had been sheltered from the wind by the great wall; now suddenly a blast of air made him stumble backward. In front of him a huge fault split the black stone, creating a sort of giant door. Jon entered.

Between the walls of the fault, large blocks of basalt had fallen in great disordered heaps, and he had to climb slowly, using every notch, every crack. He climbed up the blocks one after the other, without pausing to catch his breath. He felt a sort of haste inside him; he wanted to get to the top of the fault as quickly as possible. Several times he nearly fell backward, because the stone blocks were damp and covered with lichen. Jon grasped the stone with both hands, and at one point he broke the nail of his index finger without feeling a thing. The warmth continued to flow in his blood, despite the chill of the shade.

At the top of the fault, he turned around. The great valley of lava and moss stretched below him as far as he could see, and the sky was immense, rolling gray clouds. Jon had never seen anything so beautiful. It was as if the earth had become far away and empty, without men, without animals, without trees, as vast and solitary as the ocean. Here and there above the valley, a cloud broke apart, and Jon could see the oblique rays of rain and halos of light.

Without moving, his back against the wall of stone, Jon gazed at the plain. He searched for the spot of his red bicycle, and the outline of his father's house at the far end of the valley. But he could not see them. Everything he knew had disappeared, as if the green moss had risen up and covered everything. Only the stream shone at the foot of the mountain, like a long azure snake. But it too disappeared, in the distance, as if it were flowing into a cave.

Suddenly, Jon stared at the dark fault above him, and he shivered; he had not realized, while he was climbing up the blocks, that each piece of basalt formed the step of a giant stairway.

Once again Jon felt the strange gaze enveloping him. The unknown presence weighed on his head, his shoulders, his entire body, a dark and powerful gaze that covered the entire earth. Jon raised his head. Above him, the sky was filled with an intense light that shone from one horizon to the other in a single brilliance. Jon closed his eyes, as if he had been staring at lightning. Then the huge, low, smoky clouds joined together again, covering the earth with shadow. Jon stood for a long time with his eyes closed, not to feel the dizziness. He listened to the sound of the wind stealing over the smooth rocks, but the strange soft voice did not say his name. It was merely whispering, incomprehensible, in the music of the wind.

Was it the wind? Jon could hear unfamiliar sounds, women's voices murmuring, the beating of wings, the rush of waves. Sometimes from the end of the valley came strange bee buzzing noises, the humming of a motor. The sounds mingled together, resounding in an echo on the slopes of the mountain, flowing like water from a spring, to be buried in the lichen and the sand.

Jon opened his eyes. His hands clung to a rockface. There were drops of sweat on his face despite the cold. Now it was as if he were on a vessel of lava that was turning slowly, touching the clouds. Very gently, the great mountain was moving across the land, and Jon felt the swaying motion as it rocked. Like immense waves in flight, clouds unfurled across the sky, causing the light to flicker.

It lasted a long time, as long as a journey to an island. Then Jon felt the gaze moving away from him. He lifted his fingers from the rockface. Above him the mountaintop was clearly visible. It was a great dome of black stone, inflated like a balloon, smooth and shining in the light of the sky.

The flows of lava and basalt formed a gentle slope on the side of the dome, and Jon decided to continue his climb along that slope. He took small steps as he climbed, zigzagging like a goat, leaning forward. Now that the wind was free it came at him in violent gusts, causing his clothes to snap. Jon squeezed his lips, and his eyes blurred with tears. But he was not afraid, and he no longer felt dizzy. The unfamiliar gaze no longer weighed upon him. On the contrary, it seemed to be supporting his body, pushing him ever higher with all its light.

Jon had never felt such an impression of strength. Someone who loved him was walking next to him, in step, breathing at the same rhythm. The unfamiliar gaze was drawing him toward the top of the rocks, helping him to climb. Someone had come from the deepest origins of a dream, and his power was growing constantly, swelling like a cloud. Jon placed his feet on the slabs of lava exactly where he ought to, because, perhaps, he was following invisible tracks. The cold wind made him gasp for breath and blurred his sight, but he did not need to see. His body found its own way, putting the distance behind him with each step as he climbed higher and higher along the curve of the mountain.

He was alone in the middle of the sky. All around him there was no longer any earth, any horizon, only air, light, gray clouds. Jon went toward the top of the mountain, light-headed, and his gestures were slow, like a swimmer's. Sometimes his hands touched the smooth cold slate, his stomach rubbed against it, and he could feel the sharp edges of the crevices and the traces of the veins of lava. The light made the rock swell, made the sky swell; it was growing inside his body, vibrating inside his blood. The music of the voice of the wind filled his ears, resonated in his mouth. Jon did not think about anything, did not look at anything. He was climbing, a single effort; all his body was climbing, without stopping, toward the mountaintop.

Gradually, he was getting closer. The basalt slope became gentler, longer. For Jon now it was like in the valley, at the foot of the mountain, but it was a valley of stone—vast and beautiful, reaching in a long curve to the source of the clouds.

The wind and rain had worn away the rock, polished it like a millstone. Here and there were sparkling bloodred crystals, green and blue striae, yellow spots that seemed to ripple in the light. Higher up, the stone valley disappeared into the clouds as they slid over the valley, trailing filaments, streaks, behind them, and when they dissolved Jon could once again see the pure line of the curving stone.

Then Jon reached the very top of the mountain. He did not realize right away, because it had come about gradually. But when he looked around him, he saw a big black circle with himself at the center, and he understood that he had arrived. The summit of the mountain was this plateau of lava, touching the sky. Here the wind no longer blew in gusts but continuously, powerfully, slicing along the plateau like a blade. Jon took a few steps, stumbling. His heart was pounding wildly in his chest, driving the blood into his temples, into his neck. For a moment he was suffocating, as the wind pressed against his nostrils and his lips.

He searched for a shelter. The summit of the mountain was barren, not a blade of grass, not a hollow. The lava shone coarsely, like asphalt, cracked in places, wherever the rain had carved its rivulets. The wind ripped away motes of the gray dust that drifted out of the crust in hesitant puffs of smoke.

This was where the light was sovereign. It had called to him when he was walking at the foot of the mountain, and that was why he had left his bicycle flung onto the mound of moss at the side of the path. Here, the light of the sky swirled around, completely free. It poured incessantly out of space and struck the stone, then rebounded to the clouds. The black lava was penetrated with this heavy light, deep as the sea in summer. It was a light without heat that had come from the farthest point in space, the light of all the suns and all the invisible stars, and it relit the most ancient of embers, rekindled the fires that had burned on earth millions of years ago. The flame burned in the lava inside the mountain; it shimmered in the breath of the cold wind. Jon could now see before him, beneath the hard stone, all the mysterious moving currents. The red veins slithered, like serpents of fire; the slow bubbles frozen in the heart of matter glowed like the photogens of marine animals.

The wind suddenly dropped, as if someone were holding their breath. So Jon was able to walk to the center of the lava plain. He stopped in front of three strange marks. There were three basins carved out in the stone. One of the basins was filled with rainwater, and the other two contained moss and a scrawny bush. Scattered around the basins were black stones, and the red lava dust flowed along the grooves.

This was the only shelter. Jon sat at the edge of the basin with the bush. Here the wind did not seem to be blowing so hard. The lava was soft and smooth, warmed by the light of the sky. Jon leaned back on his elbows and looked at the clouds.

He had never seen the clouds this close. Jon liked the clouds. Down in the valley he had often looked at them, lying on his back behind the farmyard wall. Or hidden in an inlet on the lake, he would stay for a long time with his head flung back, until the tendons in his neck grew as taut as ropes. But here, at the top of the mountain, it wasn't the same. The clouds came quickly, level with the lava plain, their immense wings widespread. They swallowed air and stone, soundlessly, effortlessly; they forced their membranes open, to the extreme. When they passed over the summit of the mountain, everything became white and phosphorescent, and the black stone was covered with pearls. The clouds passed without a shadow. On the contrary, the light shone with greater strength—it left everything the color of snow and foam. Jon looked at his white hands, his nails like pieces of metal. He threw his head back and opened his mouth to drink the tiny droplets mingled with the dazzling light. With his eyes wide open he looked at the silver glow that filled the space. And there was no more mountain, there were no more valleys of moss, or villages, nothing. Nothing left at all but the body of the cloud as it fled southward, filling every hole, every crevice. The chill mist circled for a long time over the summit of the mountain, blinding the world. Then, very suddenly, the cloud went away again the way it had come, rolling toward the far end of the sky.

Jon was happy to be there, close to the clouds. He loved their country, so high, so far from the valleys and roads of men. The sky constantly took shape and came apart again around the circle of lava, the intermittent light of the sun shifting like the beams of lighthouses. Perhaps there was nothing else, really. Perhaps everything would be in constant motion now, steaming, wide whirlwinds, slipknots, veils, wings, pale rivers. The black lava flowed too, spreading, sliding toward the valley, the cold slow lava that spilled from the lips of the volcano.

As the clouds departed, Jon looked at their round backs scurrying across the sky. Then the atmosphere of the very blue, vibrant sunlight reappeared, and the blocks of lava hardened once again.

Jon lay on his stomach and touched the lava. Suddenly he saw a strange rock lying at the edge of the basin filled with rainwater. He crawled over on all fours to look at it. It was a block of black lava that had probably become detached from the mass through erosion. Jon wanted to turn it over but was not able to. It was firmly welded to the ground by a huge weight that was not in keeping with its size.

And Jon felt the same shiver as before, when he was climbing the blocks in the ravine. The rock was exactly the shape of the mountain. There was no doubt about it: it had the same wide, angular base and the same hemispheric summit. Jon leaned in closer, and he could clearly see the fault where he had climbed up. On the rock the fault was no more than a crevice, but jagged, like the steps of the giant stairway he had climbed.

Jon brought his face closer to the black stone, until his vision blurred. The block of lava was growing bigger, filling all his gaze, spreading around him. Jon gradually began to feel that he was losing his body and his weight. Now he was floating, lying on the gray back of the clouds, and the light went right through him. Below him he could see the large sheets of lava shining with water and sunlight, the rusty stains of lichen, the blue circles of the lakes. Slowly, he slid above the earth, because now he was like a cloud, light, changing his shape. He was gray smoke, a vapor cloud, clinging to the rocks, depositing fine droplets.

Jon did not take his gaze from the stone. He was happy like that, and for a long time he stroked the smooth surface with his open hands.

The stone vibrated beneath his fingers like a skin. He felt each bump, each crevice, each mark polished by time, and the gentle heat of the light made a light carpet, like dust.

His gaze stopped at the top of the rock. There, on the rounded, brilliant surface, he saw three tiny holes. There was a strange intoxication in seeing the very place where he was at that moment. Jon looked with almost painful attention at the marks of the basins, but he could not see the strange black insect who was motionless at the top of the stone.

He stood for a long time looking at the block of lava. He felt as if he were gradually departing from himself, escaping through his gaze. He did not lose consciousness, but his body was slowly becoming numb. His hands were getting cold, placed flat on either side of the mountain. He leaned his head with his chin against the stone, and his eyes stared ahead.

All this time the sky around the mountain took shape and came apart. The clouds slid over the lava plain, the droplets fell on Jon's face, clung to his hair. The sun glowed at times, with great, burning shards. The wind blew all around the mountain for a long time, sometimes in one direction, sometimes in the other.

Then Jon heard his heart pounding but far away, deep within the earth, down into the depths of the lava, to the arteries of fire, to the root of the glaciers. The pounding shook the mountain, vibrated in the veins of lava, in the gypsum, in the cylinders of basalt. It resounded deep within the caverns, the faults, and the regular sound surely reached along the valleys of moss as far as the homes of men.

"Ta-dom, ta-dom, ta-dom, ta-dom, ta-dom, ta-dom."

It was the heavy sound that pulled you toward another world, like on the day of your birth, and Jon saw before him the great black stone, throbbing in the light. With each pulsation all the clarity of the sky vacillated, intensified by a dazzling charge. The clouds dilated, swollen with electricity, phosphorescent like the clouds that glide around the full moon.

Jon heard another sound, a sound as from the deep sea, a heavy scraping, a sound of vapor gushing, and that also pulled him farther on. It was difficult to resist sleep. Other sounds constantly emerged, new sounds, the vibrations of engines, the calls of birds, the creaking of winches, the bubbling of boiling liquids.

All the sounds were born, came, went away again, came back, and it was like a music carrying him far away. Jon no longer made an effort to come back. Completely inert, he felt himself going down somewhere, toward the summit of the black rock, perhaps, to the edge of the tiny holes.

When he opened his eyes again, he immediately saw the light-faced child standing on the lava slab, by the water reservoir. Around the child the light was intense, for there were no more clouds in the sky.

"Jon!" said the child. His voice was soft and fragile, but his light face was smiling.

"How do you know my name?" asked Jon.

The child did not reply. He stayed motionless at the edge of the basin of water, turning slightly to one side as if preparing to run away.

"And you, what's your name?" asked Jon. "I don't know you." He didn't move, for fear of frightening the child.

"Why did you come here? No one ever comes to the mountain."

"I wanted to see the view from here," said Jon. "I thought you could see everything from very high up, like the birds."

He hesitated for a moment, then said, "Do you live here?"

The child continued to smile. The light surrounding him seemed to come from his eyes and his hair.

"Are you a shepherd? You are dressed like a shepherd."

"I live here," said the child. "Everything you see here is mine."

Jon looked at the expanse of lava and sky.

"You are wrong," he said. "This doesn't belong to anybody."

Jon made as if to stand up. But the child leapt to one side, as if he were going to leave.

"I'm not going anywhere," said Jon to reassure him. "Stay, I'm not getting up."

"You must not get up now," said the child.

"Then come and sit next to me."

The child hesitated. He looked at Jon as if he were trying to guess his thoughts. Then he came closer and sat down cross-legged next to him.

"You did not answer me. What's your name?" asked Jon.

"It's not important, since you don't know me," said the child. "I didn't ask you your name."

"That's true," said Jon. But he felt he should have been surprised.

"Tell me, then, what are you doing here? Where do you live? I didn't see any houses on my way up."

"This is all my house," said the child. His hands were moving slowly, with gracious gestures that Jon had never seen.

"You really live here?" asked Jon. "And your father, your mother? Where are they?"

"I don't have any."

"Your brothers?"

"I live all alone, I just told you."

"Aren't you afraid? You're very young to be living alone."

The child smiled again.

"Why should I be afraid? Are you afraid, in your house?"

"No," said Jon. He thought it wasn't the same thing, but he didn't dare say so.

They were silent for a moment, then the child said, "I've been living here for a long time. I know every stone on this mountain better than you know your room. Do you know why I live here?"

"No," said Jon.

"It's a long story," said the child. "A long time ago, a very long time ago, many men arrived and built their houses on the shores, in the valleys, and the houses became villages, and the villages became towns. Even the birds fled. Even the fish were frightened. So I too left the shores, the valleys, and I came to this mountain. Now you have come to this mountain too, and others will come after you."

"You talk as if you were very old," said Jon. "And yet you're just a child!"

"Yes, I am a child," said the child. He stared at Jon, and his blue gaze was so full of light that Jon had to lower his eyes.

The light of the month of June was even more beautiful. Jon thought that perhaps it came from the eyes of this strange shepherd, and that it spread up to the sky, as far as the sea. Above the mountain, the sky was emptied of its clouds, and the black stone was soft and warm. Jon was not sleepy anymore. With all his strength he looked at the child sitting next to him. But the child was looking elsewhere. There was an intense silence, without a breath of wind.

The child turned to Jon again.

"Can you play music?" he asked. "I like music very much."

Jon shook his head, then he remembered that he had a little Jew's harp in his pocket. He took it out and showed it to the child.

"You can play music with that?" asked the child. Jon handed him the Jew's harp, and the child examined it for a moment.

"What do you want me to play for you?" asked Jon.

"Whatever you know how to play, it doesn't matter! I like all music."

Jon placed the Jew's harp against his lips and made the little metal blade vibrate with his index finger. He played an air that he liked very much, *Draumkvaedi*, an old air that his father had taught him a long time ago.

The nasal twang of the Jew's harp echoed far into the lava plain, and the child listened, cocking his head slightly to one side.

"That's pretty," said the child, when Jon had finished. "Play some more for me, please."

Without really understanding why, Jon felt happy that the young shepherd liked his music.

"I also know how to play *Manstu ekki vina*," said Jon. "It's a foreign song."

As he was playing, he beat the rhythm with his foot on the slab of lava.

The child listened, and his eyes shone with happiness.

"I like your music," he said finally. "Can you play anything else?"

Jon thought for a moment.

"My brother sometimes lends me his flute. He has a lovely flute; it's all silver, and sometimes he lends it to me to play."

"I'd like to hear that music, too."

"I'll try to borrow his flute from him, next time," said Jon. "Maybe he'd like to come, too, to play you some music."

"I'd like that," said the child.

Then Jon began to play the Jew's harp again. The metal blade vibrated loudly in the silence of the mountain, and Jon thought that perhaps you could hear it to the end of the valley, as far as the farm. The child came closer. He was moving his hands in time, his head slightly to one side. His light eyes shone, and he began to laugh when the music became really too nasal. So Jon slowed the rhythm and made the long notes sing and tremble in the air, and the child's face again became serious, and his eyes again took on the color of the deep sea.

At the end, he stopped, out of breath. His teeth and lips were hurting.

The child clapped his hands and said, "It's beautiful! That's fine music you know how to play!"

"I also know how to speak with the Jew's harp," said Jon.

The child looked surprised.

"Speak? How can you speak with that thing?"

Jon put the Jew's harp back in his mouth, and very slowly, he said a few words while he vibrated the metal blade.

"Do you see?"

"No," said the child.

"Listen carefully."

Jon began again, even more slowly. The child's face lit up.

"You said, 'Hello my friend!'"

"That's right."

Jon explained: "Where I live, down in the valley, all the boys know how to do that. When summer comes, we go into the fields, behind the farms, and we talk like that to the girls, with our Jew's harps. When we find a girl we like, we go behind her house, in the evening, and we talk to her like that, so that her parents won't understand. The girls like it. They look out the window and listen to what we tell them with the music."

Jon showed the child how they said, "I love you, I love you, I love you," just by scratching the metal blade of the Jew's harp and wiggling their tongues in their mouths.

"It's easy," said Jon. He handed the instrument to the child, who tried in turn to speak by twanging the metal blade. But it didn't sound at all like a language, and they both burst out laughing.

The child was not the least bit wary now. Jon also showed him how to play tunes, and the nasal sounds echoed in the mountain for a long time.

Then the light began to fade. The sun was very close to the horizon, in a red haze. There was a strange light in the sky, as if there were a fire. Jon looked at his companion's face, and it seemed to him that it had changed color. His skin and hair were becoming gray as ash, and his eyes were the color of the sky. The gentle warmth was waning. A chill arrived, like a shiver. At one point, Jon wanted to get up and leave, but the child placed his hand on his arm.

"Don't go, I beg you," he said simply.

"I have to go back down now. It must be late already."

"Don't leave. The night will be clear; you can stay here until tomorrow morning."

Jon hesitated.

"My mother and father are waiting at home," he said.

The child thought. His gray eyes were shining forcefully.

"Your father and mother have fallen asleep," he said. "They won't wake up until tomorrow morning. You can stay here."

"How do you know that they're asleep?" asked Jon. But he understood that what the child said was true. The child smiled.

"You know how to play music and speak with music. I know other things."

Jon took the child's hand and squeezed it. He did not know why, but he had never felt such happiness before.

"Teach me some other things," he said. "You know so many things!"

Instead of answering, the child leapt up and ran toward the reservoir.

He took a bit of water in his cupped hands and brought it to Jon. He lifted his hands to Jon's mouth.

"Drink," he said.

Jon obeyed. The child poured the water gently between his lips. Jon had never tasted water like that before. It was sweet and cool but also thick and heavy, and it seemed to run through his entire body like a spring. It was water that quelled both thirst and hunger, moving through his veins like a light.

"It's good," said Jon. "What is this water?"

"It comes from the clouds," said the child. "No one has ever looked at it."

The child was standing before him on the slab of lava.

"Come, I'll show you the sky now."

Jon put his hand in the child's, and they walked together along the top of the mountain. The child stepped lightly, slightly ahead of him, his bare feet hardly touching the ground. They walked like this to the end of the plateau of lava, where the mountain overlooked the earth like a promontory.

Jon looked at the sky open before them. The sun had completely disappeared below the horizon, but the light continued to illuminate the clouds. Very far away, down in the valley, lay a light shadow that concealed the terrain. You could no longer see the lake, nor the hills, and Jon could not recognize the countryside. But the immense sky was full of light, and Jon saw all the clouds—long, the color of smoke, spread across the pink and yellow air. Higher up began the blue, a deep, dark blue that vibrated with light, too, and Jon could see the white dot of Venus, shining alone like a lighthouse.

Together they sat on the edge of the mountain and looked at the sky. There was not a breath of wind, not a sound, not a movement. Jon felt the space enter him and swell his body, as if he were holding his breath. The child did not speak. He was immobile, sitting very straight, his head thrown back slightly, and he was looking at the center of the sky.

One by one, the stars appeared, spreading their eight sharp beams. Again Jon felt the regular pulsing in his chest, in the arteries of his neck, because it was coming from the center of the sky and through him and resounding throughout the mountain. The light of day was also pounding, very near the horizon, answering the palpitations of the nocturnal sky. The two colors, one dark and deep, the other light and warm, had joined at the zenith and moved together with one single swinging motion.

Jon sat farther back on the stone and lay on his back, his eyes open. Now he could hear the sound distinctly, the great sound that was coming from all the corners of space and united above him. It was not words, nor even music, and yet it seemed to him that he understood what it meant, like words, like the lyrics of a song. He could hear the sea, the sky, the sun, the valley, crying like animals. He could hear the heavy sounds that were prisoners of the abyss, the murmurs hidden in the depths of wells, in the depths of the faults. Somewhere, out of the north, came the smooth, continuous sound of the glaciers, the crackling sound moving and creaking over the base of stones. The vapors poured forth from the solfatara, making hissing sounds, and the tall flames of the sun roared like forges. Everywhere the water flowed, the mud burst clouds of bubbles, the hard seeds split open and sprouted beneath the earth. There were the vibrations of the roots, the steady drip of sap in the trunks of the trees, the Aeolian song of the sharp grasses. Then there came other sounds, which Jon knew better—the motors of the vans and the pumps, the clanking of metal chains, electric saws, the hammering of pistons, ships' sirens. An airplane tore the air with its four jet engines far above the Ocean. A man's voice was speaking somewhere in a schoolroom, but was he really a man? It was the song of an insect, rather, now changing into a deep susurration, a rumbling, or it split into strident whistling. Seabirds' wings purred above the cliffs, gulls squawked. All the sounds bore Jon away; his body was floating above the lava slab, gliding as if on a raft of moss, spinning in invisible eddies while in the sky, at the limit of day and night, the stars shone with their immovable brilliance.

Jon stayed like that for a long time, flat on his back, watching and listening. Then the sounds began to fade, to move on, one after the other. The thudding of his heart became gentler, more even, and the light was veiled with a gray opacity.

Jon turned on his side and looked at his companion. On the black slab, the child was curled up with his head on his arm. His chest rose and fell slowly, and Jon understood that he was asleep. So he closed his eyes, too, and waited for sleep.

Jon awoke when the sun appeared above the horizon. He sat up and looked around him, failing to understand. The child was no longer there. There was only the expanse of black lava and, as far as the eye could see, the valley, where the first shadows were beginning to form. The wind was blowing again, sweeping space. Jon stood up and looked for his companion. He followed the lava slope as far as the basins. In the reservoir, the water was the color of metal, ruffled by gusts of wind. In the hole covered with moss and lichen the old dry shrub shuddered and trembled. On the slab, the rock shaped like the mountain was still in place. So Jon stood for a moment at the summit of the mountain and called out, several times, but not even an echo came in reply:

"Hey!"

"Hey!"

When he understood that he would not find his friend, Jon felt so alone that it hurt to the core of his body, as if he had a stitch in his side. He began to go down the mountain, as quickly as he could, leaping over the rocks. Quickly, he looked for the fault where he found the giant stairway. He slid down the huge wet stones, toward the valley, without looking back. The beautiful light was expanding in the sky, and it was fully day when he arrived at the foot of the mountain.

Then he began running across the moss, and his feet bounced and propelled him forward ever quicker. He leapt over the sky-colored stream without looking at the rafts of moss as they made their way downstream, turning in the eddies. Not far from there he saw a herd of sheep bolt from him, bleating, and he understood that he was once again in the territory of man. Near the dirt path his fine new bicycle was waiting, its chrome handlebars covered in dew. Jon straddled his bike and began to ride along the dirt path as it led ever lower. He wasn't thinking; all he felt was the emptiness, the boundless solitude, as he pedaled along the dirt path. When he arrived at the farm, Jon leaned his bicycle against the wall and went into the house without making a sound, not to wake his father and mother, who were still sleeping.

The Waterwheel

THE SUN HAS NOT YET RISEN ABOVE THE RIVER. THROUGH THE narrow door of the house, Juba looks at the smooth water already shimmering on the far side of the gray fields. He sits up on his mattress, tosses off the sheet wrapped around him. The cold morning air makes him shiver. In the dark house, there are other shapes wrapped in sheets, other sleeping bodies. Juba recognizes his father on the other side of the door, his brother, and all the way at the back his mother and two sisters huddled beneath the same sheet. A dog has been barking somewhere for a long time, a strange barking that sings a bit and then chokes. But there are not many sounds on the earth, or on the river, because the sun has not yet risen. The night is gray and cold, carrying the air of the mountains and deserts, and the pale light of the moon.

Juba looks out at the night and shivers, without moving from his bed. The chill of the earth rises through the mat of woven reeds, and dew drops form on the dust. Outside, the grasses shine faintly like damp blades. The tall, thin acacia trees are black, motionless in the cracked earth.

Juba gets up without making a sound. He folds his sheet and rolls up his mat, then heads off down the path that crosses the deserted fields. He looks at the sky, toward the east, and he guesses the day is about to appear. He can feel the light coming, deep inside his body, and the earth knows it too—the plowed earth of the fields and the dusty earth between the thorny bushes and the acacia trunks. It is like a restlessness, like a doubt passing over the sky, drifting on the slow waters of the river and spreading all across the level ground. The spiderwebs tremble, the grasses vibrate, the midges hover above the ponds, but the sky is empty, because there are no more bats and not yet any birds. Under Juba's bare feet, the path is hard. The faraway vibration is walking alongside him, and the huge gray grasshoppers begin to leap through the grasses. Slowly, while Juba heads away from the house, the sky grows lighter downstream. At the speed of a raft, the mist settles between the riverbanks, stretching out its white membranes.

Juba stops on the path. For a moment he looks at the river. Wet reeds bend over the sandy shores. A huge black trunk bobs in the current, immersing then waving its branches like the neck of a swimming serpent. The river is still in shadow, the water heavy and dense, flowing with slow ripples. But beyond the river the dry earth can already be seen. The dust is rough beneath Juba's feet, the red earth is broken like old pottery, the ruts zigzag like ancient crevices.

Gradually the night opens in the sky, over the earth. Juba crosses the deserted fields, moving away from the last of the peasants' houses; he can no longer see the river. He climbs a mound of dry stones where a few acacias cling. Juba picks up a handful of acacia flowers from the ground and chews on them as he scrambles up the mound. The sap spreads through his mouth and dissolves the drowsiness of sleep. On the other slope of the hill of stones, the oxen are waiting. When Juba approaches them, the big beasts stamp their hooves, limping, and one of them throws his head back to bellow.

"Tssht! Outta! Outta!" says Juba, and the oxen recognize him. With a constant clicking of his tongue, Juba removes their fetters and leads them to the top of the hill of stones. The two oxen have trouble moving forward; they limp, because the fetters have numbed their hind legs. Steam comes from their nostrils.

When they arrive at the noria, the oxen stop. They breathe heavily and pull backward, making a noise in their throats while their hooves beat against the ground and scatter the pebbles. Juba attaches the oxen to the end of the long shaft. While he harnesses the beasts to the yoke, he continues to click his tongue against his palate. Forest flies begin to hover around the oxen's eyes and nostrils, and Juba swats away the ones that land on his face and hands.

The animals wait by the well, and the heavy shaft of wood creaks and groans as they step forward. Juba pulls on the rope tied to the yoke, and the wheel begins to creak, like a boat setting sail. The gray oxen walk heavily along the circular path. Their hooves land in the tracks they made the day before, digging the ancient holes in the red earth among the pebbles. At the end of the long shaft is the big wooden wheel that turns along with the oxen, and its axis moves the gear of the other vertical wheel. The long strap of boiled leather goes right down to the bottom of the well, carrying the buckets into the water.

Juba goads the oxen, clicking his tongue relentlessly. He talks to them, too, in a low voice, gently, because the fields and river are still in shadow. The heavy wooden mechanism creaks and cracks, resists, moves off again. The oxen stop from time to time, and Juba has to run behind them, switching their rumps with a short stick, pushing on the shaft. The oxen set off on their circular walk again, their heads low, their breath heavy.

When at last the sun rises, it lights the fields all of a sudden. The red earth is furrowed, revealing blocks of dry clay, sharp shining pebbles. Above the river, at the other end of the fields, the mist parts, the water is illuminated.

A flock of birds rises suddenly from the riverbanks, from among the reeds, bursting into the clear sky with a clamor. They are sandgrouse, partridges of the desert, and their shrill cry makes Juba start. Standing on the rocks of the well, he follows them for a moment with his gaze. The birds climb high in the sky, then swing again toward the earth and disappear into the river grasses. Far away, across the fields, women are coming out of their houses. They light the braziers, but the sunlight is still so new that it fails to tarnish the red glow of the burning charcoal. Juba hears the children's cries, men's voices. Someone somewhere is calling, a shrill voice echoing for a long time in the air:

"Ju-uuu-baa!"

The oxen are moving more quickly now. The sun warms their bodies and gives them strength. The waterwheel groans and creaks, each cog in the gear cracks as it presses against another, the leather strap stretched tight with the weight of the buckets makes a continuous vibration. The buckets come back up to the edge of the well, spill into the tin gutter, and go back down, banging against the sides of the well. Juba watches as the water flows in waves along the gutter, ripples in the acequia, and drops in regular splashes toward the red earth of the fields. The water slides like a long swallow, and the dry earth drinks it up avidly. The bottom of the ditch turns muddy, and the regular flow moves forward, foot by foot. Juba never tires of observing the water, sitting on a stone at the side of the well. Next to him the wooden wheel turns very slowly, creaking, and the continuous thrumming of the belt rises in the air; the buckets bump against the tin gutter, one after the other, spilling the water that gushes forward with a rushing sound. It is a slow, keening music, like a human voice, filling the empty sky and the fields. It is a music that Juba has learned well, day after day. The sun rises slowly above the horizon; the daylight shimmers on the stones, on the stems of the plants, on the water flowing in the acequia. In the distance men are walking over the curve of the fields, black silhouettes against the pale sky. The air is gradually getting warmer, the stones seem to swell, the red earth glows like a man's skin. There are shouts from one end of the earth to the other, men shouting, and dogs barking, and the sound echoes in the sky, endlessly, while the wooden wheel turns and creaks. Juba is no longer watching the oxen. He has his back to them, but he hears their breath rasping in their throats, now close, now farther away. The beasts' hooves constantly strike the same stones on their circular path and sink into the same holes.

Juba wraps his head with a white cloth and stops moving. He might be looking into the distance, to the far side of the fields of red earth, to the far side of the metallic river. He cannot hear the sound of the wheel turning. He cannot hear the heavy sound of the wooden shaft pivoting around its axis.

"Hey-ho!"

He too sings from his throat, slowly, his eyes half closed.

"Eeeh-oooh, oooh-oooh!"

His hands and face hidden beneath the white cloth, his body motionless, he sings out as the wheel turns. He hardly opens his mouth, and his song emerges slowly from his throat, like the oxen's breathing, like the continuous humming of the leather belt.

"Eeh-eeh-eyaah-oh!"

The oxen's breathing recedes, returns, moves endlessly around the circular path. Juba sings to himself, and no one can hear him, while the water flows in mouthfuls along the acequia. The rain, the wind, the heavy water of the great river running to the sea are in his throat, in his motionless body. The sun, unhurried, rises in the sky; the heat causes the wooden wheels and the shaft to vibrate. Perhaps this is the same movement that draws the star to the center of the sky, while the oxen move heavily around the circular path.

"Eya-oooh-eya-oooh, ooo-oh ooo-oh!"

Juba hears the song rising inside him, through his belly and his chest, the song that comes from the depths of the well. The water flows in waves, earth-colored, running down to the bare fields. The water turns too, slowly, a circle of rivers, a circle of walls, a circle of clouds around the invisible axis. The water slides, cracking, creaking, running endlessly toward the dark chasm of the well, where the empty buckets will lift it out again.

It is music that cannot end, because it is in all the world, in the very sky, where the disc of the sun is rising along its curved path. The deep, regular, monotonous sounds rise from the large wooden wheel with its moaning gears, the winch pivots around its axis with its lament, the metal buckets drop down into the well, the leather belt vibrates like a voice, and the water continues to flow along the gutter in waves, drowning the channel of the acequia. No one speaks, no one moves, and the water cascades, swells like a waterfall, gushes into the furrows, across the fields of red earth and stone.

Juba tilts his head back and looks at the sky. He sees the slow circular movement marking its phosphorescent wake; he sees the transparent spheres, the gears of light in space. The sound of the waterwheel fills the entire atmosphere, turns interminably with the sun. The oxen pace at the same rhythm, their heads bent, their necks stiff beneath the weight of the yoke. Juba hears the heavy thud of their hooves, the sound of their breathing in and out, and he calls to them again, speaks grave words that linger for a long time, words that mingle with the moaning of the shaft, with the sounds of effort coming from the gears of the wheels, the ringing of the buckets as they rise incessantly, pouring out their water.

"Eeeya-ayaaah, eyaaa-oh! eyaaa-oh!"

And then, while the sun is slowly rising, pulled by the wheel and the oxen's footsteps, Juba closes his eyes. The heat and light make a gentle whirlwind that carries him away in their current, along a circle so vast that it seems it will never close. Juba is on the wings of a white vulture, very high in the cloudless sky. He is sliding on himself, across the layers of air, and the red earth turns slowly beneath his wings. The bare fields, the paths, the houses with their leafy roofs, the river the color of metal all pivot around the well, making a clicking, creaking sound. The monotonous music of the waterwheels, the breathing of the oxen, the gurgling of the water in the acequia—all of it is turning, lifting him, carrying him away. The light is vast, the sky is open. There are no more men, now; they have disappeared. There is nothing but water, earth, sky, mobile surfaces passing each other, crossing over each other, each element like a cogged wheel biting into its gear.

Juba is not asleep. He has opened his eyes again, and he is looking straight ahead, beyond the fields. He does not move. The white cloth covers his head and his body, and he is breathing gently.

That is when Yol appears. Yol is a strange town, very white in the middle of the deserted land and the red stones. Its tall monuments are still moving, vague, unreal, as if they had not yet been finished. They are like the glinting of the sun on great salt lakes.

Juba knows this town well. He has often seen it, in the distance, when the light of the sun is very strong and his eyes are slightly veiled with fatigue. He has often seen it, but no one has ever gone close, because of the spirits of the dead. One day he asked his father the name of the town, so white, so beautiful, and his father told him that the town was called Yol, that it was not a town for men but only for the spirits of the dead. His father also talked to him about the young king who reigned over the town, very long ago, a young king who had come from the far side of the ocean and who bore the same name.

Now, in the slow music of the wheels, in the dazzling light, when the sun is at its highest point in the sky, Yol has appeared yet again. It is growing before Juba's eyes, and he can clearly see its great edifices trembling in the hot air. There are high, windowless towers, white villas in the middle of palm gardens, palaces, temples. Blocks of marble glow as if they have just been cut. The city turns slowly around Juba, and the monotonous music of the waterwheel is like the murmur of the sea. The city floats above deserted fields, as light as the glinting of the sun upon the great salt lakes, and before it the waters of the river Azan flow like a road of light. Juba listens to the murmur of the sea on the far side of the city. It is a very heavy sound, mingled with the rolling of the drum and the deep lowing of trumpets and tubas. The people of Himyar hurry through the city streets. There are black slaves who have come from Nubia, troops of soldiers, horsemen with red capes, and copper helmets on their heads, the blond children of the mountain dwellers. The dust rises in the air above the roads and the houses, creating a great gray cloud that swirls outside the gates to the city walls.

"Eya! Eya!" cries the crowd, while Juba strides forward along the white way. The people of Himyar are calling him, reaching out their arms to him. But he strides ahead without looking at them, along the royal way. At the top of the city, above the villas and the trees, the temple of Diana is immense, its marble columns like petrified trunks. The light of the sun illuminates Juba's body, intoxicates him, and he hears the ever-increasing, constant murmur of the sea. The city around him is light, vibrating and undulating like the glinting of the sun on the great salt lakes. Juba walks and his feet do not seem to touch the ground, as if he were being carried by a cloud. The people of Himyar, the men and women, are walking with him, the hidden music echoes in the streets and over the squares, and sometimes the murmur of the sea is muffled by the shouts calling,

"Juba! Eya! Ju-uuu-baa!"

There is a sudden flash of light when Juba reaches the top of the temple. It is the immense blue sea, stretching to the horizon. The slow circular movement traces the pure line of the horizon, and the monotonous voice of the waves echoes against the rocks.

"Juba! Juba!"

The people of Himyar are shouting, and his name resonates throughout the city, above the earth-colored ramparts, along the peristyles of the temples, in the courtyards of the white palaces. His name fills the red fields, to the boundaries of the Azan river.

Then Juba climbs the last steps of the temple of Diana. He is dressed in white, his black hair circled with a headband of golden thread. His fine copper-colored face is turned toward the city, and his dark eyes are looking, but it is as if they could see through the bodies of men, through the white walls of the buildings.

Juba's gaze looks through the ramparts of Yol and beyond; it follows the meanders of the river Azan, crosses the expanse of the deserted fields, until it reaches the Amour mountains, the source of Sebgag. He sees the clear water springing from between the rocks, the precious cold water that flows with a regular sound.

The crowd is silent now, while Juba watches with his dark eyes. His face is like that of a young god, and the light of the sun seems to increase tenfold on his white clothing and his copper-colored skin.

The music surges like a clamor of birds, rebounding against the city walls. It inflates the sky and the sea, spreading in waves for a long time.

"I am Juba," thinks the young king, then he says it out loud, forcefully: "I am Juba, the son of Juba, the grandson of Hiempsal!"

"Juba! Juba! Eya-oooh!" cries the crowd.

"I am Juba, your king!"

"Juba! Ju-uuu-baa!"

"Today I have returned, and Yol is the capital of my kingdom!"

The murmur of the sea grows ever louder. Now, on the steps of the temple, comes a young woman. She is beautiful; she is wearing a white robe that moves in the wind, and her fair hair is full of sparks. Juba takes her hand and walks with her to the edge of the temple.

"Cleopatra Selene, the daughter of Anthony and Cleopatra, your queen!" says Juba.

The noise of the crowd spreads all through the city.

The young woman stands motionless looking at the white villas, the ramparts, and the expanse of red earth. She hardly smiles.

But the slow movement of the wheels continues, and the sound of the sea is louder than the voices of men. In the sky, the sun is gradually beginning its descent along its circular path. Its light changes color on the marble walls, lengthens the shadows of the columns.

It is as if they were alone now, sitting at the top of the steps to the temple, next to the marble columns. Around them the earth and the sea turn, making their regular groaning sound. Cleopatra Selene looks at Juba. She admires the young king's face, his high forehead, his hook nose, his almond eyes accentuated by the black line of eyelashes. She leans over to him and speaks softly, in a language Juba cannot understand. Her voice is gentle, and her breath is sweet. Juba looks at her in turn, and he says, "Everything is beautiful here. I have wanted to return for so long. Every day, since my childhood, I have been thinking of the moment when I could see all this again. I would like to be eternal, so that I would never have to leave this city and this land again, so that I could see it forever."

His dark eyes shine with all he sees around him. Juba cannot stop looking at the city, the white houses, the terraces, the palm gardens. Yol shimmers in the afternoon light that is pale and unreal like the glinting of the sun on the great salt lakes. The wind ruffles Cleopatra Selene's golden hair; the wind carries the monotonous sound of the sea to the top of the temple.

The young woman questions him, merely by uttering his name: "Juba . . . Juba?"

"My father died, defeated in this very place," says Juba. "I was taken as a slave to Rome. But today the city is beautiful, and I want it to be more beautiful still. I want it to be the most beautiful city on earth. Here we will teach philosophy, the science of the stars, the science of numbers, and men will come from every corner of the earth to learn."

Cleopatra Selene listens to the young king's words, not understanding. But she is also looking at the city, listening to the murmur of music circling the horizon. Her voice seems to sing as she calls the king, "Juba! Eyaaa-oh!"

"On the square, in the heart of the city, the masters will teach the language of the gods. The children will learn to honor knowledge, the poets will read their works, the astronomers will predict the future. No land will be more prosperous, no nation more peaceful. The city will be radiant with the treasures of the spirit, radiant with this light."

The handsome face of the young king shines in the clarity of the temple of Diana. His eyes see far into the distance, beyond the ramparts, beyond the hills, to the center of the sea.

"The wisest men in the nation will come here, to this temple, with the scribes, and with them I will establish the history of this land, the history of mankind, of wars, of the great exploits of civilization, and the history of the towns, the rivers, the mountains, and the shores of the sea, from Egypt to the island of Cerne."

Juba looks at the men of the nation of Himyar crowding through the city streets around the temple, but he cannot hear the sound of their voices; he can only hear the monotonous murmur of the sea.

"I have not come for revenge," says Juba.

He looks too at the young queen seated next to him.

"My son Ptolemy will be born," he says. "He will reign here, in Yol, and his children will reign after him, so that everything shall continue."

Then he stands up on the platform of the temple, squarely facing the sea. The dazzling light is in him, the light that comes from the sky that causes the marble walls to sparkle, and the houses, and the fields, and hills. The light comes from the center of the sky, immobile above the sea.

Juba is no longer speaking. His face is like a mask of copper, and the light shines on his forehead, on the curve of his nose, on his cheekbones. His dark eyes see what is there, beyond the sea. Around him the white walls and the calcite steles tremble and vibrate, like the glinting of the sun on the great salt lakes. Cleopatra Selene's face too is unmoving—illuminated, peaceful, like the face of a statue.

Together, standing next to each other, the young king and his spouse are on the platform of the temple, and the city is turning slowly around them. The monotonous music of the large hidden wheels fills their ears and mixes with the sound of waves on the rocks of the shore. It is like a chant, like a human voice shouting from very far away, calling, "Juba! Ju-uuu-baa!"

The shadows are growing longer across the earth, while the sun slowly declines in the west, to the left of the temple. Juba sees the buildings tremble and dissolve. They slide over one another like clouds, and the song of the wheels, in the sky and the sea, grows deeper, groaning. There are great white circles in the sky, great swimming waves. Human voices grow fainter, more distant, then vanish. There are still traces of music now and again, the sound of tubas, shrill flutes, a drum. Or the guttural cry of camels braying, near the gates to the ramparts. The gray and purple shadow expands at the foot of the hills, moves across the river valley. The temple alone is lit by the sun, rising above the city like a vessel of stone.

Juba is alone now in the ruined city of Yol. Slow waves pass over the broken marble, rippling the surface of the sea. Columns lie beneath the water, the great petrified trunks sunken deep in the seaweed, the buried staircases. There are no more men or women here, no more children. The city is like a cemetery trembling at the bottom of the sea, and the waves come to beat against the last steps of the temple of Diana, as against a reef. There is still the monotonous sound, the murmur of the sea. It is the movement of the large cogged wheels, still creaking, still groaning, while the pair of oxen harnessed to the shaft slow their circular march. In the dark blue sky, a crescent moon has appeared, and it radiates a light without heat.

Then Juba removes the white cloth covering his head. He is shivering, because the chill of night comes very quickly. His limbs are numb, and his mouth is dry. He scoops some water from a motionless bucket into the hollow of his hand. His fine face is very dark, almost black, because of the heat given by the sun. His eyes take in the expanse of red fields, where there is no one now. The oxen have stopped on their circular path. The huge waterwheels are no longer turning, but they crack and creak, and the long belt of boiled leather is still vibrating.

Without hurrying, Juba unfastens the oxen's straps, removes the heavy wooden shaft. Night is rising at the far side of the land, downstream from the river Azan. Near the houses, embers have been lit, and the women stand around the braziers.

"Ju-uuu-baa! Ju-uuu-baa!"

It is the same voice calling, sharp and singing, somewhere on the far side of the deserted fields. Juba turns around and looks for a moment, then he goes down the mound of stones, guiding the oxen with their tether. When he comes to the bottom of the mound, he ties the fetters around the oxen's hocks. The silence in the river valley is immense; it has covered earth and sky like a calm water where not a single wave is moving. It is the silence of stones.

Juba looks all around him for a long time and listens to the sound of the oxen's breathing. The water has stopped flowing in the acequia; the earth drinks the last drops in the crevices of the furrows. The gray shadow has covered over the white city with its light temples, its ramparts, its palm gardens. Perhaps somewhere there is still a monument in the shape of a tomb, a dome of broken stones where grass and bushes grow, not far from the sea? Perhaps tomorrow, when the big waterwheels begin to turn, when the oxen set off again, slowly, breathing heavily, on their circular path, perhaps then the city will reappear, very white, trembling and unreal like the glinting light of the sun? Juba turns slightly, looks only at the expanse of fields resting from the light, bathing in the mist of the river. Then he moves on; he walks quickly along the path, toward the houses where the living wait.

Daniel Who Had
Never Seen the Sea

HIS NAME WAS DANIEL, BUT HE WOULD HAVE LIKED TO HAVE been called Sindbad, because he had read of Sindbad's adventures in a big book with red binding that he carried everywhere with him, in class and in the dormitory. In fact, I believe he had never read any other book. He didn't talk about it, except sometimes when people asked him about it. And then his black eyes would shine more brightly, and his knife-blade face seemed suddenly to grow animated. But he was not a boy who spoke a great deal. He did not join in other people's conversations, except when it was something about the sea or traveling. Most men are land dwellers—that's the way it is. They are born on land, and it is land and the things of the land that interest them. Even sailors are often people of the land; they love houses and women, and they talk about politics and cars. But Daniel—it was as if he belonged to another race. The things of the land bored him—stores, cars, music, films, and naturally classes at his high school. He didn't say anything; he didn't even yawn to show how bored he was. But he would stay in one place, sitting on a bench or on the stairs by the schoolyard, staring into space. He was a mediocre student, earning just enough points each semester to make it through. When a teacher would call his name, he would get up and recite his lesson, then sit back down and it was over. It was as if he were sleeping with his eyes open.

Even when they were talking about the sea, it did not interest him for long. He would listen for a moment, ask two or three questions, then he would realize it wasn't really about the sea that they were talking but about swimming, or underwater fishing, beaches and sunburn. So he would go away to sit back down on his bench or on his steps on the stairway, and stare into space. He didn't want to hear about that sea. There was another sea—it wasn't clear which one, but it was another sea.

All that was before he disappeared, before he went away. No one could have imagined he would leave one day, I mean *really*, without coming back. He was very poor; his father had a little farm a few miles from town, and Daniel wore the gray smock the boarders wore, because his family lived too far away for him to go home every evening. He had three or four older brothers, but we didn't know them.

He had no friends—he knew no one and no one knew him. Maybe he liked it better that way, so he wouldn't grow attached. He had a strange sharp face like a knife blade, and fine indifferent black eyes.

He didn't say anything to anyone. But by then he had prepared everything, that is for sure. He prepared everything in his mind, remembering the roads and the maps and the names of the cities he would go through. Maybe he had dreamt about a lot of things, day after day and every night, lying in his bed in the dormitory, while the others were joking around and smoking cigarettes on the sly. He had thought about the rivers that go gently down to the estuaries, about the seagulls' cries, about the wind, the storms whistling in the boats' masts, and the sirens on the buoys.

It was at the beginning of winter that he left, around the middle of the month of September. When the boarders woke up, in the big gray dormitory, he had vanished. They noticed right away, as soon as they opened their eyes, because his bed had not been slept in. The blankets were carefully tucked in and everything was in order. All they said was, "Hey! Daniel is gone!" without really being surprised, because after all they did know in a way that this would happen. But nobody said anything else, because they didn't want him to get caught.

Even the most talkative of the fifth-year students said nothing. And anyway, what could anyone have said? They didn't know anything. For a long time, they whispered in the schoolyard or during French class, but these were just bits of sentences that only we knew the meaning of.

"Do you think he's gotten there by now?"

"You think so? Not yet. It's a long way, you know . . ."

"Tomorrow?"

"Yes, maybe . . ."

The most daring among them said, "Maybe he's in America, already . . ."

And the pessimists, "Naw, maybe he'll come back today."

But even if we didn't say much, in high places the matter was getting a lot of attention. The teachers and supervisors were regularly summoned to the headmaster's office, and even to the police. From time to time inspectors came and questioned the students one after the other to try to worm something out of them.

Naturally we would talk about everything except what we knew, about the sea. We talked about mountains, and cities, and girls, and treasures, even about gypsies who kidnapped children, and the Foreign Legion. We said all that to get them confused, and the teachers and supervisors got more and more annoyed, and that made them nasty.

The big fuss lasted several weeks, several months. There were two or three missing-person notices in the newspapers, with a description of Daniel and a photo that didn't look like him. Then everything calmed down all of a sudden, because we were all getting a little tired of this business. Maybe we'd all understood that he wouldn't come back, ever.

Daniel's parents got over their loss as best they could, because they were very poor and what else could they do. The police closed the case—that's how they put it—and they added something that the teachers and supervisors repeated as if it were just normal, but to the rest of us it seemed absolutely extraordinary. They said that every year tens of thousands of people disappeared, just like that, without a trace, and they were never found. The teachers and supervisors repeated that little sentence, shrugging their shoulders as if it were the most banal thing on earth, but for us, when we heard it, it made us dream, planted a secret deep inside us, a spellbinding dream that has not yet ended.

WHEN DANIEL GOT THERE, IT MUST HAVE BEEN AT NIGHT, on board a long freight train that had traveled day and night for ages. Freight trains run mainly at night, because they're very long and go very slowly, from one rail hub to another. Daniel lay on the hard floor, wrapped in an old piece of sacking. He looked through the slats in the door while the train slowed down and stopped, creaking along the tracks. Daniel opened the door, jumped out onto the track, and ran along the embankment until he found a passageway. He had no baggage, just a navy blue beach bag that he always took with him and where he had put his old red book.

Now he was free, and he was cold. His legs hurt after all the hours spent in the railroad car. It was night time, and it was raining. Daniel walked as quickly as he could to get away from the city. He did not know where he was going. He walked straight ahead, between the warehouses, along the road that shone in the yellow light of the streetlamps. There was no one here, and no names were written on the walls. But the sea was not far. Daniel guessed it must be somewhere on his right, hidden by the huge cement buildings, on the far side of the walls. The sea was there, in the night.

After a while, Daniel grew tired of walking. He was out in the countryside now, and the city twinkled far behind him. The night was black, and the earth and sea were invisible. Daniel looked for a place to shelter from the rain and the wind, and he went into a wooden shack by the roadside. There he settled in to sleep until morning. He hadn't slept for several days, nor had he eaten much at all, because he'd had to keep a constant watch out from the door of the railroad car. He knew he mustn't run into any policemen. So he hid himself well inside the wooden shack, and he nibbled a bit of bread and fell asleep.

When he woke up, the sun had already risen. Daniel came out of the shack and took a few steps, blinking. There was a path that led to the dunes, and that was where Daniel began to walk. His heart began to beat harder, because he knew that it was on the other side of the dunes, scarcely two hundred yards away. He ran along the path, climbing the sandy slope, and the wind was blowing stronger and stronger, bringing unfamiliar sounds and smells. Then he arrived at the top of the dune, and all of a sudden he saw it.

It was there, everywhere, in front of him, vast, swollen like the slope of a mountain, shining with its deep blue color, very near, its tall waves rolling toward him.

"The sea! The sea!" thought Daniel, but he didn't dare say anything out loud. He stood there unable to move, his fingers slightly spread, and found it hard to realize that he had slept next to the sea. He heard the slow sound of the waves moving against the shore. Suddenly there was no more wind, and the sun shone on the sea, lighting a fire on the crest of each wave. The sand on the beach was the color of ashes, smooth, crisscrossed by rivulets and covered with large puddles that reflected the sky.

Deep inside himself, Daniel said the beautiful name several times, like this, "The sea, the sea, the sea . . . ," his head full of sound and dizziness. He felt like talking, even shouting, but his throat restrained his voice. So he had to run off if he were to let out a shout, throwing his blue bag far ahead of him, where it rolled in the sand; he had to run on, waving his arms and legs like someone crossing a freeway. He leapt over the strands of kelp, and he stumbled in the dry sand at the top of the beach. He took off his socks and shoes and, barefoot, he ran even faster, and he did not feel the spines of the thistles.

The sea was far away, on the other side of a field of sand. It was shining in the light, changing color and aspect, an expanse of blue, then gray, green, almost black, banks of ochre sands, the white hem of the waves. Daniel had not thought that it would be so far. He continued to run, his arms tight against his body, his heart pounding with all its strength in his chest. Now he could feel the sand as hard as asphalt, damp and cold beneath his feet. The closer he came, the greater the sound of the waves, filling everything like a hissing of steam. It was a very slow and gentle sound, then violent and distressing like a train crossing over an iron bridge; or else it seemed to be fleeing backward, like a river's flow. But Daniel was not afraid. He continued to run as fast as he could, straight ahead in the cold air, without looking anywhere else. When he was only a few yards from the fringe of foam, he smelled the odor of the depths and he stopped. He had a stitch in his side, burning, and with the powerful smell of salt water he could not catch his breath.

He sat down on the damp sand and looked at the sea rising before him almost to the center of the sky. He had thought so often of this moment, had so often imagined the day when he would see it at last, truly—not the way it was in photographs or in the cinema but the way it really was, all the sea, there all around him, swollen, the round backs of the waves rushing forward, breaking, the clouds of spume, the showers of spindrift like dust in the light of the sun, and above all, in the distance, the curve of the horizon like a wall before the sky! He had desired this instant so greatly that he had no more strength, as if he were going to die, as if he were going to fall asleep.

It really was the sea now, his sea, for him alone, and he knew he would never be able to leave again. Daniel lay for a long time on the hard sand; he waited so long, stretched out on his side, that the sea began to rise along the slope and came to touch his bare feet.

It was the tide. Daniel leapt to his feet, all his muscles straining to flee. In the distance, against the black breakwater, the waves crashed with the sound of thunder. But the water had no strength yet. It was breaking, churning at the edge of the beach, only crawling just yet. The light foam circled Daniel's legs, forming little wells around his heels. At first the cold water only nibbled at his toes and ankles, then it numbed them.

With the tide came the wind. It blew in from the horizon; there were clouds in the sky. But they were unfamiliar clouds, like the foam of the sea, and the salt traveled on the wind like grains of sand. Daniel no longer thought of running away. He began to walk along the sea in the fringe of foam. With each wave, he felt the sand running out through his widespread toes then coming in again. In the distance the horizon rose and fell as if breathing, striving toward the land.

Daniel was thirsty. He took a bit of water and foam in his palm and swallowed it. The salt burned his mouth and his tongue, but Daniel continued to drink, because he liked the taste of the sea. He had been thinking for so long about all this water, free, without boundaries, all the water you could drink in an entire lifetime! On the shore, the last tide had discarded roots and pieces of wood, like huge bones. Now the water was slowly lifting them again, then depositing them a bit farther up, mixing them with the huge black seaweed.

Daniel walked at the water's edge and looked at everything eagerly, as if he wanted to know in an instant everything that the sea could show him. In his hand he took the slimy seaweed and pieces of shells, he dug for worms where they had tunneled in the silt, he looked everywhere, walking or crawling in the wet sand. The sun was harsh and strong in the sky, and the sea rumbled endlessly.

From time to time Daniel stopped, facing the horizon, and he looked at the tall waves as they tried to pass over the breakwater. He breathed in to the bottom of his lungs, to feel the air, and it was as if the sea and the horizon were inflating his lungs, his belly, his head, and he was becoming a sort of giant. He looked at the dark water in the distance, where there was neither land nor foam but only the open sky, and it was to that sea that he was speaking, in a low voice, as if the sea could hear him. He said, "Come on! Come up here, come on!"

"You are beautiful. You are going to come and you are going to cover all the earth, all the cities; you are going to reach to the top of the mountains!"

"Come, with your waves, higher, higher! This way, this way!"

Then he stepped backward, one step after the other, toward the top of the beach. That was how he learned the way of the water that rises, swells, spreads like hands along the little valleys of sand. The gray crabs ran ahead of him, their nippers raised, light as insects. The white water filled the mysterious holes, drowned the secret tunnels. It rose, slightly higher with each wave; it spread its moving layers. Daniel danced before it like the gray crabs, running sideways and raising his arms, and the water came to nip at his heels. Then he went back down and dug trenches in the sand for the water to rise more quickly, and he sang his words to help it come:

"Come on, rise, come on, waves, higher, higher, come on!"

He was in the water up to his waist now, but he did not feel the cold; he wasn't frightened. His clothes were soaking and stuck to his skin, and his hair fell in his eyes like seaweed. The sea was churning all around him, withdrawing with so much force that he had to cling to the sand not to be towed backward, then it rushed forward again and pushed him toward the top of the beach.

The dead seaweed whipped at his legs, wound itself around his ankles. Daniel tore it off as if it were snakes, throwing it into the sea and shouting, "Aaah! Aaah!!"

He did not look at the sun or the sky. He did not even see the faraway strip of land nor the outlines of the trees. There was no one here, no one but the sea, and Daniel was free.

Suddenly the sea began to rise more quickly. It swelled up over the breakwater, and now the waves were coming in from the open sea, and nothing was holding them back. They were high and wide and came in at a slight angle, their crests foaming and their dark blue bellies hollowed out beneath them and edged with foam. The waves came in so quickly that Daniel did not have time to find shelter. He turned his back to them to flee, and the first wave touched him on his shoulders and went over his head. Instinctively, Daniel clawed with his nails at the sand and held his breath. The water fell on him with a sound of thunder, whirling, penetrating his eyes, ears, mouth, nostrils.

Daniel crawled toward the dry sand with a great effort. He was so stunned that he stayed for a moment lying on his stomach in the fringe of foam, unable to move. But other waves were coming, roaring. They raised their crests even higher, and their bellies were dug deep as caves. So Daniel ran to the top of the beach and sat in the sand dunes on the other side of the barrier of wrack. For the rest of the day, he did not go near the sea. But his body was still trembling, and all over his skin and even inside him he had the burning taste of salt, and in the depths of his eyes was the dazzled splashing of the waves.

AT THE FAR END OF THE BAY THERE WAS A BLACK HEADLAND, pitted with caves. That was where Daniel lived the first days, when he arrived by the sea. His cave was a small breach in the black rocks, with a carpet of pebbles and gray sand. That was where Daniel lived all through those days, scarcely once taking his eyes from the sea.

When the light of the sun appeared, very pale and gray, and the horizon was like a thread barely visible between the mingled colors of sky and sea, Daniel would rise and go out of his cave. He climbed to the top of the black rocks to drink the rainwater in the puddles. The huge seabirds came there, too; they flew around him giving their long shrill cries, and Daniel greeted them with a whistle. In the morning when the sea was low, the mysterious seabed lay revealed. There were great pools of dark water, small torrents rushing between the stones, slippery paths, hills of living algae. So Daniel would leave the headland and go down along the rocks to the center of the plain left bare by the sea. It was as if he were arriving in the very center of the sea, in a strange land that existed only for a few hours.

He had to hurry. The black foam of the small breakers was very near, and Daniel heard the waves grumbling in a low voice and deep currents murmuring. Here the sun did not shine for long. The sea would soon return to cover them in shadow, and the light glinted off them violently, unable to warm them. The sea would share a few secrets, but you had to learn them quickly, before they disappeared. Daniel ran over the rocks from the depths, between the forests of seaweed. A powerful odor rose from the pools and the black valleys, a smell that men do not know, an intoxicating smell.

In the big puddles right by the sea, Daniel hunted for fish, shrimp, shells. He would plunge his arms into the water, among the clusters of seaweed, and he waited for the shellfish to come and tickle the tips of his fingers; then he would catch them. In the puddles there were sea anemones—purple, gray, bloodred—opening and closing their corollas.

On the flat rocks there lived blue and white limpets, orange dog whelks, mitre shells, ark shells, and clams. In the hollows of the ponds the light would sometimes shine on the wide backs of sea snails or on the opaline mother-of-pearl of a moon snail. Or sometimes between the blades of seaweed appeared the empty shell of an old abalone, iridescent as a cloud or a knife blade, or the perfect form of a scallop. Daniel looked at them for a long time where they lay, through the glass pane of water, and it was as if he were living in the tidepool too, at the bottom of a tiny crevice, dazzled by the sun and waiting for the nocturnal sea.

To eat, he hunted for limpets. He had to approach them without making any noise so they would not cling to the stone. Then he would kick them to make them come unstuck, with the tip of his big toe. But often the limpets heard the sound of his feet or the gentle hiss of his breathing, and they would stick to the flat rocks, making a series of clacking noises. When Daniel had gathered enough shrimp and shellfish, he deposited his catch in a little puddle in the hollow of a rock, so that he could cook it later in a tin can on a fire of kelp. Then he went to look farther along, all the way at the end of the plain of the seabed, where the waves broke. For that was where his friend the octopus lived.

Daniel had met the octopus right away, the first day he arrived by the sea, before he even knew the seabirds and the anemones. He'd come to the edge of the waves that broke, tumbling over each other when the sea and the horizon no longer move, no longer swell, and the great deep currents seem to hold back before leaping. This was surely the most secret place in the world, there where the light of day shines only a few minutes. Daniel had walked very gently, holding himself against the wall of slippery rock, as if he were going down into the center of the earth. He had seen the great pond of heavy water, where the long tendrils of seaweed moved slowly, and he stood motionless, his face almost touching the surface. Then he saw the octopus's tentacles floating by the walls of the pond. They came out of the crevice near the bottom, just like smoke, and they slid gently on the seaweed. Daniel held his breath, looking at the almost motionless tentacles mingling with the filaments of seaweed.

Then the octopus came out. Its long cylindrical body moved cautiously, its tentacles waving. In the broken light of the ephemeral sun, the octopus's yellow eyes shone like metal beneath its prominent brows. The octopus let its long tentacles with their purple discs float for a moment, as if it were looking for something. But then it saw Daniel's shadow leaning over the pond, and it leapt backward, squeezing its tentacles and releasing a strange gray-blue cloud.

Now, just as every day, Daniel arrived by the edge of the pool near the waves. He leaned over the transparent water and quietly called to the octopus. He sat on the rock, letting his bare legs hang into the water in front of the crevice where the octopus lived, and he waited without moving. After a while, he felt the tentacles lightly touching his skin, curling around his ankles. The octopus caressed him cautiously, sometimes between his toes or on the soles of his feet, and Daniel began to laugh.

"Hello Wiatt," said Daniel. The octopus was called Wiatt, but it didn't know its name, of course. Daniel spoke to it in a quiet voice, so as not to frighten it. He asked it questions about what happens at the bottom of the sea, about what you can see when you're under the waves. Wiatt did not reply but continued to caress Daniel's feet and ankles, very gently, as if with strands of hair.

Daniel liked it. He could never see it for very long, because the sea rose quickly. When his catch had been good, Daniel would bring Wiatt a crab or shrimp, and he released them into the tidepool. The gray tentacles lashed out like whips, seizing their prey and taking it back to the rock. Daniel never saw the octopus eating. It almost always stayed hidden in its black crevice, motionless, with its long tentacles floating in front of it. Maybe it was like Daniel; maybe it had traveled for a long time to find its house at the bottom of the pool, and it looked at the clear sky through the transparent water.

When the tide was out, there was something like an illumination. Daniel walked among the rocks, on the bed of seaweed, and the sun began to reverberate on the water and on the stones, creating a fierce blaze. There was no wind at that moment, not a breath of air. Above the expanse of the seabed, the blue sky was very big, shining with an exceptional light. Daniel could feel the heat on his head and on his shoulders, and he closed his eyes so as not to be blinded by the terrible reflection. There was nothing else then, nothing at all: the sky, the sun, the salt, which began to dance on the rocks.

One day when the sea was so far out that you could see nothing more than a thin blue strip toward the horizon, Daniel set off across the rocks on the seabed. He suddenly felt the intoxication of those who have entered virgin territory and who know that they may not be able to come back. There was nothing else like it, that day; everything was unknown, new. Daniel turned around and saw land far behind him, like a lake of mud. He also felt the solitude, the silence of the bare rocks worn by the seawater, the unquiet fear that emerged from all the crevices, all the secret wells, and he began to walk more quickly, then to run. His heart was pounding in his chest, like on the day he first arrived by the sea. Daniel was running, without catching his breath, leaping above the pools in the valleys of seaweed, following the rocky crests, his arms spread wide to keep his balance.

Sometimes there were wide slimy slabs covered with microscopic algae, or boulders sharp as blades, strange stones that looked like shark skins. Everywhere the puddles of water sparkled, shimmered. The shells embedded in the rocks crackled in the sun, and the rolls of seaweed made a strange hissing noise.

Daniel ran without knowing where he was going, in the middle of the plain of the seabed, not stopping to see how far the waves had gone. The sea had disappeared now, had withdrawn to the horizon, as if it had run out through a hole leading to the center of the earth.

Daniel was not afraid, but he was no longer quite himself. He did not call to the sea; he no longer spoke to it. The light of the sun reverberated on the water in the puddles as if they were mirrors; it broke against the tips of the rocks, leapt like quicksilver, flashing again and again. The light was everywhere at once, so close he could feel the passage of the harsh rays over his face, or it was very far away, like the cold spark of the planets. It was because of the light that Daniel ran in zigzags across the plain of rocks. The light had made him free, made him crazy, and he leapt as if he were light, blindly. The light was not gentle and calm, the way it had been on the beaches or the dunes. It was a wild whirlwind, constantly leaping, rebounding between the twin mirrors of sky and rock.

Above all, there was the salt. For days it had been accumulating everywhere on the black stones, on the pebbles, in the shells and the mollusks, and even on the pale little blades of the succulent plants at the foot of the cliff. The salt had entered Daniel's skin, had left its marks on his lips, in his eyebrows and eyelashes, in his hair and clothes, and now it had formed a hard, burning carapace. The salt had even gone inside his body, into his throat, his belly, to the center of his bones; it was gnawing and scraping like a dust made of glass, lighting sparks upon his painful retinas. The sunlight had set the salt ablaze, and now each prism scintillated around Daniel and inside his body. And there was a sort of intoxication, a vibrant electricity, because the sun and the light did not want him to stay in one place; they wanted him to dance and run, to leap from one rock to the next. They wanted him to flee across the seabed.

Daniel had never seen so much whiteness. Even the water in the pools, even the sky, were white. It burned his retinas. Daniel closed his eyes completely and stood still, because his legs were trembling and would not carry him any farther. He sat down on a flat rock before a lake of seawater. He listened to the sound of the light leaping over the rocks, all the dry cracking sounds, clacking, susurrant, and close to his ears, there came a shrill murmur like the humming of bees. He was thirsty, but it was as if no water could ever quench that thirst. The light continued to burn his face, his hands, his shoulders; it singed him with a thousand white-hot, prickling needles. Salt tears began to run from his closed eyes, slowly, leaving warm tracks across his cheeks. He opened his eyelids slightly, with an effort, and looked at the plain of white rocks, the great wilderness where the pools of cruel water shone. The marine animals and shellfish had disappeared; they hid in the crevices, beneath the curtains of seaweed.

Daniel leaned forward on the flat rock, and he put his shirt on his head so he would no longer see the light and the salt. He stayed motionless for a long time, with his head between his knees, while the burning dance went back and forth across the seabed.

Then the wind came, weak at first, moving with difficulty in the thick air. The wind grew, the cold wind that came out of the horizon, and the tidepools shivered and changed color. The sky had clouds, and the light was once again coherent. Daniel heard the rumbling of the sea nearby, the great waves striking their bellies against the rocks. Drops of water dampened his clothes, and he emerged from his torpor.

Already the sea was there. It was coming very quickly, hastily surrounding the first rocks like islands, drowning the crevices, flowing with the sound of a river at high water. Every time it engulfed a piece of rock, there was a dull sound that shook the base of the earth, and a rumbling in the air.

Daniel leapt to his feet. He began to run toward the shore without stopping. He was no longer sleepy; he no longer feared the light and the salt. He felt a sort of anger deep inside his body, a strength he did not understand, as if he could break the rocks and dig into the crevices, just like that, with a kick of his heel. He was running before the sea, following the route of the wind, and behind him he heard the roar of the waves. From time to time he too shouted, to imitate them:

"Ram! Ram!"

Because he was the one who commanded the sea.

He had to run quickly! The sea wanted to take everything—the rocks, the seaweed, and also anyone running ahead of it. Sometimes it reached forward with an arm to the left or to the right, a long gray arm speckled with foam, barring Daniel's way. He leapt to the side, he found a way up onto the rocks, and the water receded, sucking the holes in the crevices.

Daniel swam across several lakes that were already rough. He no longer felt tired. On the contrary, there was a sort of joy in him, as if the sea, the wind, and the sun had dissolved the salt and set him free.

The sea was beautiful! The white spray burst into the sunlight, very high and very straight, then fell in clouds of wind-tossed vapor. The new water filled the hollows in the rocks, washed the white crust, tore away clumps of algae. Far away near the cliffs shone the white road of beach. Daniel thought about Sindbad's shipwreck, when he was carried by the waves to the islands of King Mihrage, and it was just like that, now. He was running quickly over the rocks, his bare feet choosing the best passage, and he didn't even have time to think about it. No doubt he had always lived there, on the plain of the seabed, among the shipwrecks and the storms.

He was going as fast as the sea, never stopping, never catching his breath, listening to the sound of the waves. They came from the other side of the earth, tall waves, straining forward, carrying their foam; they slid over the smooth rocks and crashed into the crevices.

The sun was shining with a steady brilliance near the horizon. It was from the sun that all this strength came, its light driving the waves against the earth. It was a dance that could not end—the dance of the salt when the sea was low, the dance of the waves and wind when the waters rose against the shore.

Daniel went into the cave when the sea reached the barrier of kelp. He sat on the pebbles to look at the sea and the sky. But the waves were rising higher than the seaweed, and he had to withdraw farther inside the cave. The sea was still pounding, tossing out its white sheets that trembled on the pebbles like boiling water. The waves continued to rise, like that, one after the other, up to the last barrier of seaweed and twigs. It found the driest seaweed, the salt-whitened tree branches, anything that had piled up at the entrance to the cave over the months. The water pounded against the debris, pulled it apart, took it into the undertow. Now Daniel was up against the very back of the cave. He could not go back any farther. So he looked at the sea to stop it. Not speaking, he looked at the sea with all his strength, and he sent the waves back, a wall of counter-breakers that stopped the sea in its forward motion.

Several times, the waves leapt above the barriers of seaweed and debris, splashing against the back of the cave and swirling around Daniel's legs. Then suddenly the sea stopped rising. The terrible sound grew calmer, and the waves became gentler, slower, as if weighed down by foam. Daniel knew it was over.

He lay on the pebbles at the entrance to the cave, his head turned toward the sea. He was shivering with cold and fatigue, but he had never known such happiness. He fell asleep like that, in a becalmed peace, and the light of the sun faded slowly, like a flame going out.

WHAT BECAME OF HIM AFTER THAT? WHAT DID HE DO ALL THOSE days, all those months, in his cave by the sea? Perhaps he really did leave for America, or China, on a cargo ship that sailed slowly from port to port, from island to island. Dreams that begin in this way must not stop. Here, for those of us who are far from the sea, everything was impossible and easy. All that we knew was that something strange had happened.

It was strange, because there was something illogical about it that contradicted everything that serious people were saying. They had gone to such lengths to try to find a trace of Daniel Sindbad—teachers, supervisors, policemen; they had asked so many questions, and then one day on a certain date, they acted as if Daniel had never existed. They no longer talked about him. They sent all his belongings, even his old notebooks, to his parents, and there was nothing left of him at the school apart from his memory. And even that, nobody wanted it anymore. They began talking about other things, about their wives and their houses, their cars and their local elections, like before, as if nothing had happened.

Or maybe they weren't pretending. Maybe they really had forgotten Daniel, because they had thought about him so much, for months. Perhaps if he had come back and had shown up at the door to the school, people would not have recognized him, and they would have asked, "Who are you? What do you want?"

But we hadn't forgotten him. Nobody had forgotten him, in the dormitory, in the classrooms, in the schoolyard, even those who never knew him. We talked about school, about math problems and translations, but we still thought about him a great deal, as if he truly were Sindbad and was still traveling all around the world. From time to time we would stop talking, and someone would ask the question, always the same, "Do you think he is there?"

Nobody knew exactly where *there* was, but it was as if we could see that place—the vast sea, the sky, the clouds, the wild reefs and waves, the great white birds gliding on the wind.

When a breeze shook the branches of the chestnut trees, we would look at the sky and say, a bit worried, the way sailors do, "There's a storm coming."

And when the winter sun shone in the blue sky, we would say, "It's a good day for him today."

But we never said much more than that, because it was like a pact we had made with Daniel without knowing it, an alliance of secrecy and silence that we had made with him one day. Or maybe it was like the dream that had begun simply one morning, when we opened our eyes and in the half-light of the dormitory saw Daniel's bed that he had prepared for the rest of his life, as if he would never sleep again.

Hazaran

FRENCHMAN'S DIKE WASN'T REALLY A TOWN, BECAUSE THERE WERE no houses or streets, only shacks made of planks and tarpaper and dirt floors. Maybe they called it that because the people who lived there were Italians, Yugoslavs, Turks, Portuguese, Algerians, Africans, masons, earthmovers, and peasants, people who weren't sure of finding work and who never knew if they were going to stay for a year or two days. They arrived there at the Dike, near the swamps along the estuary, they settled where they could, and built their shacks in a few hours. They bought planks from the people who were leaving, planks that were so old and full of holes that you could see the daylight through them. For the roofs they used planks too, and big sheets of tarpaper, or if they were lucky enough to find any, pieces of corrugated iron held in place with bits of wire and stones. They plugged up the holes with rags.

That's where Alia lived, in the western part of the Dike, not far from Martin's house. She'd come there at the same time as he had, right at the beginning, when there were only a dozen shacks or so, and the earth was still soft, with huge fields of grass and reeds by the edge of the swamp. Her father and mother had died in an accident, and all she knew how to do was to play with the other children, and her aunt had taken her in. Now, four years later, the Dike had grown and covered the left bank of the estuary, from the embankment by the highway to the sea, with hundreds of dirt lanes and so many shacks that you couldn't count them. Every week, several trucks would stop outside the Dike to drop off new families and pick up the ones who were leaving. On her way to get water at the pump or to buy rice and sardines at the co-op, Alia would stop and look at the newcomers settling in wherever there was room. Sometimes the police also came to the entrance of the Dike to perform inspections, and they wrote down the departures and arrivals in a notebook.

Alia remembered the day Martin arrived very clearly. The first time she saw him, he was getting out of the truck with other people. His face and clothes were gray with dust, but she noticed him right away. He was a funny man, tall and thin, his face darkened by the sun, like a sailor. You might have thought he was old because of the wrinkles on his forehead and his cheeks, but his hair was very black and thick, and his eyes shone as bright as mirrors. Alia thought he had the most interesting eyes of anyone in the Dike—maybe in the entire country—and that's why she had noticed him.

She stood still when he walked by her. He walked slowly, looking all around him, as if he had simply come to visit the place and the truck was going to pick him up again in an hour. But he stayed.

Martin did not move into the center of the Dike. He went all the way to the edge of the swamp, where the pebbles of the beach began. That's where he built his shack, all alone on a plot of earth that no one else would have wanted, because it was too far from the road and the freshwater pumps. His house was the very last one in the town.

Martin had built it himself, without anyone's help, and Alia thought it was also the most interesting house around, in its way. It was a circular shack, with no opening except for a low door that Martin had to bend down to go through. The roof was made of tarpaper, like the roofs of the other shacks, but it had the shape of a lid. When you saw Martin's house from a distance, in the morning mist, all alone in the middle of the empty landscape between the edge of the swamp and the beach, it seemed bigger and taller, like the tower of a castle.

That was actually the name Alia had given it right from the start: the Castle. People who didn't like Martin and who made fun of him now and again, like the manager at the co-op, for example, said it was more of a doghouse, but that's because they were jealous. That's what was strange, actually, because Martin was very poor, poorer than anybody in the town, but that windowless house had something mysterious, almost majestic, about it, something you didn't understand very well, something intimidating.

Martin lived there all alone, out of the way. There was always silence around his house, especially in the evening, a silence that made everything seem far away and unreal. When the sun shone above the dusty valley and the swamp, Martin would sit there on a crate, outside the door of his house. People didn't go that way very often, maybe because the silence intimidated them or because they did not want to disturb Martin. In the morning and the evening there were sometimes women looking for dead wood, and children coming back from school. Martin liked children. He spoke to them gently, and they were the only ones who could get a real smile out of him. It was then that his eyes became very beautiful, shining like mirrors of stone, full of a clear light that Alia had never seen anywhere else. The children liked him too, because he knew how to tell stories and he would ask them riddles. The rest of the time, Martin didn't really work, but he knew how to repair little things—the gears of a watch, radio sets, the pistons of kerosene heaters. He did it all for nothing, because he didn't want to take any money for his trouble.

So, from the time he arrived there, every day people would send their children to him with a bit of food on a plate—potatoes, sardines, rice, bread, or a bit of hot coffee in a glass. The women also came sometimes to bring him food, and Martin thanked them, exchanging a few words. Then, when he had finished eating, he gave the plate back to the children. That was how he wanted to be paid.

Alia liked to visit Martin, to hear his stories and see the color of his eyes. She would take a piece of bread from the cupboard and go through the Dike to the Castle. When she got there, she saw the man sitting on his crate outside his house repairing a gas lamp, and she sat on the ground beside him to look at him. The first time she brought him some bread, he looked at her with his eyes full of light and said, "Hello, Moon."

"Why are you calling me Moon?" asked Alia.

Martin smiled, and his eyes grew even brighter.

"Because I like the name. Don't you want me to call you Moon?"

"I don't know. I didn't think it was a name."

"It's a pretty name," said Martin. "Have you ever looked at the moon when the sky is very pure and black, on a night when it's very cold? It's all round and gentle, and I think that's what you are like."

And from that day on, Martin had always called her by that name: Moon, Little Moon. And he had a name for each of the children who came to see him—the name of a plant, or a fruit, or an animal, and it made them laugh. Martin never talked about himself, and no one would have dared to ask him anything. In the end, it was as if he had always been there in the Dike, long before the others, even long before they had built the road, or the iron bridge, or the landing strip. He surely knew things that people from there did not know, very ancient and beautiful things that he kept inside his head and that caused the light in his eyes to shine.

That was what was strange, above all, because Martin owned nothing, not even a chair or a bed. In his house there was only a mat for sleeping on the floor and a bucket of water on a crate. Alia didn't really understand, but she sensed it was something he wanted, as if he didn't want to keep anything. It was strange, because it was like a fragment of clear light always shining in his eyes, like those pools of water that are more transparent and more beautiful when there is nothing at the bottom.

The moment she finished work, Alia went out of her aunt's house clutching the piece of bread in her shirt, and she went to sit across from Martin. She liked to look at his hands while he was repairing things. He had big sun-blackened hands with broken fingernails, like the hands of the earthmovers and the masons, but Martin's were lighter and more agile; they knew how to make knots with tiny strings or turn screws you could hardly see. His hands worked for him, and he didn't need to pay attention to them or look at them, and his eyes stared off into the distance, as if he were thinking about something else.

"What are you thinking about?" asked Alia.

He looked at her with a smile.

"Why are you asking me that, Little Moon? And you, what are you thinking about?"

Alia concentrated and thought.

"I'm thinking it must be beautiful, where you come from."

"What makes you think that?"

"Because—"

She could not find the answer, and she blushed.

"You're right," said Martin. "It's very beautiful."

"And I think that life here is sad," said Alia.

"Why do you say that? I don't think so."

"Because there is nothing here, it's dirty, you have to go get water at the pump, there are flies and rats, and everybody is so poor."

"And I'm poor, too," said Martin. "And yet I don't think that's a reason to be sad."

Alia thought some more.

"If it's so beautiful, where you come from, then why did you leave? Why did you come here where everything is so—so dirty, so ugly?"

Martin looked at her carefully, and Alia searched in the light of his eyes for whatever beauty she could find—the beauty that this man had once gazed upon, the immense countryside with its deep and golden splashes of light that still lived in his eyes. But Martin's voice was softer, like when he was telling a story.

"Would you be happy eating everything you like best, Little Moon, if you knew that next to you there was a family who had not eaten in two days?"

Alia shook her head.

"Would you be happy looking at the sky, the sea, the flowers, or listening to the birds singing if you knew that next to you, in the next house, there was a child who was locked up for no reason and who could see nothing, hear nothing, feel nothing?"

"No," said Alia. "I would go and open the door to his house, so he could go out."

As she was saying this, she understood that she had just answered her own question. Martin was still looking at her with a smile, then he went on fixing his object, somewhat distractedly, not looking at his hands as they moved.

Alia was not sure she was completely convinced. So she said, "All the same, it must be really very beautiful, where you come from."

When he had finished working, he stood up and took Alia by the hand.

He led her slowly to the far side of the empty lot, next to the swamp.

"Look," he said then. He pointed to the sky, the flat earth, the estuary opening out onto the sea. "There you are. It's all of this, the place I come from."

"All of this?"

"Yes, all of this, everything you can see."

Alia stood for a long time, not moving, looking all she could until her eyes hurt. She was looking with all her strength, as if the sky were finally going to open and show her all the palaces, and castles, and gardens full of fruit and birds, and she grew so dizzy she had to close her eyes.

When she looked behind her, Martin had gone. His tall, thin figure was walking between the rows of shacks, toward the far end of town.

IT WAS FROM THAT DAY ON THAT ALIA HAD BEGUN TO LOOK AT the sky, to really look at it, as if she had never seen it. When she was working in her aunt's house, sometimes she would go out for a moment to lift her head toward the sky, and when she went back in, she felt something that continued to vibrate in her eyes and in her body, and she would bump into the furniture sometimes, because her retinas were dazzled.

When the other children learned where Martin came from, they were very surprised. In those days there were a lot of children there, at the Dike, who would wander around with their heads lifted toward the sky, and they would bump into poles, and people wondered what on earth could have happened to them. Maybe they thought it was a new game.

Sometimes, no one knew why, Martin would stop eating. The children brought him his food on a plate, just like every morning, and he would refuse politely, saying, "No thank you, not today."

Even when Alia came, with her piece of bread held tightly in her shirt, he would smile gently and shake his head. Alia did not understand why the man refused to eat, because all around the house, on the ground, in the sky, everything was as it usually was. In the blue sky there was the sun, one or two clouds, and from time to time a jet airplane was landing or taking off. In the lanes of Frenchman's Dike, the children played and shouted, and the women called to them and gave them orders in all sorts of languages. Alia did not see what could have changed. But she would sit down next to Martin all the same, with two or three other children, and they would wait for him to talk to them.

Martin wasn't like he was on other days. When he didn't eat, his face seemed older, and his eyes would shine in a different way, with the worrying glow of someone who has a fever. Martin looked elsewhere, above the children's heads, as if he could see farther than the earth and the swamp, to the far side of the river and the hills, so far away that it would have taken months and months to go that far.

On those days, he almost never spoke, and Alia did not ask him any questions. People came, as on other days, to ask him for a favor: to glue a pair of shoes together, fix a clock, or simply write a letter. But Martin would hardly reply; he would shake his head and say in a low voice, almost without moving his lips, "Not today, not today."

Alia understood that on those days he was not there—he really was elsewhere, even if his body remained motionless, lying on his mat inside his house. Perhaps he had gone back to the country he came from, where everything was so beautiful and where everybody was a prince or princess, that country with the road that crossed the sky, the road that he had shown them one day.

Every day, Alia came back with a new piece of bread to wait for his return. Sometimes it lasted a very long time, and she was a bit frightened to see his face growing gaunt, turning gray as if the light had stopped burning and there was nothing left but ash. Then, one morning, he'd come back so weak that he could hardly walk from his bed to the empty lot outside his house. When he saw Alia, he finally looked at her with a feeble smile, and his eyes were dull with fatigue.

"I'm thirsty," he said. His voice was slow and hoarse.

Alia put the piece of bread on the ground, and she ran through the town to fetch a bucket of water. When she came back, breathless, Martin drank for a long time from the bucket. And he washed his face and his hands, sat on his crate in the sun, and he ate a piece of bread. He took a few steps around the house and looked all around him. The sunlight warmed his face and hands, and his eyes again began to shine.

Alia looked at him eagerly. She dared to ask him, "How was it?"

He did not seem to understand.

"How was what?"

"How was it, that place where you went?"

Martin did not reply. Maybe he remembered nothing, as if he had simply gone through a dream. He began to live again and to speak as before, sitting in the sun outside the door of his house, repairing the broken machines, and walking along the lanes of the Dike and greeting people as they went by.

Later, Alia asked him again, "Why is it, sometimes you don't want to eat?"

"Because I have to fast," Martin said.

Alia grew thoughtful.

"What does that mean, fast?" She added, "Is it like traveling?"

But Martin laughed. "What a strange idea! No, fasting is when you don't want to eat."

How could anyone not want to eat? thought Alia. Nobody had ever said anything so strange to her. In spite of herself, she also thought about all the children in the Dike who spent their days looking for something to eat, even the ones who weren't hungry. She thought about the ones who went to steal from the supermarkets near the airport, and the ones who went to pilfer fruit and eggs from the neighboring gardens.

Martin answered right away, as if he had heard what Alia was thinking.

"Have you ever been very thirsty?"

"Yes," said Alia.

"And when you were very thirsty, did you want to eat?"

She shook her head.

"You didn't, did you? You just wanted to drink, you were so thirsty. You felt like you could have drunk all the water at the pump, and if somebody had given you a huge plate of food at that point, you would have refused, because it was water you needed."

Martin stopped talking for a moment. He smiled.

"And the same goes for when you were very hungry. You wouldn't have wanted someone to give you a jug of water. You would have said no, not now, I want to eat first, eat as much as I can, and then afterward, if there's room, I'll drink some water."

"But you don't eat or drink!" exclaimed Alia.

"That's what I wanted to tell you, Little Moon," said Martin. "When you fast, you don't feel like having food or water, because what you feel like is something else, and it is more important than eating or drinking."

"And what is it you feel like having, then?" asked Alia.

"God," said Martin.

He said it very simply, as if it were obvious, and Alia didn't ask any more questions. It was the first time that Martin talked to her about God, and it frightened her a bit—well, not exactly frightened, but it made her feel farther away all of a sudden, pushed far back, as if the entire expanse of the Dike with its wooden shacks and the swamp by the river were separating her from Martin.

But Martin did not seem to notice. He got up and looked at the plain of swampland where the reeds were swaying. He ran his hand over Alia's hair and set off slowly down the path that led through the town, while the children ran ahead of him, shouting to celebrate his return.

IN THOSE DAYS, MARTIN HAD ALREADY BEGUN HIS TEACHING, but nobody knew it. It wasn't really teaching—I mean, like that of a priest or a teacher—because there was nothing solemn about it, and you learned without really knowing what you had learned. The children had gotten into the habit of going to the ends of the Dike, outside Martin's castle, and they sat on the ground to talk and play or to listen to stories. As for Martin, he did not move from his crate; he went on repairing what he was repairing—a saucepan, the valve on a pressure cooker, or a lock—and the teaching began. It was mostly the children who came, after their noontime meal or after school. But sometimes there were women and men, too, when work was over and it was too hot to sleep.

The children sat toward the front, right next to Martin, and that was where Alia liked to sit, too. They made a lot of noise—they couldn't sit still for long—but Martin was happy to see them. He spoke to them, and he asked them what they had done and what they had seen, in the Dike or by the seashore. There were some people who liked to talk, who would have told you anything for hours. Others remained silent and hid behind their hands when Martin spoke to them.

Then Martin would tell a story. The children really liked to hear stories—that was why they came. When Martin began his story, even the rowdiest children remained seated and stopped talking.

Martin knew a lot of stories—long, strange stories that were set in unknown countries that he had surely visited in the old days.

There was the story about the children who went down a river on a raft made of reeds, and in that way they went through extraordinary kingdoms, forests, mountains, mysterious cities, all the way to the sea. There was the story about the man who had discovered a well that led to the center of the earth, where the States of Fire were found. There was the story about the merchant who thought he would get rich selling snow, and he brought bagfuls of it down from the top of the mountain, but when he got to the bottom, all that he owned was a puddle of water. There was the story about the boy who came to the castle where the princess of dreams lived, the one who sends dreams and nightmares down to earth, and the story of the giant who sculpted the mountains, and the child who tamed dolphins, and the one about Captain Tecum, who saved the life of an albatross, and to thank him the bird taught him the secret of flight. They were beautiful stories, so beautiful that sometimes you fell asleep before you'd heard the end. Martin told them very softly, moving his hands, or pausing from time to time so you could ask questions. While he talked, his eyes shone brightly, as if he were having a good time, too.

Of all the stories that Martin told, it was the one about Hazaran that the children liked best. They didn't understand it very well, but all of them would hold their breath when he began to tell it.

To begin with, there was the little girl whose name was Clover, and it was a funny name they'd given her, no doubt because of a little mark she had on her cheek near her left ear that looked like a clover. She was poor, very poor, so poor that she had nothing to eat but a crust of bread and the fruit she gathered from the bushes. She lived alone in a shepherd's hut, lost among the brambles and the rocks, with no one to take care of her. But when they saw that she was so alone and sad, all the little animals that lived in the fields became her friends. They often came to see her in the morning or in the evening, and they talked to her to amuse her. They showed her tricks and told her stories, because Clover knew how to speak their language. There was an ant called Zöe, a lizard called Zoot, a sparrow called Pipit, a firefly called Zelle, and all sorts of butterflies—yellow, red, brown, blue. There was also a wise beetle called Kepr and a big green grasshopper that sunbathed on the leaves. Little Clover was kind to them and that was why they liked her.

One day when Clover was even sadder than usual, because she had nothing to eat, the big green grasshopper called out to her. Do you want to change your life? it asked, whistling. How could I change my life, replied Clover, I have nothing to eat and I'm all alone. You can change it if you want, said the grasshopper. All you need to do is go to the country of Hazaran. What country is that? asked Clover. I've never heard of such a place. To enter, you have to answer the question the guard at the gates of Hazaran will ask you. But you have to be knowledgeable, very knowledgeable, to be able to reply. So Clover went to see the beetle Kepr, who lived on the branch of a rose bush, and she said to it, Kepr, teach me what I must know, because I want to go to Hazaran. For a long time, the beetle and the big green grasshopper taught the little girl everything they knew. They taught her how to guess what the weather would be like, and what people were thinking when they didn't say it out loud, and how to cure fevers and illnesses. They taught her how to ask the praying mantis if the baby about to be born would be a girl or a boy, because the praying mantis knows that and answers by raising its pincers for a boy and lowering them for a girl. Little Clover learned all of that and many other things besides—secrets and mysteries.

After the beetle and the big green grasshopper had finished teaching her what they knew, a man arrived in the village one day. He was wearing splendid clothes, and he looked like a prince or a minister. The man went through the village and said, *I am looking for someone.* But the people did not understand. So Clover went up to the man, and she said, I am the person you are looking for. I want to go to Hazaran. The man was a bit surprised because little Clover was very poor and seemed very ignorant. Do you know how to answer questions? asked the minister. If you cannot answer, you will never be able to go to the country of Hazaran. I will answer the questions, said Clover. But she was afraid, because she was not sure she could answer. Then you must answer the questions I am going to ask you. If you know the answers, you will be the Princess of Hazaran. Here are the questions, and there are three of them.

Martin stopped talking for a moment, and the children waited.

Here is the first question, said the minister. At the meal to which I have been invited, my father gives me three very good things to eat. That which my hand can hold, my mouth cannot eat. That which my hand can hold, my hand cannot keep. That which my mouth can hold, my mouth cannot keep. The little girl thought for a moment, then she said, I can answer this question. The minister looked at her with surprise, because to that date no one had ever given the answer. Here is the second question, continued the minister. My father has invited me into his four houses. The first is to the north—it is poor and sad. The second is to the east—it is full of flowers. The third is to the south—it is the most beautiful. The fourth is to the west, and when I go into that house, I am given a present and yet I am poorer. I can answer this question, said Clover again. The minister was even more astonished, because no one had been able to answer that question, either. Here is the third question, said the minister. My father's face is very handsome, and yet I cannot see him. My servant dances for him every day. But my mother is even more beautiful—her hair is very black and her face is white as snow. She is covered in jewels, and she watches over me when I sleep. Clover thought again, and she signaled that she was ready to answer the questions. Here is the first answer, she said: The meal I have been invited to is the world where I was born. The three excellent foods that my father gives me are earth, water, and air. My hand can hold the earth, but I cannot eat it. My hand can lift the water, but it cannot hold it. My mouth can take in the air, but I must let go of it again when I breathe out.

Martin stopped for a moment, and the children lifted the earth in their hands and made the water run through their fingers. They breathed the air before them.

Here is the answer to the second question: The four houses where my father has invited me are the four seasons of the year. The one that faces north, and that is sad and poor, is the house of winter. The one that is to the east, where there are many flowers, is the house of spring. The one that is to the south, which is the most beautiful, is the house of summer. And the one that is to the west is the house of autumn, and when I go in there, I receive the gift of the new year, which leaves me weaker in strength, because I am older. The minister nodded in agreement, because he was surprised at the little girl's great knowledge. The last answer is easy, said Clover. The one you call my father is the sun I cannot look at. The servant who dances for it is my shadow. The one you call my mother is the night, and her hair is very black and her face is as white as the moon. Her jewels are the stars. That is the meaning of the questions. When the minister heard Clover's answers, he gave orders, and all the birds in the sky came to carry the little girl away to the country of Hazaran. It is a very distant country, very far away, so far that the birds had to fly for days and for nights, but when Clover arrived she was filled with wonder, because she had not imagined anything so beautiful, even in her dreams.

Then Martin paused again for a while, and the children grew impatient and said, What was it like? What was the country of Hazaran like?

Well, everything was big and beautiful, and there were gardens filled with flowers and butterflies, and rivers so clear you would have thought they were silver, and trees that were very tall and covered with fruit of all sorts. That was where the birds lived, all the birds in the world. They flew from one branch to the next, they sang all the time, and when Clover arrived, they surrounded her to welcome her. They had garments of feathers and all the colors, and they also danced for Clover, because they were happy to have a princess like her. Then the blackbirds came, and they were the ministers of the king of birds, and they led her to the palace of Hazaran. The king was a nightingale who sang so beautifully that everyone stopped speaking to listen to him. It was in his palace that Clover would live thereafter, and because she could speak the language of animals, she learned to sing, too, to reply to the king of Hazaran. She stayed in that country, and perhaps she is living there still, and when she wants to visit the earth, she takes the shape of a chickadee, and she flies down to see her friends who have stayed on the earth. Then she goes back to her home, to the big garden where she became a princess.

When the story was finished, the children left one after the other and went home. Alia always stayed until last outside Martin's house. She would not leave until the man went back into his castle and rolled out his mat to go to sleep. She walked slowly down the lanes of the Dike, while the gas lamps were being lit inside the shacks, and she wasn't sad anymore. She thought of the day when, perhaps, a man dressed like a minister would come, and he would look all around him and say, *I am looking for someone*.

IT WAS AT AROUND THAT TIME THAT THE GOVERNMENT BEGAN to come there, to Frenchman's Dike. Strange people, who showed up once or twice a week in black cars and orange vans that stopped up on the road, a short ways before the town began; they did all sorts of things for no reason, like measuring the distances in the lanes and between the houses, or taking away a bit of soil in a tin can, a bit of water in glass tubes, or a bit of air in little yellow balloons. They also asked a lot of questions of the people they met, of the men above all, because the women didn't understand what they were saying, and in any case, they did not dare reply.

When she went to get water at the pump, Alia stopped to watch them go by, but she knew very well that they had not come there to look for someone. They weren't there to ask the questions that meant you could go to the country of Hazaran. And anyway, they weren't interested in children—they never asked them any questions. There were men who looked serious and who were dressed in gray suits and carried little leather suitcases, and there were students, boys and girls wearing thick sweaters and parkas. The students were the oddest of all, because they asked questions that everyone could understand, about the weather or the family, but the thing was you couldn't figure out why they were asking these questions. They wrote their answers down in notebooks as if it were something very important, and they took a lot of photos of the wooden shacks as if they were worth something. They even photographed what was inside the houses, using a little lamp that lit up and was brighter than the sun.

It was a bit later that we understood, when we found out that these gentlemen and these students were from the government and that they had come to take everything away, the town and the people, to another place. The government had decided that the Dike should no longer exist, because it was too close to the road and the landing strip, or maybe because they needed the land to build apartment buildings and offices. We found out because they handed out fliers to all the families to say that everybody had to leave and that the town was going to be razed by machines and trucks. The government students showed the men some drawings representing the new town that they were going to build upstream, along the river. They were very strange drawings, too, with houses that didn't look like anything you'd ever seen—big flat houses with windows all the same, like the holes in a cinder block. At the center of each house there was a big courtyard and trees, and the streets were very straight like railroad tracks. The students called it Future City, and when they talked about it to the men and women of the Dike, they seemed very pleased and their eyes shone, and they waved their arms around. It was probably because they had made the drawings.

When the government decided to destroy the Dike and that nobody could stay there, they had to get the agreement of the person in charge. But there wasn't a person in charge of the Dike; people had always lived just like that, without anyone in charge, because nobody had needed a person in charge up to now. The government looked for someone who would agree to be in charge, and the manager of the co-op was appointed. So the government often went to his place to talk with him about Future City, and sometimes they even took him with them in a black car so that he could go to their offices and sign papers so everything would be in order. Maybe the government should have gone to see Martin in his castle, but nobody had mentioned him, and he lived too far away, all the way at the end of the Dike, near the swamp. And in any case, he wouldn't have wanted to sign anything, and people would have thought he was too old.

When Martin heard the news, he didn't say anything, but you could tell that he didn't like it. He had built his castle where he wanted it, and he really didn't want to go and live anywhere else, especially not in one of the houses in Future City, which looked like a slice of cinder block.

And then he began to fast, but it wasn't a fast just for a few days, the way he usually fasted. It was a terrifying fast that seemed as if it would never end and lasted for weeks.

Every day, Alia came to his house with some bread, and the other children came too with plates of food, hoping that Martin would get up. But he stayed there, lying on his mat, his face turned toward the door, and a sickly pallor had replaced the burnish of the sun on his skin. His dark eyes shone with a bad light, because they were tired and hurt from constantly looking. At night he didn't sleep. He stayed like that, without moving, lying on the ground, his face turned toward the opening by the door to look at the night.

Alia sat down beside him; she wiped his face with a damp towel to remove the dust that the wind left on him like on a stone. He drank a little water from the jug, just a few swallows for the entire day. Alia said, "Don't you want to eat something now? I brought you some bread."

Martin tried to smile but his mouth was too tired, and only his eyes managed to smile. Alia felt a pang in her heart because she thought that Martin would die soon.

"Is it because you don't want to leave that you're not hungry?" asked Alia.

Martin didn't reply, but his eyes did, with their light full of weariness and pain. He looked outside, through the opening of the low door, at the earth, the reeds, the blue sky.

"Maybe you shouldn't go with us there, to the new town. Maybe you should go back to your country that is so beautiful, where you came from, where everybody is like a princess or a prince."

The government students came less often now. Then they stopped coming altogether. Alia looked out for them when she was working in her aunt's house, or when she went to get water at the pump. She looked to see if their cars were parked on the road by the entrance to the town. Then she ran to Martin's castle.

"They didn't come today either!" She was trying to speak, but she was out of breath. "They won't come here anymore! Do you hear? It's over, they won't come anymore, we're going to stay here!"

Her heart was pounding, because she thought that it was Martin who had managed to make the students go away, just by fasting.

"Are you sure?" asked Martin. His voice was very slow, and he lifted himself slightly on his mat.

"They haven't come for three days!"

"Three days?"

"They won't come here anymore, I'm sure of it!"

She broke off a piece of bread and handed it to Martin.

"No, not right away," he said. "I have to wash first."

Leaning on Alia, he took a few steps outside, staggering. She led him to the river, through the reeds. Martin knelt down and slowly washed his face. Then he shaved his beard and combed his hair, without hurrying, as if he had simply just woken up. Then he went to sit on his crate, in the sun, and he ate Alia's piece of bread. Now the children were coming one after the other bringing food, and Martin took everything they gave him, saying thank you. When he had eaten enough, he went back inside his house and lay down on his mat.

"I'm going to sleep now," he said.

But the children stayed sitting on the ground outside his door to watch him sleep.

It was while he was sleeping that the new cars came back. First there were the men in gray suits with their black suitcases. They went straight to the house of the manager of the co-op. Then the students arrived, more numerous than the first time.

Alia stood there motionless, her back against the wall of the house, while they went by her and walked quickly to the square where the freshwater pump was. They gathered there and they seemed to be waiting for something. Then the men in gray came too, and the manager of the co-op was walking with them. The men in gray were speaking to him, but he was shaking his head; in the end, it was one of the government men who made the announcement to everybody in a clear voice that carried far. He said simply that the departure would take place tomorrow at eight o'clock in the morning. The government trucks would come to transport everybody to the new terrain, where they were soon going to build Future City. He also said that the government students would act as volunteers to help the population load their furniture and belongings onto the trucks.

164

Alia did not dare move, even when the men in gray and the students in their parkas left again in their cars. She was thinking about Martin, who would surely die now, because he would never want to eat again.

So she went to hide as far away as she could, among the reeds, near the river. She stayed there sitting on the pebbles, and she watched as the sun went down. This time tomorrow, when the sun reached the same place, there would be nobody left in the Dike. The bulldozers would have already gone back and forth over the town, shoving the houses ahead of them as if they were mere matchboxes, and all that would be left would be their tire tracks, their caterpillar tracks, over the crushed earth.

Alia stayed there for a long time, not moving, amidst the reeds near the river. Night fell, a cold night lit by the round, white moon. But Alia did not want to go back to her aunt's house. She began to walk through the reeds, along the river, until she came to the swamp. A bit higher up, she could just make out the round shape of Martin's castle. She listened to the croaking of the toads and the regular sound of the river water, on the other side of the swamp.

When she came up to Martin's house, she saw him standing there, motionless. His face was lit by the moonlight, and his eyes were like the water of the river, dark and shining. He was looking toward the swamp, toward the wide estuary, with its great expanse of phosphorescent pebbles.

Martin turned to her and his gaze was full of a strange strength, as if it were truly giving light.

"I was looking for you," said Martin simply.

"Are you going to leave?" Alia spoke in a low voice.

"Yes, I'm going to leave right away."

He looked at Alia as if something were amusing him.

"Do you want to come with me?"

Alia suddenly felt her lungs and throat swell with joy. She said, almost shouting, "Wait for me! Wait for me!"

Now she was running through the streets of the town and knocking on all the doors, shouting, "Come quickly! Come! We are leaving right away!"

The children and the women came out first, because they had understood. Then the men came too, one after the other. The residents of the Dike crowded into the lanes, ever greater in number. They took what they could in the beam of their flashlights—bags, boxes, kitchen utensils. The children were shouting and running through the lanes repeating the same thing, "We are leaving! We are leaving!"

When they had all arrived outside Martin's house, there was a moment of silence, almost of hesitation. Even the manager of the co-op did not dare say anything, because it was a mystery they could all feel.

Martin stood by the path that opened between the reeds. Then, without saying a word to the waiting crowd, he began to walk along the path in the direction of the river. Then the others set off behind him. He walked ahead with his regular steps, without turning back, without hesitating, as if he knew where he was going. When he began to walk in the water of the river, over the ford, the people understood where he was going, and they were no longer afraid. The black water sparkled around Martin's body while he moved ahead across the ford. The children took the hands of the women and the men, and very slowly the crowd moved into the cold water of the river. Ahead of them, from the other side of the black river with its banks of phosphorescent stones, as she walked along the slippery riverbed with her dress sticking to her stomach and her thighs, Alia looked back at the dark strip of the other shore, where not a single light was shining.

People of the Sky

LITTLE CROSS LIKED THIS BETTER THAN ANYTHING: TO GO ALL the way to the end of the village and sit down, making a very straight angle with the hard earth, when the sun was very hot. She did not move, or hardly, for hours, her torso very straight, her legs stretched out in front of her. Sometimes her hands moved, as if they were independent, pulling on strands of grass to weave baskets or ropes. It was as if she were looking at the ground below her, not thinking about anything, not waiting, but simply sitting at a right angle to the hard earth, all the way at the end of the village, there where the mountains stopped all of a sudden to make room for the sky.

It was a land without people, a land of sand and dust bordered only by the rectangular mesas. The earth was too poor to feed the people, and rain did not fall from the sky. The paved road crossed the country from one side to the other, but it was a road for going along without stopping, without looking at the dust villages, a road for going straight ahead of oneself amidst the mirages, in the damp swish of overheated tires.

The sun was very strong there, much stronger than the earth. Little Cross was sitting, and she could feel its strength on her face and her body. But she was not afraid of the sun. It went on its way across the sky without paying her any mind. It burned the stones, it dried the streams and the wells, it caused the bushes and spiny shrubs to crack. Even the snakes, even the scorpions feared the sun and stayed in the shelter of their little hiding places until night.

But Little Cross was not afraid. Her unmoving face had become almost black, and she covered her head with a length of her blanket. She liked her place at the top of the cliff, where the rocks and the earth were broken in a single blow and sliced the cold wind like the stem of a ship. Her body knew its place well and was made for it. A little place, just the right size, in the hard earth, carved out for the shape of her buttocks and her legs. That way she could stay there for a long time, sitting at a right angle to the ground, until the sun grew cold and old Bahti came to take her by the hand for the evening meal.

She touched the ground with the palms of her hands, and slowly with her fingertips she followed the little creases left by the wind and the dust, the furrows, the bumps. The sand dust made a powder soft as talc that slid beneath the palms of her hands. When the wind blew, the dust escaped from her fingers, but it was light as smoke and vanished in the air. The hard earth was warm beneath the sun. Little Cross had been coming to this place for days, for months. She herself no longer remembered very well how she had found this spot. She only remembered the question she had asked old Bahti, about the sky, the color of the sky.

"What is *blue*?"

That was what she had asked the first time, and then she had found this place, with a hollow in the hard earth, ready to receive her.

THE VALLEY PEOPLE ARE FAR AWAY, NOW. THEY LEFT LIKE insects in their shells along the road in the middle of the desert, and you can no longer hear their sound. Or they are driving along in vans, listening to music on the radio that hisses and squeaks like insects. They go straight on the black road, across the dry fields and the lakes of mirages, without looking around them. They go away as if they will never come back again.

Little Cross likes it when there is no one left around her. Behind her back, the village streets are empty, so smooth that the wind can never stop there, the cold wind of silence. The walls of the half-ruined houses are like rocks, motionless and heavy, worn by the winds, without noise, without life.

And the wind, it doesn't speak—it never speaks. It is not like people and children, or even like animals. It is only passing through, between the walls, over the rocks, over the hard earth. It comes to Little Cross and envelops her; for a moment it removes the burning of the sun from her face and makes her blanket flap.

If the wind were to stop, then perhaps you could hear the voices of the men and women in the fields, the sound of the pulley near the reservoir, the children's cries outside the prefabricated school building down there in the village with its sheet metal houses. Perhaps Little Cross would be able to hear farther than the freight trains screeching on the rails, the trucks with their eight wheels roaring down the black road toward the cities that are even noisier, toward the sea.

Now Little Cross can feel the cold inside, and she doesn't resist. She only touches the earth with the palms of her hands, and she touches her face. Somewhere behind her, dogs are barking for no reason, then they lie down again curled at the foot of the wall, their noses in the dust.

This is the moment when the silence is so great that anything can happen. Little Cross remembers the question she has been asking for so many years, the question she would like so much to know, about the sky and its color. But she no longer says it out loud: "What is *blue*?"

Because no one knows the right answer. She stays motionless, sitting at a right angle at the end of the cliff, before the sky. She knows very well that something must come. Every day is waiting for her, as she sits in her place on the hard earth; every day is for her alone. Her face, nearly black, is burned by the sun and the wind, and she raises it slightly so that there is not a single shadow on her skin. She is calm, and she is not afraid. She knows that the answer must come someday, even if she does not understand how. Nothing bad can come from the sky, that much is sure. The silence of the empty valley, the silence of the village behind her: that is so she can better hear the answer to her question. Only she can hear it. Even the dogs are sleeping, unaware of what is coming.

IT BEGINS WITH THE LIGHT. IT MAKES A VERY GENTLE SOUND on the ground, like the rustling of a broom made of leaves, or a curtain of raindrops approaching. Little Cross listens with all her strength, holding her breath somewhat, and she can distinctly hear the noise as it comes. It goes *shshshsh* and *dtdtdt!* everywhere—on the ground, on the rocks, on the flat roofs of the houses. It is the sound of fire but very gentle and fairly slow, a tranquil fire that does not hesitate, does not throw off sparks. It comes mainly from above, across from her, and scarcely flies through the atmosphere, rustling its tiny wings. Little Cross hears the murmur growing louder, expanding all around her. It is coming from everywhere now, not just from above but also from the earth, the rocks, the village houses. It is splattering in every direction like drops; it makes knots, stars, rosettes. It forms long curves that leap above her head, immense arcs, sprays.

That is the first noise, the first word. Before the sky is even filled, she hears the passage of the rays, gone mad with light, and her heart begins to beat harder and harder.

Little Cross does not move her head or her torso. She lifts her hands from the dry earth and extends them in front of her, her palms turned outward. That is how you must do it; then she feels the heat passing over her fingertips, like a caress that comes and goes. The light crackles on her thick hair, on the threads of her blankets, on her eyelashes. The skin of the light is gentle, and it shimmers as it slides its immense back and belly over the little girl's open palms.

It's always like that, in the beginning, with the lights turning all around her and rubbing against the palms of her hands like old Bahti's horses. But these horses are even bigger and gentler, and they come straight to her as if she were their mistress.

They come from the depths of the sky; they have leapt from mountain to mountain, over the big cities, over the rivers, soundlessly, with only the silky quiver of their short-haired coats.

Little Cross likes it when they come. They come only for her, to answer her question perhaps, because she is the only one who understands them, the only one who loves them. Other people are afraid, and the horses from the blue frighten them, and that is why they never see them. Little Cross calls to them; she speaks gently, in a low voice, humming a bit, because the horses of light are like the horses of the earth—they like gentle voices and songs.

"Horses, horses,
Little horses of the blue

Fly me away
Fly me away
Little horses of the blue."

She says "little horses" just to please them, because surely they would not like to know that they are enormous. That's the way it is in the beginning. Later, the clouds come. The clouds are not like the light. They do not caress the palms of hands with their back and their belly, because they are so fragile and light that they might lose their fleece and drift away as floss-silk, like the flowers of the cotton plant.

Little Cross knows them well. She knows that the clouds don't like anything that might dissolve them and make them melt, so she holds her breath and takes short little puffs, like dogs when they've been running for a long time. It makes her throat and lungs cold, and she feels herself becoming weak and light, too, like the clouds. Then the clouds can come.

At first they are far above the earth, stretching, dissolving, changing shape, passing back and forth before the sun, and their shadow glides over the hard earth and over Little Cross's face like the gentle waving of a fan.

On the dark, almost black skin of her cheeks, her forehead, her eyelids, her hands, the shadows collide, extinguish the light, create cold, empty spots. That's what white is, the color of clouds. Old Bahti and the schoolteacher, Jasper, told Little Cross: white is the color of snow, the color of salt, of clouds, and of the north wind. It is the color of bones and teeth, too. Snow is cold and melts in your hands, and wind is cold and no one can grasp it. Salt burns your lips, bones are dead, and teeth are like stones in your mouth. But that is because white is the color of emptiness, for there is nothing after white, nothing that remains.

The clouds are like that. They are so far away, they come from so far, from the heart of the blue; they are cold like the wind, light as snow, and fragile. They make no sound as they arrive; they are completely silent, like the dead, still more silent than the children walking barefoot in the rocks around the village.

But they like to come and see Little Cross—they are not afraid of her. They swell around her now, by the steep cliff. They know that Little Cross is a person of silence. They know she will not hurt them. The clouds are swollen and they go right by her, surround her, and she feels the soft chill of their fleece, the millions of droplets that dampen the skin on her face and her lips like the dew at night. She hears the very smooth sound that floats around her, and she sings some more, for them:

"Clouds, clouds,
Little clouds of the sky
Fly me away
Fly me away
Away
In your flock."

She also says "little clouds," but she knows that they are very, very big because their cool fleece covers her for a long time, hiding the heat of the sun for so long that she shivers.

She moves slowly when the clouds are upon her, not to frighten them. The local people don't really know how to talk to clouds. They make too much noise, they wave their arms, and the clouds stay high in the sky. Little Cross slowly lifts her hands to her face and presses her palms to her cheeks.

Then the clouds drift apart. They go elsewhere, where they have things to do, farther than the ramparts of the mesas, farther than the towns. They go as far as the sea, where everything is always blue, to make the rain, because that's what they like best of all on earth, to rain on the blue expanse of the sea. The sea, said old Bahti, is the most beautiful place in the world, a place where everything is truly blue. There are all sorts of blue in the sea, said old Bahti. How can there be several sorts of blue, asked Little Cross. But that's the way it is—there are several blues. It's like the water you drink that fills your mouth and flows down to your tummy, sometimes cold, sometimes hot.

Little Cross waits some more, for the others who have yet to come.

She waits for the scent of grass, the smell of fire, the golden dust that dances on itself, spinning on one leg, and the bird that croaks just once, brushing her face with the tip of his wing. They always come when she is there. They are not afraid of her. They listen to her question, always, about the sky and its color, and they go so near to her that she can feel the air moving on her eyelashes and in her hair.

THEN THE BEES COME. THEY LEFT THEIR HOME EARLY, THE HIVES down in the valley. They went to visit all the wildflowers, in the fields, between the piles of rocks. They know the flowers well, and they carry their powder on their legs, which dangle with the weight.

Little Cross hears them coming, always at the same time, when the sun is very high above the hard earth. She hears them from all sides at once, because they come out of the blue of the sky. Then Little Cross digs into the pockets of her jacket, and she takes out the grains of sugar. The bees vibrate in the air, and their high-pitched song drifts across the sky, reverberates against the rocks, brushes by Little Cross's ears and cheeks.

They come every day at the same time. They know that Little Cross is waiting for them, and they like her too. They come by the dozen, from every side, playing their music in the yellow light. They land on Little Cross's open hands, and they eat the grains of sugar greedily. Then they wander across her face, her cheeks, her mouth, stepping very gently, and their little feet tickle her skin and make her laugh. But Little Cross does not laugh too hard, not to frighten them. The bees vibrate on her black hair, near her ears, and make a monotonous chant that speaks of flowers and plants, all the flowers and all the plants they visited that morning. "Listen to us," say the bees, "we've seen a lot of flowers, in the valley—we went all the way to the end of the valley without stopping, because the wind carried us, then we came back, from one flower to the next." "What did you see?" asks Little Cross. "We saw the yellow sunflower, and the red flower of the thistle, and the ocotillo flower that looks like a snake with a red head. We saw the big purple flower of the pitaya cactus, the lacy flower of the wild carrots, the pale flower of the laurel. We saw the poison flower of the senecio, and the curled flower of the indigo, and the light flower of red sage." "And what else?" "We flew to the faraway flowers, the one that shines on wild phlox, the one that devours bees, and we saw the red star of the Mexican catchfly, the wheel of fire, the flower of milk. We flew above the agarita shrubs, and we drank for a long time from the nectar of yarrow and the water of bergamot. We even went to the most beautiful flower on earth, the one that springs very high above the sword-blade leaves of the yucca tree and that is white as the snow. All these flowers are for you, Little Cross. We have brought them to you to thank you."

That is what the bees say, and many other things, too. They talk about the red and gray sand that shines in the sun, the drops of water that are held prisoner in the down of the euphorbia, or that balance on the spines of the agave. They talk about the wind that blows over the ground and flattens the grasses. They talk about the sun that rises in the sky then rolls back down again, and the stars that pierce the night.

They do not speak the language of men, but Little Cross understands what they are saying, and the shrill vibrations of their thousands of wings make spots and stars and flowers appear on her retinas. Bees know so many things! Little Cross opens her palms so that they can eat the last grains of sugar, and she sings them a song, too, scarcely parting her lips, and her voice resembles the humming of insects:

"Bees, bees,
Blue bees in the sky
Fly me away
Fly me away
Away
In your flock."

There is silence again, silence for a long time once the bees have gone.

The cold wind blows over Little Cross's face, and she turns her head slightly to one side to breathe. Her hands are joined over her belly under her blanket, and she stays motionless, at a sharp right angle to the hard earth. Who is going to come now? The sun is high in the blue sky, casting shadows on the little girl's face, beneath her nose, beneath her eyebrows.

Little Cross thinks about the soldier who is surely on his way here now. He has to walk along the narrow path that climbs the headland to the old abandoned village. Little Cross listens, but she cannot hear his footsteps. And the dogs have not barked. They are still sleeping in old neglected corners, their noses in the dust.

The wind whistles and moans over the stones, on the hard earth. There are sleek, quick animals, animals with long noses and little ears; they make a faint sound as they leap through the dust. Little Cross knows these animals well. They come out of their lairs at the far end of the valley, and they run, they gallop, they sport as they jump over cascades, ravines, crevices. From time to time they stop, panting, and the light shines on their golden fur. Then they begin leaping skyward again, chasing this way and that. They brush against Little Cross, they ruffle her hair and her clothes, their tails whip the air with a whistling sound. Little Cross reaches out her arms to try to stop them, to catch them by the tail.

"Stop! Stop! You're going too fast! Stop!"

But the animals don't obey. They leap playfully all around her, slip past her arms, breathe against her face. They make fun of her. If she could catch one of them, just one, she would not let it go. She knows very well what she would do. She would jump on its back, like on a horse, and squeeze her arms tight around its neck—and giddy up! With one leap the animal would carry her up to the heart of the sky. She would fly; she would run with it so quickly that no one could see her. She would go high above the valleys in the mountains, above the cities, even as far as the sea; she would go into the blue of the sky, all the time. Or she would glide along the ground or in the tree branches and the grass, making a very soft sound like running water. That would be good.

But Little Cross can never grasp the animals. She feels their fluid skin slipping through her fingers, whirling through her clothes and hair. Sometimes the animals are very slow and cold like snakes.

There is no one up on the headland. The village children no longer come here, except from time to time to chase grass snakes. One day they came, and Little Cross did not hear them. One of them said, "We've brought you a present." "What is it?" asked Little Cross. "Open your hands, you'll see," said the child. Little Cross opened her hands, and when the child placed the grass snake in her palms she quivered, but she did not cry out. She shivered from head to toe. The children laughed, but Little Cross simply let the snake slide onto the ground, without saying a word, and she hid her hands beneath her blanket.

Now they are her friends, those creatures who glide soundlessly over the hard earth with their long bodies cold as water: snakes, slow worms, lizards. Little Cross knows how to speak to them. She calls to them gently, whistling through her teeth, and they come to her. She doesn't hear them coming, but she knows when they are approaching, slithering along from one fissure to another, from one pebble to another, and they raise their heads the better to hear her soft whistling, and their throats palpitate.

"Snakes, snakes," sings Little Cross. They are not all snakes, but that's what she calls them.

"Snakes, snakes,
Fly me away
Fly me away."

They come confidently, they climb onto her knees, they stay for a moment in the sun, and she likes to feel their light weight upon her legs. Then suddenly they go away again, because they are afraid when the wind blows or when the earth cracks.

Little Cross listens to the sound of the soldier's footsteps. He comes every day at the same time, when the sun is beating down directly overhead and the hard earth is warm beneath her hands. Little Cross does not always hear him arrive, because he makes no sound with his rubber soles. He sits on a rock next to her and looks at her for a long time without speaking. But Little Cross feels his gaze upon her, and she asks, "Who's there?"

He is a stranger and does not speak the language of her region very well, like those who come from the big towns near the sea. When Little Cross asked him who he was, he told her he was a soldier, and he talked about the war there had been long ago, in a faraway country. But perhaps he's no longer a soldier now.

When he arrives, he brings her a few wildflowers that he gathered while walking along the path that climbs to the top of the cliff. The flowers are long and thin, their petals widespread, and they smell like sheep. But Little Cross likes them and squeezes them in her hands.

"What are you doing?" asks the soldier.

"I'm looking at the sky," says Little Cross. "It is very blue today, isn't it?"

"Yes," says the soldier.

Little Cross always gives the same answer, because she cannot forget her question. She lifts her face and turns it, and she slowly passes her hands over her forehead, her cheeks, her eyelids.

"I think I know what it is," she says.

"What?"

"The blue. It's very hot on my face."

"That's the sun," says the soldier.

He lights an English cigarette and smokes unhurriedly, looking straight ahead. The smell of the tobacco envelops Little Cross and makes her feel slightly dizzy.

"Tell me . . . what's it like."

She always asks this. The soldier speaks to her gently, breaking off from time to time to inhale his cigarette.

"It's very beautiful," he says. "First of all, there is a vast plain with yellow crops—it must be corn, I think. There's a footpath of red earth that goes right across the middle of the fields, and a wooden cabin . . ."

"Is there a horse?" asks Little Cross.

"A horse? Wait . . . No, I don't see any horses."

"Then that's not my uncle's house."

"There is a well next to the cabin, but I think it might be dry . . . Black rocks that have a funny shape—they look like sleeping dogs . . . Farther along there is a road and telegraph poles. After that there is the washland, but it must be dry because you can see the pebbles at the bottom . . . Gray, full of loose stones and dust . . . And then there's the big plain that goes far, far to the horizon, to the third mesa. There are hills to the east, but everywhere else the plain is very flat and smooth like a landing field. To the west there are the mountains, dark red and black—they also look like sleeping animals, elephants . . ."

"Don't they move?"

"No, they don't. They sleep for thousands of years, without moving."

"And here too, is the mountain sleeping?" asks Little Cross. She places her hands flat onto the hard earth.

"Yes, it is sleeping too."

"But sometimes it moves," says Little Cross. "It moves a little bit, shakes itself a little bit, and then it goes back to sleep."

The soldier doesn't say anything for a while. Little Cross sits facing the landscape, straight on, to feel what the soldier has told her. The great plain is long and gentle against her cheek, but the ravines and the red footpaths burn her a little, and the dust dries her lips.

She raises her face and feels the heat of the sun.

"What is up there?" asks Little Cross.

"In the sky?"

"Yes."

"Well . . . ," says the soldier. But he doesn't know how to tell it. He squints his eyes because of the light of the sun.

"Is there a lot of blue today?"

"Yes, the sky is very blue."

"There isn't any white at all?"

"No, not the least little white spot."

Little Cross reaches her hands out before her.

"Yes, it must be very blue. It is burning so strong today, like a fire."

She lowers her head because the burning hurts her.

"Is there a fire in the blue?" asks Little Cross.

The soldier does not seem to understand.

"No . . . ," he says finally. "Fire is red, not blue."

"But the fire is hidden," says Little Cross. "The fire is hidden all the way in the depths of the blue of the sky, hidden like a fox, and it's looking our way; it's looking and its eyes are burning."

"What an imagination you have," says the soldier. He gives a slight laugh, but he looks at the sky, too, shading his eyes with his hand.

"What you can feel is the sun."

"No, the sun isn't hidden; it doesn't burn like that," says Little Cross. "The sun is gentle, but the blue—it's like stones in the oven. It hurts your face."

Suddenly, Little Cross gives out a faint cry, and she starts.

"What's the matter?" asks the soldier.

The little girl runs her hands over her face and moans. She bends her head toward the ground.

"It stung me . . . ," she says.

The soldier spreads Little Cross's hair and runs his rough fingertips over her cheek.

"What stung you? I don't see anything . . ."

"A light . . . a wasp," says Little Cross.

"There is nothing, Little Cross," says the soldier. "You've been dreaming."

They stay for a long while without speaking. Little Cross is still sitting at right angles to the hard earth, and the sun lights her bronze-colored face. The sky is calm, as if it were holding its breath.

"Can't you see the sea today?" asks Little Cross.

The soldier laughs.

"Oh, no! It's much too far away from here."

"So here, there are only the mountains?"

"The sea is days and days away from here. Even by plane, it would take you hours before you could see it."

Little Cross would like to see it all the same. But it's hard, because she doesn't know what the sea is like. Blue, of course, but in what way?

"Does it burn like the sky, or is it cold like water?"

"That depends. Sometimes it burns your eyes like the snow in the sun. At other times, it is sad and dark, like the water in a well. It's never the same."

"And do you like it better when it is cold or when it burns?"

"When the clouds are very low, and it is all spotted with yellow shadows that move over it like great islands of seaweed—that's how I like it."

Little Cross concentrates, and on her face she feels the low clouds passing over the sea. But only when the soldier is there can she imagine all of this. Perhaps it is because he looked at the sea so often in the old days that now it comes out of him, and flows all around him.

"The sea isn't like here," says the soldier. "It's alive. It's like a very big living animal. It moves, it leaps, changes shape and mood, it talks all the time, it never stops for a single second without doing something, and you cannot get bored with it."

"Can it be cruel?"

"Sometimes, yes. It catches people and boats and swallows them, hup! But only on days when it is very angry, and then it is better to stay home."

"I will go to see the sea," says Little Cross.

The soldier looks at her for a moment, not speaking.

Then he says, "I'll take you there."

"Is it bigger than the sky?" asks Little Cross.

"It's not the same. There is nothing bigger than the sky."

As he has had enough of talking, he lights another English cigarette and starts smoking again. Little Cross likes the sweet smell of the tobacco. When the soldier has almost finished his cigarette, he gives it to Little Cross so that she can take a few puffs before he puts it out. Little Cross smokes, taking deep breaths. When the sun is very hot and the blue of the sky is burning, the cigarette smoke forms a very gentle screen and makes the void in her head whistle, as if she were falling from the top of the cliff.

When she has finished the cigarette, Little Cross tosses it in front of her, into the void.

"Do you know how to fly?" she asks.

The soldier laughs again.

"What do you mean, fly?"

"In the sky, like the birds."

"Come now, nobody knows how to do that."

All of a sudden he hears the sound of the airplane crossing the stratosphere, so high that all you can see is a dot of silver at one end of a long white trail dividing the sky. The sound of the jet engines echoes, with a delay, over the plain and in the hollow of the torrents, just like faraway thunder.

"That's a Stratofortress. It's very high," says the soldier.

"Where is it going?"

"I don't know."

Little Cross raises her face to the sky and follows the slow progression of the airplane. Her face is somber, her lips squeezed tight, as if she were afraid or hurting somewhere.

"It's like the sparrowhawk," she says. "When the sparrowhawk flies over in the sky, I can feel its shadow. It's very cold, and it turns slowly, slowly, because the sparrowhawk is looking for its prey."

"So, you are like the hens. They all squeeze together when the sparrowhawk flies overhead." The soldier is joking, and yet he too can feel it, and the sound of the jet engines in the stratosphere makes his heart beat faster.

He watches the flight of the Stratofortress above the sea, toward Korea, long hours ahead; the waves on the sea are like wrinkles, and the sky is smooth and pure, dark blue at the zenith, turquoise blue on the horizon, as if the twilight were never-ending. In the hold of the giant plane, the bombs are stored one next to the other, death by the ton.

Then the airplane moves away toward the desert, slowly, and the wind gradually sweeps away the white vapor trail. The silence that follows is heavy, almost painful, and the soldier has to make an effort to get up from the stone where he is sitting. He remains standing for a moment and looks at the little girl sitting at right angles to the hard earth.

"I'm going," he says.

"Come back tomorrow," says Little Cross.

The soldier hesitates to tell her that he won't be coming back the next day, nor the day after that, nor any other day perhaps, because he too has to fly away, toward Korea. But he doesn't dare say anything; he simply says one more time, in an awkward voice, "I'm going."

Little Cross listens to the sound of his steps as they grow fainter on the dirt path. Then the wind returns, cold now, and she trembles a bit beneath her woolen blanket. The sun is low, almost on the horizon, and its heat comes in waves, like breath.

Now is the time when the blue grows thin and fades. Little Cross can feel it on her chapped lips, her eyelids, her fingertips. The earth itself is not as hard, as if the light had gone through it and worn it down.

Once again, Little Cross calls the bees, her friends, and the lizards too, and the salamanders drunk with sunshine, and the leaf-insects, the stick-insects, the ants in their serried ranks. She calls them all, singing the song that old Bahti taught her:

"Animals, animals,
Take me away
Fly me away
Fly me away
In your flock."

She holds her hands out before her, to hold back the air and the light. She does not want to leave. She wants everything to stay, to stay here, and not go back into hiding places.

It is the hour when the light burns and hurts, the light bursting from the depths of the blue space. Little Cross does not move, and the fear grows inside her. Instead of the sun there is a very blue star watching her, and its gaze presses against Little Cross's forehead. It is wearing a mask of scales and feathers; it comes to her, dancing, striking the earth with its feet. It comes flying like the airplane and the sparrowhawk, and its shadow covers the valley like a cloak.

He is alone—Saquasohuh they call him—and he is walking toward the abandoned village, along the blue road in the sky. His single eye is watching Little Cross with a terrible gaze that burns and freezes at the same time.

Little Cross knows him well. He is the one who stung her earlier, like a wasp, through the vastness of the empty sky. Every day at the same time, when the sun goes down and the lizards go back into the cracks in the rock, when the flies become heavy and land wherever they can, that is when he comes.

He is like a giant warrior, standing at the other side of the sky, and he looks at the village with his terrible burning, icy gaze. He looks Little Cross in the eyes, in a way that no one has ever looked at her.

Little Cross feels the clear, pure, blue light that goes deep within her body like fresh water from a spring, intoxicating her. It is a gentle light like the southerly wind, which brings the smells of plants and wildflowers.

Now, today, the star is no longer immobile. It is moving slowly across the sky, gliding, flying, as if traveling the length of a powerful river. Its clear gaze does not leave Little Cross's eyes, and it shines with a glow so intense that she must protect herself with both hands.

Little Cross's heart is beating very quickly. She has never seen anything more beautiful.

"Who are you?" she cries.

But the warrior does not answer. Saquasohuh is standing on the stone headland before her.

All at once, Little Cross understands that he is the blue star that lives in the sky, and that he has come down to earth to dance on the village square.

She wants to get up and run away, but the light coming from Saquasohuh's eye is within her and prevents her from moving. When the warrior begins his dance, men and women and children will begin to die, all over the world. The airplanes turn slowly in the sky, so high that you can scarcely hear them, but they are looking for their prey. Fire and death are everywhere, around the headland, the very sea burning like a lake of pitch. The big cities are set ablaze by the intense light bursting from the depths of the sky. Little Cross hears the thunder rolling, and the explosions, and the cries of children, the cries of the dogs that will die. The wind is turning on itself with all its strength, and it is no longer a dance—it is like the running of a horse gone mad.

Little Cross puts her hands before her eyes. Why do men want this? But it is already too late, perhaps, and the giant of the blue star will not go back into the sky. He came to dance on the village square, just the way old Bahti said he had done in Hotevilla, before the great war.

The giant Saquasohuh hesitates, standing by the cliff, as if he did not dare to come in. He looks at Little Cross, and the light of his gaze enters and burns so strong inside her head that she can no longer bear it. She cries out, leaps to her feet, and stands still, her hands thrown behind her, her breath caught in her throat, a pain in her heart, because suddenly, as if the single eye of the giant had opened incredibly wide, she sees the blue sky before her.

Little Cross says nothing. Tears fill her eyes, because the light of the sun and the blue sky is too strong. She stumbles at the edge of the cliff of hard earth, and she sees the horizon turning slowly around her, exactly the way the soldier had said: the great yellow plain, the dark ravines, the footpaths of red earth, the enormous outlines of the mesas. Then she rushes forward, running through the streets of the abandoned village, in shadow and in light, beneath the sky, without letting out a single cry.

The Shepherds

1

THE LONG, STRAIGHT ROAD WENT THROUGH THE COUNTRY OF dunes. There was nothing else there, only sand, thorny bushes, dried grasses that cracked beneath our feet, and, above all that, the vast black night sky. You could hear all the sounds distinctly in the wind, mysterious and somewhat frightening night noises. Like the little cracking sounds made by stones crunching together, or the crushing of sand beneath soles, or twigs snapping. The earth seemed immense because of these sounds, because of the black sky, too, and the stars shining with their steady brightness. Time seemed immense, very slow, with moments of strange incomprehensible acceleration, a dizziness, like crossing a river current. You were walking in space, as if suspended in a void among clusters of stars.

From all around came the sounds of insects, a continuous grating that echoed in the sky. Perhaps it was the sound of the stars, strident messages arriving from the void. There were no lights on land, except the fireflies zigzagging above the road. In the night as black as the depths of the sea, dilated pupils searched for the faintest source of light.

Everything was on the lookout. The desert animals ran among the dunes: sand hares, rats, snakes. Sometimes the wind blew in from the sea, and you could hear the rumbling of the waves breaking on the shore. The wind drove against the dunes. At night they glowed faintly, like a ship's sails. The wind blew, lifting up clouds of sand that burned the skin on your face and hands.

There was no one, and yet everywhere you could sense the presence of life, of gazes. It was like being in a great sleeping city at night and walking by all those windows where people are hidden.

The sounds echoed together. In the night they were stronger, more precise. The chill made the land vibrant, sonorous, great stretches of sand humming, great slabs of stone that spoke. The insects rustled, and the scorpions, and caterpillars, and desert snakes. From time to time you could hear the sea, the dull roar of the ocean waves that came to expire on the sand of the beach. The wind brought the voice of the sea this far, in gusts, with a bit of spindrift.

Where were you, now? There were no landmarks. Only the dunes, the rows of dunes, the invisible expanse of sand where clumps of grass quivered and the leaves on the bushes rustled—all of this, as far as the eye could see. Not far from there, however, there must have been houses, the flat city, streetlamps, the headlights of trucks. But you no longer knew where that was. The cold wind had swept everything away, washed everything, worn everything with its grains of sand.

The great black sky was absolutely smooth, hard, pierced with tiny faraway lights. It was the cold that reigned over this land, that made its voice heard.

Perhaps where you were going, you could never come back from there, ever. Perhaps the wind would cover your tracks, just like that, with the sand, and it would close all the paths behind you. And the dunes moved slowly, imperceptibly, like a long swell from the sea. The night enveloped you. It emptied out your head, made you go round in circles. The roaring sound of the sea arrived as if through a fog. The chirring of the insects faded, returned, left again, came from all sides at once, and it was the entire world and the sky that were calling loudly.

How long the night was in that land! It was so long that you forgot what it was like when it was daylight. The stars revolved slowly in the void, dropping to the horizon. Sometimes a shooting star streaked the sky. It slid above the others, very quickly, then was extinguished. The fireflies also flew by on the wind, catching on the branches of bushes. They would stay there, causing their bellies to twinkle. From the top of the dunes, you could see the desert as the light passed over it and vanished, and came again, incessantly, on all sides.

Perhaps it was because of this that you could feel that presence, those gazes. And then there were those sounds, all those strange, tiny sounds of life all around. Unfamiliar little animals scurried along a hollow in the sand, went into their burrows. This was where they lived; we were in their country. They gave out their alarm signals. The nightjars flew from one bush to the next. Jerboas followed their tiny paths. Grass snakes poured their bodies between slabs of cold stone. These were the inhabitants, running, stopping, their hearts racing, their necks raised, their eyes staring straight ahead. This was their world.

Shortly before dawn, as the sky was gradually turning gray, a dog began to bark, and the wild dogs answered. They let out long, shrill cries, their heads thrown back. It was strange; it made your skin crawl.

There were no more sounds of insects, now. The stones no longer cracked. The fog was coming in from the sea, following the beds of dried-up gullies. It passed very slowly over the dunes and wafted away like smoke.

The stars were fading from the sky. A light made a spot to the east, above the desert. The earth began to appear, not at all beautiful but gray and dull, because it was still sleeping. The wild dogs wandered among the dunes, hunting for food. They were thin little dogs, with arched backs and long paws. They had pointed ears, like foxes.

The light was growing, and you could begin to make out shapes. There was a plain, scattered with burned rocks and a few adobe huts with roofs made of palm leaves. The huts were in ruins; they had probably been abandoned for months, except for one, where the children lived. Around the houses was the great plain of stones, the dunes. Behind the dunes, the sea. A few paths crossed the plain, made by the children's bare feet and the hooves of the goats.

When the sun appeared above the earth, far away to the east, the light caused the plain to shine all of a sudden. The sand of the dunes shone like copper dust. The sky was smooth and clear like water. The wild dogs went closer to the houses, to the herd of goats.

This was their world, on the great expanse of stone and sand.

SOMEONE WAS COMING ALONG THE PATH, BETWEEN THE DUNES. It was a young boy, dressed like a city dweller. Slung over his shoulder was a slightly wrinkled linen jacket, and his white canvas shoes were covered in dust. From time to time he stopped and hesitated, because the paths diverged. He located the sound of the sea on his left, then he began to walk again. The sun was already high above the horizon, but he could not feel its heat. The light reverberating on the sand obliged him to close his eyes. His face was not used to the sun; it was red in places, on his forehead and, above all, his nose, where the skin was beginning to peel. Nor was the young boy very used to walking in the sand; you could tell by the way he twisted his ankles as he walked on the slopes of the dunes.

When he came to the wall of dry stones, the boy stopped. It was a very long wall across the plain. At either end, the wall disappeared into the dunes. You had to make a huge detour to find a way through. The boy hesitated. He looked behind him, thinking he might have to retrace his steps.

That was when he heard the sound of voices. It was coming from the other side of the wall, muffled cries, calls. They were children's voices. The wind carried the sound above the wall, somewhat unreal, mingled with the rumbling of the sea. The wild dogs were barking louder, because they had sensed the newcomer's presence.

The young boy climbed the wall and looked down on the other side. But he didn't notice the children. On this side of the wall, it was still the same plain of stones, the same bushes, and, in the distance, the gentle line of the dunes.

The young boy really wanted to go and have a look on the other side. There were a lot of tracks along the ground—footpaths, openings through the undergrowth that showed that people had passed there. On the rocks, patches of mica glittered in the sunlight.

The young boy was drawn to this place. He jumped down from the wall and felt lighter, freer. He listened to the sound of the wind and the sea, and he saw the hollows where lizards lived, the bushes where the birds made their nests.

He began to walk across the stone plain. Here the bushes were taller. Some of them had red berries.

All of a sudden he stopped, because very near he heard: "Frrtt! Frrtt!"

A strange sound, as if someone were tossing little pebbles over the ground. But no one was there.

The young boy began walking forward again. He followed a little path that led to a cluster of rocks, at the center of the enclosure of dry stones.

Once again he heard, very near: "Frrtt! Frrtt!"

It came from behind him now. But all he could see was the wall, the bushes, the dunes. There was no one.

But the young boy sensed that someone was looking at him. It came from all sides at once, an insistent gaze, watching him, that knew every one of his movements. This gaze had been upon him like that for a long time, but the young boy had only just realized. He was not afraid; it was broad daylight now, and besides, there was nothing frightening about the gaze.

To see what would happen, the boy crouched near a bush and waited, as if he were looking for something on the ground. After a minute had gone by, he heard the sound of running. He stood up and saw shadows hiding behind the bushes, and he heard stifled laughter.

So he took a small mirror from his pocket and aimed the reflection toward the bushes. The little white circle fluttered here and there and seemed to set the dry leaves on fire.

Suddenly, in the middle of the branches, the white disc lit up a face and caused a pair of eyes to shine. The young boy kept the reflection of the sun on the face, until the stranger emerged, dazzled by the light.

They came out together, all four of them: they were children. The young boy looked at them with astonishment. They were small, barefoot, dressed in clothes made of old canvas. Their faces were the color of copper, and their hair was the color of copper, too, falling in large curls. In the middle was a wild-looking little girl, dressed in a blue shirt that was too big for her. The eldest of the four children held in his right hand a long green strap, which seemed to be made of braided straw.

As the young boy did not move, the children came nearer. They were speaking in quiet voices and laughing, but the young boy could not understand what they were saying. He asked them where they came from and who they were, but the children shook their heads and continued to laugh now and again.

His voice somewhat hoarse, the young boy said, "My name is Gaspar."

The children looked at each other and burst out laughing. They repeated: "Gash pa! Gash pa!" just like that, their voices shrill. And they laughed as if they had never heard anything so funny.

"What is it?" said Gaspar. He took in his hands the green strap that the eldest boy held out to him. Taking it back, the boy knelt down and picked up a little stone from the ground. He placed it in the hollow of the strap and twirled it above his head. He opened his hand, the strap went slack, and the pebble flew high in the sky with a whistle. Gaspar tried to follow it with his gaze, but the pebble disappeared in the air. When it landed on the ground, twenty yards farther along, a small cloud of dust showed the spot where it had landed.

The other children shouted and clapped their hands. The eldest boy handed the strap to Gaspar and said, "Goum!"

The young boy chose a pebble for himself from the ground and placed it in the loop of the sling. But he did not know how to hold the strap. The child with the copper-colored hair showed him how to slip one end of the strap around his wrist, and he bent Gaspar's fingers back over the other end. Then he took a few steps back and said again, "Goum! Goum!"

Gaspar began to whirl his arm above his head. But the strap was heavy and long, and it was not nearly as easy as he had thought. He whirled the strap several times, faster and faster, and just as he was about to open his hand, he did something wrong. The braided strap whistled and slashed his back, so hard that it tore his shirt.

It hurt, and Gaspar was angry, but the children were laughing so hard that he could not help but laugh, too. The children were clapping their hands and shouting, "Gash pa! Gash pa!"

Then they sat on the ground. Gaspar showed them his little mirror. The oldest boy played with the sun's reflection for a moment, then he looked in the mirror.

Gaspar would have liked to know their names. But the children didn't speak his language. They spoke a funny language, voluble and somewhat guttural, but it made a music that went well with the landscape of stones and dunes. It was like the cracking of the stones at night or the rustling of the dry leaves, like the sound of the wind over the sand.

Only the little girl remained to one side. She was squatting on her heels, her knees and feet covered by her huge blue shirt. Her hair was the color of pink copper and fell in thick curls over her shoulders. Her eyes were very black, like the boys', but shone even brighter. There was a strange light in her eyes, like a smile that hesitated to come out. The eldest indicated the little girl to Gaspar and said, several times over, "Khaf . . . Khaf . . . Khaf . . ."

So Gaspar called her that, too: Khaf. It was a name that suited her well.

The sun was strong, now. It lit all the sharp rocks with sparks, little flashing shards of light, like tiny mirrors.

The sound of the sea had stopped, because now the wind was blowing from inland, from the desert. The children went on sitting there. They looked over toward the dunes, squinting. They seemed to be waiting.

Gaspar wondered how they lived there, far from the town. He would have liked to ask the oldest boy some questions, but it wasn't possible. Even if they had spoken the same language, Gaspar would not have dared to ask him questions. That's the way it was. This was a place where you mustn't ask questions.

When the sun was high in the sky, the children left to join the herd. Without a word to Gaspar, they headed in the direction of the great burning rocks, there in the east, and they walked in single file along the narrow footpath.

Sitting on a pile of rocks, Gaspar watched them go. He wondered what he should do. Perhaps he should turn around and go back along the road toward the houses in the town, toward the people who were waiting for him on the other side of the wall and the dunes.

When the children were quite far away, hardly any bigger than black insects against the plain of rocks, the eldest one came back to Gaspar.

He whirled his grass sling above his head. Gaspar did not see anything coming, but he heard something whistle by his ear, and the pebble struck behind him. He stood up straight, pulled out his little mirror, and flashed a reflection in the children's direction.

"Haa-hoo-haa!"

The children shouted in their shrill voices. They made signs with their hands. Only little Khaf kept on walking along the path, without turning back.

Gaspar leapt up and began to run as fast as he could across the plain, jumping over the stones and bushes. In a few seconds he had reached the children, and together they went on their way.

It was very hot now. Gaspar opened his shirt and rolled up his sleeves. To protect himself from the sun, he put the cloth jacket on his head. The burning air was crisscrossed by swarms of tiny flies that buzzed all around the children's hair. The sun magnified the stones and made the branches of the bushes crackle. The sky was absolutely pure, but now it was the pale color of overheated gas.

Gaspar walked behind the eldest child, his eyes half closed because of the light. No one spoke. The heat had dried their throats. Gaspar had been breathing through his mouth, and his throat was so painful that he was choking. He stopped and said to the oldest boy, "I'm thirsty . . ."

He said it several times over, pointing to his throat. The boy shook his head. Perhaps he hadn't understood. Gaspar saw that the children were no longer as they had been before. Now their faces were hard. The skin on their cheeks was dark red, a color that looked like the earth. Their eyes were dark, shining with a hard mineral brilliance.

Little Khaf came up to him. She felt through the pockets of her blue shirt and pulled out a handful of seeds that she gave to Gaspar. They were seeds that looked like beans, green and dusty. As soon as Gaspar put one in his mouth, it burned him like pepper, and his throat and nose immediately grew moist.

The oldest child pointed to the seeds and said, "Lula."

They began walking again and climbed over a first range of hills. On the other side, there was a plain identical to the one they had just left behind. It was a vast plain full of rocks, with grass growing at the center.

That was where the herd was grazing.

IN ALL, THERE WERE A DOZEN BLACK SHEEP, A FEW GOATS, AND A big black billy goat who kept off to one side. Gaspar stopped to rest, but the children did not wait for him. They ran down the ravine that led to the plain. They let out strange cries, "Hawa! Hahoowa!" like barking. And they whistled between their fingers.

The dogs got up and answered, "Woof! Woof! Woof!"

The big billy goat shook himself and struck the earth with his hooves. Then he joined the herd and all the animals moved aside. A cloud of dust began to swirl around the herd. It was the wild dogs, circling rapidly around them. The billy goat circled as they did, his head down, showing his long, sharp horns.

The children drew closer, barking and whistling. The oldest boy twirled his braided sling. Every time he opened his hand, a pebble struck one of the animals in the herd. The children ran and waved their arms, constantly shouting, "Ha! Hawa! Hawap!"

When the herd had gathered around the billy goat, the children threw stones to chase the dogs away. Now Gaspar came down the ravine. A wild dog growled, showing his fangs, and Gaspar twirled his jacket, shouting, too, "Ha! Haaa!"

He was no longer thirsty. His fatigue had disappeared. He ran over the rocky plain, twirling his jacket. The sun was very high in the white sky, burning violently. The air was saturated with dust, and the smell of sheep and goats enveloped everything, penetrated everything.

The herd moved slowly across the yellow grass toward the hills. The animals squeezed close together and called in their plaintive voices. At the back of the herd, the billy goat walked heavily, sometimes lowering his pointed horns. The oldest child was keeping an eye on him. Without stopping, he picked up a pebble and made his sling whistle. The billy goat was snorting angrily, then he leapt forward when the pebble hit his back.

The wild dogs continued to run around the herd, barking, as if they were mad. The children answered back and threw stones at them. Gaspar imitated them; his face was gray with dust, his hair stuck to his scalp with sweat. He had forgotten everything now, everything he had known before coming here. The streets of the town, the dark classrooms, the tall white buildings of the boarding school, the lawns: it had all disappeared like a mirage in the overheated air of a desert plain.

It was the sun above all that was the cause of what was happening there. It was at the center of the white sky, and beneath the sky the animals circled in their cloud of dust. The dark shadows of the dogs crossed the plain, came back, went off again. Hooves drummed on the hard earth, and they made a sound that rolled and roared like the sea. The howling of the dogs, the voices of the sheep, the calls and whistles of the children did not stop.

In this way, slowly, the herd began to climb the second range of hills, following the bed of the waterfalls. The sand rose in the air and, caught by gusts of wind, came whirling back down toward the plain.

The ravines became narrower, bordered by spiny bushes. The sheep left clumps of dark fleece as they passed through. Gaspar tore his clothes on the branches. His hands were bleeding, but the hot wind stopped the blood right away. The children climbed the hills and did not tire, but Gaspar fell several times, slipping on the rocks.

When they reached the top, the children stopped to look. Gaspar had never seen anything so beautiful. Below them, the plain and the dunes sloped gently down, in waves, to the edge of the horizon. It was a vast undulating expanse, with huge blocks of dark rocks and little hills of red and yellow sand. Everything was very slow, very calm. To the east, a white cliff cast a black shadow as it looked down on the plain. A valley snaked its way down through the hills and dunes, each level dropping lower as if it were part of a stairway. And in the distance at the far end of the valley, so far that it seemed almost unreal, you could see the land between the hills: faintly gray, blue, green, light as a cloud—the faraway land, the plain of grass and water. Light, gentle, delicate, like the sea viewed from a distance.

The sky there was big, the light more beautiful, more pure. There was no dust. The wind blew intermittently along the valley, the cool wind that was calming.

Gaspar and the children looked without moving at the faraway plain, and they felt a sort of happiness in their bodies. They would have liked to fly as quickly as their gaze, to land there, at the heart of the valley.

The herd had not waited for the children. With the big black billy goat in the lead, they were rushing down the slopes, according to their usual routine. The wild dogs no longer barked; they went trotting behind the herd.

Gaspar looked at the children. They stood on an overhanging rock and contemplated the landscape, not speaking. The wind was shaking their clothing. Their faces were not as hard. The yellow light shone on their foreheads, on their hair. Even little Khaf had lost her fierce air. She gave the boys handfuls of peppery seeds. She held out her hand and showed Gaspar the valley shimmering near the horizon, and she said, "Genna."

The children took the road again, in the tracks of the sheep. Gaspar brought up the rear. As they were going back down the hills, the faraway valley disappeared behind the dunes. But they no longer needed to see it. They followed the ravine, in the direction of the rising sun.

It was already not so hot. The day had gone by, and they had not noticed. The sky was golden now, and the light no longer reverberated on the patches of mica.

The herd was half an hour ahead of the children. When they got to the top of a hill, they could see the animals climbing up the next one, causing a small slide of stones.

THE SUN SET QUICKLY. THERE WAS A SHORT TWILIGHT, AND THE shadows began to cover the ravine. So the children sat in a hollow, and they waited for night. Gaspar sat there with them. He was very thirsty and his mouth was swollen because of the peppery seeds. He took off his shoes and saw that his feet were bleeding; the sand had gotten inside his shoes and rubbed away at his skin.

The children made a fire with twigs. Then one of the little boys left in the direction of the herd. He came back at nightfall carrying a goatskin full of milk. One after the other, the children drank. Little Khaf drank last, then she brought the goatskin to Gaspar. Gaspar took three long swallows. The milk was sweet and warm, and right away it calmed the fire in his mouth and throat.

The chill arrived. It rose out of the earth, like the breath of a cellar. Gaspar went close to the fire and stretched out in the sand. Next to him, little Khaf was already sleeping, and Gaspar spread his cloth jacket over her. Then, with his eyes closed, he listened to the sounds of the wind. With the crackling of the fire, it was a good music for falling asleep. And in the distance you could hear the bleating of the goats and sheep.

GASPAR AWOKE WITH A FAINT ANXIETY. HE OPENED HIS EYES, and first of all he saw the starry black sky that seemed very near. The full, white moon with its light like a lamp. The fire had gone out, and the children were sleeping. When he turned his head, Gaspar saw that the oldest boy was standing next to him. Abel (Gaspar had heard his name several times when the children were talking) was motionless, his long braided sling in his hand. The light of the moon lit his face and shone in his eyes. Gaspar sat up, wondering how long he had slept. It was Abel's gaze that had woken him. Abel's gaze said, "Come with me."

Gaspar got up and walked behind the boy. The chill of the night was sharp, and it woke him thoroughly. After they had gone a few steps, he noticed he had forgotten to put on his shoes; but his scratched feet felt better like this, and he went on.

Together they went up the slope of the ravine. In the moonlight, the rocks were white, slightly blue. His heart pounding, Gaspar followed Abel to the top of the hill. He did not even wonder where he was going. Something mysterious was drawing him, something in Abel's gaze perhaps, an instinct guiding him, helping him to walk barefoot over the sharp pebbles without making a sound. Ahead of him, Abel's slim figure leapt from one rock to the next, silent and agile as a cat.

At the top of the ravine, they were caught in the wind, a cold wind that took your breath away. Abel stopped and looked all around. They were on a sort of stone plateau. A few black bushes moved in the wind. The smoothest slabs shone in the lunar light, separated by cracks.

Noiselessly, Gaspar went to Abel's side. The young boy was watching. On his face nothing moved, only his eyes. Despite the wind that was blowing, it seemed to Gaspar that he could hear Abel's heart beating in his chest. He could see a little cloud of steam shining in front of his face, every time Abel took a breath.

Without taking his eyes from the illuminated plateau, Abel picked up a pebble and placed it in his sling. Then, suddenly, he whirled the strap above his head. Faster and faster, the sling turned like a propeller. Gaspar stood to one side. He also looked all over the plateau, examining every stone, every crack, every black bush. The sling turned, making a continuous whistling, first deep like the howling of the wind, then shrill like the sound of a siren.

The music of the grass sling seemed to fill all the space. All the sky was echoing, and the earth, the rocks, the bushes, the grasses. It went as far as the horizon—it was a voice that was calling. What did it want? Gaspar did not lower his eyes; he looked at the same point, straight ahead on the lunar plateau, and his eyes burned with weariness and desire. Abel's body was shivering. It was as if the whistling of the grass sling came out of him, through his mouth and eyes, to cover the earth and go into the depths of the black sky.

Suddenly, someone appeared on the stone plateau. It was a large desert hare, the color of sand. It was standing on its paws, its long ears erect. Its eyes shone like little mirrors while it looked at the children. The hare remained motionless, frozen at the edge of the stone slab, listening to the music of the rush sling.

There was a crack of the strap and the hare lay on its side, because the stone had hit it right between its eyes.

Abel turned to his companion and looked at him. His face was bright with contentment. Together the children ran to pick up the hare. Abel took a little knife from his pocket, and without hesitating he cut the animal's throat, then held it by its hind paws to drain it of its blood. He gave the hare to Gaspar, and with both hands he tore the skin off right to the head. Then he gutted it and ripped out its bowels and threw them into a fissure.

They went back down to the ravine. When they went by a bush, Abel picked a long branch that he trimmed with his knife.

When they were back at the camp, Abel woke up the children. They lit the fire again with new twigs. Abel skewered the hare on the branch and knelt by the fire to roast it. When the hare was cooked, Abel shared it out with his fingers. He handed a thigh to Gaspar and kept the other one for himself.

The children ate quickly, and they threw the bones to the wild dogs. Then they lay back down around the embers and fell asleep. Gaspar stayed for a few minutes with his eyes open, staring at the white moon that looked like a lighthouse above the horizon.

2

THE CHILDREN HAD BEEN LIVING IN GENNA FOR SEVERAL DAYS now. They had arrived there shortly before the sunset; they had gone into the valley at the same time as the herd. Suddenly, as the footpath rounded a corner, they had seen the great green plain shining gently, and they had stopped for a moment, unable to move—it was so beautiful.

It was truly beautiful! Below them, the expanse of tall grasses undulated in the wind, and the trees swayed from side to side, many long, tall trees, with black trunks and dense green foliage: almond trees, poplars, giant bay-trees; there were also tall palm trees, their branches waving. All around the plain, the hills of stone cast wide their shadow, and over toward the sea, the sand dunes were the color of gold and copper. This was where the herd was going—this was their land.

The children looked at the grass without moving, as if they didn't dare walk there. In the middle of the plain, surrounded by palm trees, the lake shone like a mirror, and Gaspar felt a vibration in his body. He turned around and looked at the children. Their faces were lit by the gentle light that rose from the grassy plain. Little Khaf's eyes were no longer dark; they had become transparent, the color of grass and of water.

She was the one who left first. She threw her bundles, shouting a strange word at the top of her lungs, "Mouya-a-a-a!" and she began to run through the grass.

"It's water! It's water!" thought Gaspar. But he called out the strange word with the others and began to run toward the lake.

"Mouya! Mouya-a-a-a!"

Gaspar ran quickly. The tall grasses stung his hands and his face, rustling as his body pushed them aside. Gaspar ran across the plain, his bare feet striking the damp earth, his arms slashing the sharp blades of grass. He heard the sound of his heart, the rush of the grasses folding back behind him. A few feet off to his left, Abel was running just as quickly, shouting. Sometimes he disappeared beneath the grass, then reappeared, leaping above the stones. Their paths crossed, parted, and the other children ran behind them, jumping to see where they were going. They called, and Gaspar answered, "Moya-a-a-a!"

They could smell the odor of damp earth, the sharp odor of crushed grass, the odor of the trees. The blades of grass stung their faces like whips, and they went on running without pausing for breath, they shouted, not seeing each other, they called to each other, found their way to the water.

"Mouya! Mouya!"

Gaspar saw the surface of water ahead of him, sparkling among the grasses. He thought he would get there first, and he ran even faster. But suddenly he heard Khaf's voice behind him. She was shouting with distress, like someone who is lost, "Mouya-a-a-a!"

So Gaspar turned back and looked for her among the grasses. She was so small that he could not see her. Running in circles, he called, "Mouya!"

He found her far behind the other children. She took short strides as she ran, protecting her face with her forearm. She must have fallen down several times, because her shirt and her legs were covered with dirt. Gaspar picked her up and put her on his shoulders, and he ran ahead. She was guiding him now. Clinging to his hair, she drove him in the direction of the water, and she cried out, "Mouya! Mouya-a-a-a!"

In a few strides, Gaspar caught up. He went past the two youngest boys. He arrived at the water's edge at the same time as Abel. All three fell into the cold water, breathless, and they began to drink, laughing.

BEFORE NIGHTFALL, THE CHILDREN BUILT A HOUSE. ABEL WAS the architect. He cut long reeds and grasses. With the help of the other boys, he formed a frame, bending the reeds in an arc and tying them together at the top with blades of grass. Then he filled the gaps with little branches. During that time, little Khaf and Augustin, one of the younger boys, crouched by the edge of the lake and made mud.

When the mud paste was ready, they spread it on the walls of the house, tapping with the palms of their hands. The work went quickly, and by sunset the house was finished. It was a sort of earthen igloo, with one side open for an entrance. Abel and Gaspar could only get in on all fours, but little Khaf could stand up. The house was by the edge of the lake, in the middle of a sandy beach. Around the house, the tall grasses made a sort of green wall. On the other side of the lake lived the tall palm trees. They provided the leaves for the roof of the house.

After they had drunk, the herd went farther away across the grassy plain. But the children didn't seem concerned. From time to time, they listened to the bleating that came on the wind, from the far side of the grassy plain.

When it was evening, the youngest boy went off to milk the goats. Together they drank the sweet, warm milk, then they lay down, snuggled together inside the house. A sort of light mist rose from the lake, and the wind had dropped. Gaspar smelled the scent of the damp earth on the walls of the house. He listened to the sound of the frogs and the nocturnal insects.

THIS WAS WHERE THEY HAD BEEN LIVING FOR DAYS; THIS WAS where their house was. The days were very long, the sky was always vast and pure, the sun moved slowly along its path from one horizon to the other.

Every morning, when he woke up, Gaspar saw the grassy plain streaming with little drops that shone in the light. Above the plain, the hills of stone were the color of copper. The sharp rocks stood out against the clear sky. In Genna there were never any clouds except, sometimes, the white vapor trail of a jet plane slowly crossing the stratosphere. You could stay for hours looking at the sky, doing nothing else. Gaspar walked across the grassy plain and went to sit by Augustin, near the herd. Together they looked at the big black billy goat as he tore up clumps of grass. The goats and sheep walked behind him. The goats had long heads like antelopes, their slanting eyes the color of amber. Midges buzzed constantly through the air.

Abel showed Gaspar how to make a sling. He chose several blades of a special dark-green grass that he called *goum*. Holding them down with his toes, he braided them. It was difficult, because the grass was hard and slippery. The braid kept coming undone, and Gaspar had to start all over. The edges of the blades of grass were sharp, and his hands were bleeding. The braids got gradually larger, making a pocket, where you put the pebble. Abel showed Gaspar how to close the braid at either end with a solid loop, which he consolidated with thinner blades of grass.

When the braid was finished, Abel examined it carefully. He pulled on either end to test how solid the strap was. It was long and supple but shorter than Abel's. Abel tried it right away. He picked up a round pebble from the ground and placed it in the center of the strap. Then he again showed Gaspar how to place the two ends: one loop around his wrist, the other between his fingers and the palm of his hand.

He began to twirl the sling. Gaspar listened to the regular whistling of the strap. But Abel didn't throw the stone. With a sudden, precise movement, he stopped the strap and handed it to Gaspar. Then he pointed to the trunk of a palm tree in the distance.

Now it was Gaspar's turn to twirl the sling. But he was going too quickly and felt his upper body being pulled by the weight of the stone. He started over several times, accelerating progressively. When he heard the strap thrum above his head like the motor of an airplane, he knew he had reached the right speed. Slowly his body spun on itself and pointed toward the palm tree at the other end of the plain. He was sure of himself now, and the sling was a part of him. It seemed to him he could see a great arc of a circle uniting him with the tree trunk. Just as Abel cried out, "Gia!" Gaspar opened his hands and the strap of grass whipped the air. The invisible pebble leapt toward the sky, and two seconds later Gaspar heard the sound of its impact against the trunk of the palm tree.

FROM THEN ON, GASPAR KNEW HE WAS NO LONGER THE SAME. Now he went with the eldest boy when he led the herd back to the center of the plain. The two of them would leave at dawn and make their way through the tall grasses. Abel guided him, making the sling whistle above his head, and Gaspar replied with his own sling.

In the distance, on the first dunes, the wild dogs had found a stray goat. Their shrill barking pierced the silence. Abel ran across the stones. The biggest dog had already attacked the goat. His black fur on end, he was circling around the goat, and from time to time he attacked her with a growl. The goat recoiled, lowering her horns; but there was blood flowing from her neck.

When Abel and Gaspar arrived, the other dogs ran away. But the dog with the black coat turned against them. He was foaming at the mouth, and his eyes shone with anger. Quickly, Abel loaded his sling with a sharp rock and twirled it. But the wild dog knew the sound of a sling, and when the stone flew off, he leapt to one side and avoided it. The stone hit the ground. Then the dog attacked. With a bound he jumped on the young boy. Abel cried out to Gaspar, who immediately understood. He in turn loaded his sling with a sharp stone and whirled it with all his might. The black dog stopped and turned to face Gaspar with a growl. The sharp stone hit him in the head and split his skull. Gaspar ran over to Abel and helped him to walk, because he was trembling on his legs. Abel squeezed Gaspar's arm very tight, and together they led the goat back to the herd. As they were walking away, Gaspar turned around and saw the wild dogs devouring the body of the black dog.

THAT WAS HOW THE DAYS WERE SPENT, DAYS SO LONG THEY could just as well have been months. Gaspar no longer had a very clear memory of what he had known before he came there, to Genna. Sometimes he thought of the city streets, with their strange names, and cars, and trucks. Little Khaf liked it when he made the sound of cars for her, especially the big American cars that swept along the streets blowing their horns,

iiiiaaaaoooooo!

She also laughed a lot because of Gaspar's nose. The sun had burned it, and the skin was peeling off in little flakes. When Gaspar would sit down outside the house and take his little mirror from his pocket, she would sit down next to him and laugh and say a strange word over and over: "Zezay! Zezay!"

Then the other children would laugh and say over and over again, too, "Zezay!"

Gaspar eventually understood. One day, little Khaf motioned to him to follow her. Without making a sound, she walked up to a flat slab in the stones, near the palm trees. She stopped and pointed to something on the stone. Gaspar saw it was a long gray lizard, losing its skin in the sun.

"Zezay!" she said. And she touched Gaspar's nose with a laugh.

The little girl wasn't at all afraid anymore. She liked Gaspar, perhaps because he didn't know how to speak, or because of his nose that was so red.

At night, when the chill rose from the earth and the lake, she walked over the sleeping bodies of the other children and came to snuggle up against Gaspar. Gaspar pretended that she hadn't woken him, and he stayed for a long time without moving, until the little girl's breathing became regular, because she had fallen asleep. Then he covered her with his linen jacket and fell asleep, too.

Now that there were two of them to go hunting, the children often had enough to eat. There were the desert hares that they encountered at the foot of the dunes or that came down to the edge of the lake. Or gray partridges that they went to find as night was falling, in the tall grasses. They would fly away in flocks above the plain, and the whistling stones broke their flight. There were also quails that flew low over the grass, and you had to put two or three pebbles in the slings in order to reach them. Gaspar liked the birds, and he was sorry to kill them. The ones he liked best were little gray birds with long legs that ran away across the sand, letting out strange, shrill cries, "Curleee! Curleee! Curleee!"

They brought the birds back to little Khaf, who plucked them. Then she coated them in mud and put them to cook in the embers.

Abel and Gaspar always hunted together. Sometimes Abel woke up his friend, without making a sound, like the first time, just by looking at him. Gaspar opened his eyes, got up in turn, and held the braided sling tight in his fist. They set off one behind the other through the tall grass, in the gray light of dawn. Abel stopped from time to time to listen. The wind blowing over the grass brought the faint sounds of life, and the smells. Abel listened, then changed direction slightly. The sounds became more precise. The screeching of starlings in the sky, the cooing of wood pigeons, noises you had to set apart from the sounds of insects and the rustling of the grass. The two boys slipped through the tall grass like snakes, noiselessly. Each one held his loaded sling, and a pebble in his left hand. When they reached the place where the birds were sitting, they moved apart and stood up straight, twirling their straps. Suddenly, the starlings flew up, bursting into the sky. One after the other, the boys opened their right hands, and the whistling stones brought down the birds.

When they came back to the house, the children had already lit the fire, and little Khaf had prepared the vats of water. Together they ate the birds as the sun rose above the hills at the far end of Genna.

In the morning, the water of the lake was the color of metal. Mosquitoes and water spiders ran along the surface. Gaspar went with the little girl to milk the goats. He helped her, holding the animals while she emptied their udders into large water skins. She did this calmly, without looking up, humming a song in her rather strange language. Then they went back to the house to take the warm milk to the other children.

The two young brothers (Gaspar thought they were called Augustin and Antoine, but he wasn't entirely sure) took him to check the traps. They were on the far side of the lake, where the marshlands began. In the path of the hare Antoine had placed slip knots made of braided blades of grass, fastened to curved twigs. Sometimes they found a strangled hare, but most often the snares had been torn away. Or sometimes they found rats, which they had to throw off into the distance. And sometimes the wild dogs had been by there first and had devoured their catch.

With Antoine's help, Gaspar dug a ditch to catch a fox. He covered the ditch with twigs and earth. Then he rubbed the path that led to the ditch with fresh hare skin. The trap remained intact for several nights, but then one morning, Antoine came back carrying something in his shirt. When he opened the bundle, the children saw a very young fox blinking in the sunlight. Gaspar took it by the scruff of its neck like a cat and gave it to little Khaf. In the beginning, they were a little afraid of each other, but she gave him some goat's milk to drink from the palm of her hand and they became good friends. They called the fox Mim.

In Genna, time did not go by in the same way as elsewhere. Perhaps the days did not go by at all. There were nights, and days, and the sun rose slowly into the blue sky, and shadows grew shorter, then longer across the earth, but it no longer seemed to matter in the same way. Gaspar did not think about it. He felt as if it were always the same day starting over again, a very, very long day that would never end.

Nor was there an end to the valley of Genna. They had never finished exploring. They constantly found new places where they had never been. On the far side of the lake, for example, there was an area of short yellow grass, and a sort of swamp where papyrus grew. The children went there to pick reeds for little Khaf, who wanted to weave baskets.

They stopped at the edge of the swamp, and Gaspar looked at the water glittering among the reeds. Large fireflies flew low across the surface, leaving a light trail. The sun reverberated, dazzling, and the air was heavy. Mosquitoes danced in the light around the children's hair. While Augustin and Antoine picked the reeds, Gaspar ventured into the swamp. He walked slowly, holding the plants aside, feeling the silty ground with his bare feet. Soon the water was up to his waist. It was a cool, still water, and Gaspar felt good. He went on walking through the swamp, then suddenly, far ahead, he saw a great white bird swimming on the surface of the water. Its plumage made a radiant spot amidst the gray swamp. When Gaspar came too near, the bird rose up, beat its wings, and flew a few feet away.

Gaspar had never seen such a beautiful bird. He shone like the foam on the sea, in the middle of the grasses and the gray reeds. Gaspar would have liked to call out to the bird, speak to him, but he did not want to frighten him. From time to time, the white bird stopped and looked at Gaspar. Then he flew off a ways, with an indifferent air, because this was his swamp, and he wanted to stay alone there.

Gaspar stood motionless in the water for a long time, looking at the white bird. The soft silt enveloped his feet, and the light glittered on the surface of the water. Then, after a moment, the bird came closer to Gaspar. He wasn't afraid, because the swamp really did belong to him and him alone. He just wanted to see who this stranger was standing motionless in the water.

Then he began to dance. He beat his wings, and his white body rose up slightly above the rippling water, the swaying reeds. He landed again and swam in circles around the young boy. Gaspar would have liked to talk to the bird in his language, to tell him that he admired him, tell him he did not want to harm him, that he only wanted to be his friend. But he dared not make a sound with his voice.

It was so very silent in that place. You could no longer hear the shouts of the children on the banks of the lake, or the shrill yapping of the dogs. You could only hear the light breeze blowing over the reeds, causing the papyrus leaves to quiver. There were no more hills of stone, or dunes, or grasses. There was only the water the color of metal, the sky, the bright spot of the bird gliding over the swamp.

Now he paid no attention to Gaspar. He was swimming and fishing in the silt, with the agile movements of his long neck. Then he rested, spreading his large white wings, and he really did look like a king, haughty and indifferent, reigning over his watery domain.

Suddenly he beat his wings, and the young boy saw his foam-colored body slowly rising, while his long legs skimmed along the surface of the swamp like the floats of a hydroplane. The white bird took off and made a wide turn in the sky. He flew in front of the sun and disappeared, melting into the light.

Gaspar stayed motionless in the water for a long time, hoping that the bird would return. After that, as he made his way back toward the children's voices, there was a strange spot before his eyes, a spot dazzling like the foam, that moved with his gaze and vanished amid the gray reeds.

But Gaspar was happy, because he knew that he had met the King of Genna.

3

THE BIG BLACK BILLY GOAT WAS CALLED HATROUS. HE LIVED
on the other side of the grassy plain, at the edge of the dunes, surrounded by goats and sheep. It was Augustin who looked after Hatrous.
Sometimes, Gaspar went to look for him. He would approach through
the tall grass, whistling and shouting to warn him, like this: "Ya-ha-ho!"
and he heard Augustin's voice answering from far away.

They would sit on the ground and look at the billy goat and the nan-
nies, not speaking. Augustin was much younger than Abel, but he was
more serious. He had a handsome, smooth face but he did not smile
very often, and his dark, deep eyes seemed to see far beyond you, as
far as the horizon. Gaspar liked his gaze full of mystery.

Augustin was the only one who could go anywhere near the billy
goat. He walked up to him slowly, speaking in a low voice, gentle
singing words, and the billy goat stopped eating to look at him and
perk up his ears. The billy goat had a gaze like Augustin's—the same
big slanted eyes, dark with flecks of gold, a gaze that seemed to look
right through you.

Gaspar stayed to one side, not to disturb them. He would have
liked to go up to Hatrous, to touch his horns and the thick wool on
his forehead. Hatrous knew so many things, not the things you find in
books that men like to talk about but silent, strong things, things full
of beauty and mystery.

Augustin stood there for a long time, leaning on the billy goat. He
fed him grass and roots, and all the while he spoke into his ear. The
billy goat stopped chewing on the grass to listen to the little boy's
voice, then he took a few steps, shaking his head, and Augustin walked
alongside him.

Hatrous had seen the entire earth, beyond the dunes and the hills
of stone. He knew the prairies, the fields of wheat, lakes, bushes,
footpaths. He knew the tracks of the foxes and the snakes better than

anyone. That was what he was teaching Augustin, all the things of the desert and the plains that one needs a lifetime to learn.

He stayed by the young boy, eating the grass and roots from his hand. He listened to the gentle, singing words, and the fleece on his back shivered slightly. Then he shook his head, two or three abrupt movements of his horns, and went to join his herd.

So Augustin came to sit back down next to Gaspar, and together they looked at the black billy goat moving slowly among the dancing goats. He led them over to another pasture, a little farther away, where the grass was virgin.

There was also Augustin's dog. It wasn't really his dog—it was a wild dog like the others, but this one stayed by Hatrous and the herd, and Augustin had become his friend. He had called the dog Noun. He was a big greyhound with a long coat the color of sand, and a pointed muzzle and short ears. From time to time, Augustin played with him. He would whistle between his fingers and call out his name, "Noun! Noun!"

And the tall grass parted and Noun came hurtling through at top speed, giving out short little yaps. He stopped, alert on his long legs, his belly heaving. Augustin pretended to throw a stone to him, then he called out his name again, "Noun! Noun!" and he set off at a run through the grass. The greyhound leapt behind him, barking, swift as an arrow. As he ran much faster than the child, he would make great detours on the plain, leaping over the rocks, stopping, his nose in the air, on the lookout. Then he heard Augustin's voice again and sped off. In a few leaps, he had found him in the grass, and he pretended to attack, with a growl. Augustin threw stones at him, then ran off again while the greyhound circled around him. In the end, they both emerged from the grassy plain, breathless.

Hatrous didn't like all the noise. He snorted and stamped his hoof with anger and led his herd somewhat farther along. When Augustin came back to sit next to Gaspar, the greyhound lay down on the ground, his hind legs curled to one side, his front paws stretched out straight in front of him, his head high. He closed his eyes and stayed there, not moving, just like a statue. Only his ears flicked, listening for sounds.

Augustin spoke to him as well. He didn't speak to him with words, like with the black billy goat, but by whistling between his teeth, very quietly. But the greyhound didn't like people to come near him. As soon as Augustin got up, he got up too, and remained at a distance.

When they had some meat, Augustin would cross the grassy plain and take bones to Noun. He set them down on the ground and took a few steps to the side, whistling. Then Noun would come to eat. No one was allowed to come near him at that time; the other dogs lurked around, and Noun growled, without looking up.

It was good to have these friends, in Genna. You were never alone.

In the evening, when the air, heavy with sunlight, stopped the wind, little Khaf lit the fire to chase away the midges that danced by your eyes and ears. Then she went with Gaspar to milk the goats. When they began to cross the tall grass together, the little girl stopped. Gaspar understood what she wanted, and he put her on his shoulders, like the first time when they had arrived at the lake. She was so light that Gaspar hardly felt her on his shoulders. Running, he reached the place where Hatrous lived with his herd. Augustin was still sitting in the same spot, watching the black billy goat and the distant hills.

Little Khaf went back again alone, carrying the water skin full of milk. Gaspar stayed with Augustin until nightfall. When the shadow fell, there was a strange shiver over everything. This was the time that Gaspar and Augustin liked best. The light was declining slowly, the grass on the ground turned gray, while the top of the dunes was still in the light. At that moment, the sky was so transparent that it felt like you were flying, very high, making slow circles like a vulture. There was no more wind, no more movement over the earth, and the sounds came from far away, very quiet and very calm. You could hear the dogs calling to each other from one hill to the next, and the sheep and the goats drew in closer around the big black billy goat, with their plaintive bleating. The shadow filled all the sky like smoke, and the stars came out, one by one. Augustin pointed to their lights, and he gave each of them a strange name that Gaspar tried to remember. They were the names he had to learn, the names of the stars of Genna, shining brightly in the dark blue space:

"Altaïr . . . Eltanin . . . Kochab . . . Merak . . ."

He said their names, like that, slowly, with his singing voice, and they appeared in the blue-black sky, weak at first, single points of quivering light, sometimes red, sometimes blue. Then they grew bigger, becoming steady and powerful, shooting their sharp rays, blazing from within the void. Gaspar listened closely to their magical names, and they were the most beautiful words he had ever heard:

"Fecda . . . Alioth . . . Mizar . . . Alkaïd . . ."

His head thrown back, Augustin called the stars. He paused between each name, as if the lights were obeying his gaze and growing stronger, crossing the void of the sky until they came to him, above Genna. And now between them there were new stars, smaller, hardly visible, a scattering of sand disappearing at times, then returning:

"Alderamin . . . Deneb . . . Chedir . . . Mirach . . ."

The lights were like a flotilla on the edge of the horizon. They gathered together and formed strange figures covering the sky. On the earth there was nothing left, almost nothing. The sand dunes had been covered by shadow, the grasses had vanished. All around the big black billy goat, the herd of sheep and goats walked soundlessly toward the top of the valley. Their eyes wide open, Gaspar and Augustin looked at the sky. There were a lot of people up there, they were illuminated, birds, snakes, paths winding between cities of light, rivers, bridges; there were unknown animals who had stopped there, bulls, dogs with glittering eyes, horses:

"Enif . . ."

Crows with their wings spread and their plumage gleaming, giants crowned with diamonds, motionless, looking down on the earth:

"Alnilam . . . Jouyera . . ."

Knives, lances, obsidian swords, a kite in flames hanging in the wind of the void. Above all, at the center of these magical signs, a flash of light glinting at the end of his long sharp horn, there was the great black billy goat Hatrous, standing in the night, reigning over his universe:

"Ras Alhague . . ."

Then Augustin lay on his back and gazed at all the stars shining for him in the sky. He no longer called to them; he no longer moved. Gaspar was shivering and holding his breath. He listened with all his might, to hear what the stars were saying. It was as if he were looking with his entire body, his face, his hands, to hear the gentle murmur that echoed in the depths of the sky, the sound of water and fire from faraway lights.

They could stay there all night, in the middle of the plain of Genna. They could hear the song of insects beginning, not very loud at first, then getting louder, filling everything. The sand on the dunes was still warm, and the children dug holes to sleep. Only the big black billy goat did not sleep. He was watching over his herd, his eyes shining like green flames. Perhaps he stayed awake to learn new things about the stars in the sky. Sometimes, he would shake his heavy woolen fleece and snort through his nostrils, because he had heard the slithering of a snake, or because a wild dog was lurking nearby. The goats would run away, and their hooves struck the earth, yet you didn't know where they were. Then the silence returned.

When the moon rose above the hills of stone, Gaspar woke up. The night air made him shiver. He looked around him and saw that Augustin was not there. A few feet away, the young boy was sitting next to Hatrous. He was talking to him in a low voice, always with the same singing words.

Hatrous was moving his jaw, bent over Augustin and blowing on his face. So Gaspar understood that he was teaching him new things. He was teaching him what he had learned in the desert, the days beneath the burning sun, the things of light and of the night. Perhaps he was talking to him about the crescent moon hanging above the horizon, or about the great serpent of the Milky Way crawling across the sky.

Gaspar stood there, staring with all his strength at the big black billy goat, trying to understand some of the beautiful things he was teaching Augustin. Then he crossed the field of grass and went back to the house where the children were sleeping.

He stood for a moment outside the door to the house. He looked at the thin, slightly lopsided crescent in the black sky. He felt a light breeze behind him. Without turning around, he knew it was little Khaf who had woken up. He could feel her warm hand taking his, squeezing it tight.

Then the two of them went together up into the sky, as light as feathers, and they floated toward the crescent moon. Their heads raised, they went away for a long time, a very long time, without taking their eyes from the silver-colored crescent, without thinking about anything, almost without breathing. They floated above the valley of Genna, higher than sparrowhawks, higher than jet planes. They could see the entire moon, now, the great dark disk of the dazzling crescent lying in the sky, resembling a smile. Little Khaf squeezed Gaspar's hand with all her strength, to keep from falling backward. But she was lighter, and it was she who led the young boy to the crescent moon.

When they had looked at the moon for a long time and had gotten very close to it, so close they could feel the cool radiance of the light on their faces, they went back inside the house. For a long time they did not sleep, but looked through the narrow opening of the door at the pale light and listened to the strident chirping of the crickets. The nights were beautiful and long in Genna.

4

THE CHILDREN WENT DEEPER AND DEEPER INTO THE VALLEY. Gaspar left early in the morning, when the tall grasses were still covered with dew and the sun could not yet heat all the stones and all the sand on the dunes.

He placed his bare feet in his tracks from the day before, following the footpaths. He had to look out for the thorns hidden in the sand, and the sharp flints. Sometimes Gaspar would climb up a huge rock, at the end of the valley, and look all around him. He could see the thin line of smoke rising straight into the sky. He pictured little Khaf crouching by the fire, cooking the meat and the roots.

Farther still, he saw the cloud of dust made by the herd as they walked. Led by the big billy goat Hatrous, the goats headed toward the lake. If he looked closely into every corner of the valley, Gaspar could see the other children. He greeted them from a distance, making his little mirror shine. The children answered, shouting, "Ha-hou ha!"

The farther you went from the center of the valley, the drier the earth became. It was all cracked and hardened by the sun; it resounded under your feet like the skin of a drum. Strange, twig-shaped insects lived there: beetles, centipedes, scorpions. Cautiously, Gaspar turned over the old stones, to see the scorpions scurry away, their tails erect. Gaspar was not afraid of them. He was almost one of them, thin and dry on the dusty earth. He liked the drawings they left in the dust, narrow, sinuous little paths like the barbs of the birds' feathers. There were also red ants, running quickly over the stone slabs, fleeing the deadly rays of the sun. Gaspar followed them with his gaze, and he saw that they, too, must have things to teach him. They were surely very tiny and incredible things, when pebbles became huge as mountains and clumps of grass as tall as trees. When you looked at insects, you forgot your own size and you began to understand what it was that vibrated incessantly in the air and over the earth. You forgot everything else.

Perhaps that was why the days were so long in Genna. The sun never stopped rolling across the white sky, and the wind blew for months, for years.

Farther along, when you had gone over a first hill, you came to the land of termites. Gaspar and Abel had come there one day, and they had stopped, somewhat frightened. It was a fairly large plateau of red earth, with ravines of dried up gullies, where nothing grew—not a shrub, not a blade of grass. There was only the city of termites.

Hundreds of towers were all lined up, made of red earth, with crumbling roofs and ruined walls. Some were very tall, new and solid like skyscrapers; others seemed unfinished or broken, and the walls were streaked with black, as if they had burned.

There was no sound in this city. Abel watched, leaning backward, ready to run away. But Gaspar was already moving through the streets, among the high towers, swinging his sling along his leg. Abel ran to join him. Together they wandered through the town. Around the edifices, the earth was hard and compact as if it had been stamped down by many feet. The towers had no windows. They were tall, blind buildings, standing in the violent light of the sun, worn by the wind and rain. The fortresses were hard as stone. Gaspar struck the walls with his fist, then tried to break into them with a stone. But all he managed to break off was a tiny bit of red powder.

The children walked between the towers, looking at the thick walls. They could hear their blood beating against their temples and their breath hissing in their mouths, because they felt like outsiders there, and they were afraid. They didn't dare stop. At the center of the town, there was one termites' nest that was even taller than the others. Its base was as wide as the trunk of a palm tree, and the two children standing on each other's shoulders would not have been able to reach the top. Gaspar stopped and gazed at the termites' nest. He thought about what was inside the tower, the people living all the way at the top, suspended in the sky, how they never saw the light. The heat enveloped them, but they did not know where the sun was. He thought about bats, and also about the ants, and scorpions, and beetles that left their marks in the dust. They had so much to teach him, strange and tiny things, when the days lasted as long as a lifetime. So he leaned against the red wall, and he listened. He whistled, to call to the people inside; but no one answered. There was only the sound of the wind humming as it went between the towers of the city and the sound of his own heart, echoing. When Gaspar struck the high wall with his fists, Abel was frightened and ran away. But the termites' nest remained silent. Perhaps its inhabitants were sleeping, surrounded by wind and light, in the shelter of their fortress. Gaspar took a huge stone and threw it with all his strength against the tower. The stone broke off a piece of the termites' nest, making a sound of broken glass. In the rubble of the wall, Gaspar saw some strange insects struggling. In the red dust, they looked like drops of honey. But the silence over the town had not vanished, a silence that weighed and threatened from the top of all the towers. Gaspar felt afraid, like Abel. He began to run through the streets of the city, as quickly as he could. When he had caught up with Abel, they ran together down toward the grassy plain, never turning around.

IN THE EVENING, WHEN THE SUN WAS SETTING, THE CHILDREN sat near the house to watch little Khaf dancing. Antoine and Augustin made little flutes with the reeds from the pond. They cut several tubes of differing lengths, which they tied together with blades of grass. When they blew into the reeds, little Khaf began to dance. Gaspar had never heard music like that. There were only notes that glided, rising and falling, with shrill sounds like the cries of birds. The two boys took turns playing, answering, calling to each other, always with the same sliding notes. In front of them, her head slightly to one side, little Khaf moved her hips in time, her torso very straight, her hands held out along her body. Then she struck the ground with her bare feet, making a quick movement with her soles and her heels, and it was like a rolling echo inside the earth, like the beating of a drum. Then the boys got up, and they went on playing the flutes, striking the ground with their bare feet. They played and little Khaf danced, like that, until the sun had set over the valley. Then they sat down by the blazing fire. But Augustin went off to the far side of the tall grasses, where the big black billy goat and the herd lived. There he went on playing, all alone, and at times the wind carried the light sounds of the music, the sliding, fragile notes like the cries of birds.

The children watched a jet plane pass overhead in the darkening sky. It shone high above them like a midge made of pewter, and in its wake the white vapor trail spread, splitting the sky in two.

Perhaps the airplane also had things to teach them, things that the birds did not know.

There were many things to learn, there in Genna. You did not learn them with words, as in the schools in the towns; and you were not forced to learn them, reading books or walking down streets full of noise and glowing letters. You learned them without noticing, sometimes very quickly, like a stone whistling through the air, sometimes very slowly, day by day. They were very beautiful things that lasted for a long time, that were never the same, that changed and moved all the time. You learned them, then you forgot them, and you learned them again. You didn't exactly know how they came to you: they were there, in the light, in the sky, on the earth, in the flints and the sheets of mica, in the red sand of the dunes. You only had to see them, to hear them. But Gaspar knew very well that the people from elsewhere could not learn these things. To learn them, you had to be in Genna, with the shepherds, the big billy goat Hatrous, the dog Noun, the fox Mim, and all the stars above you, and, somewhere in the great swamp, the big bird with the seafoam-colored plumage.

It was above all the sun that taught you, in Genna. Very high in the sky, it shone and gave its heat to the stones, it drew every hill, it gave everything a shadow. It was for the sun that little Khaf made plates and dishes out of mud, which she set out to dry on the leaves. She also made dolls out of mud, and she put blades of grass on their heads and dressed them with bits of rag. Then she sat down and looked at the sun baking her pottery and her dolls, and her skin turned the color of earth, too, and her hair looked like grass.

The wind itself spoke often. What it taught had no end. It came from one end of the valley, went through you, and left again toward the other end, blowing gently through your throat and your chest. Invisible and light, the wind filled you, inflated you, and you never had enough of it. Sometimes, Abel and Gaspar played at holding their breath, blocking their noses. They pretended to be diving in the sea, very deep, looking for coral. They held out for a few seconds, like that, with their mouths and noses closed. Then with a thrust of their heels they came back to the surface, and the wind again entered their nostrils, the violent, intoxicating wind. Little Khaf tried to do it, too, but it gave her the hiccups.

Gaspar thought that if he managed to understand all these teachings, he could be like the big billy goat Hatrous, so big and full of strength on the dusty earth, his eyes flashing green. He would be like the insects, too, and he could build great mud houses, tall as lighthouses, with just a window at the top, and from there you would see the entire valley of Genna.

They knew the land well, now. With the soles of their feet alone, they could have told you where they were. They knew all the sounds, the ones that went with the light of day, the ones that were born in the night. They knew where to find the roots and the grasses that were good to eat, and the bitter fruit of the bushes, the sweet flowers, grains, dates, wild almonds. They knew the paths that the hares took, the places where the birds would perch, the eggs in their nests. When Abel came back at nightfall, the wild dogs barked to demand their share of the entrails. Little Khaf tossed burning brands at them to make them go away. She held Mim the fox close inside her shirt. Only Noun the dog had the right to come near, because he was Augustin's friend.

When the flight of locusts came, it was one morning when the sun was already high in the sky. It was Mim who heard them first, long before they appeared above the valley. He paused by the door of the house, his ears cocked, his body trembling. Then the sound was upon them, and the children did not move.

It was a low cloud the color of yellow smoke that came toward them, floating above the grasses. All the children suddenly began to shout, running across the valley, while the cloud swung, hesitated, whirled in place above the grasses, and the whirring sound of thousands of insects filled the space. Abel and Gaspar ran ahead of the cloud, whistling the straps of their slings. The other children threw dried branches onto the fire, and soon huge light flames sprang up. In a few seconds, the sky was dark. The cloud of insects passed slowly in front of the sun, covering the earth with shadow. The insects struck the children's faces, scratched their skin with their jagged legs. At the far end of the grassy plain, the herd fled toward the dunes, and the big billy goat recoiled, stamping the ground with fury. Gaspar ran without stopping, his sling whirling above his head like a propeller. The continuous humming of the insects' wings echoed in his ears and he kept running, unable to see where he was going, striking the air with his sling. The cloud hovered interminably above the grassy plain, as if it were looking for a spot to fall to earth. The brown layers of insects pulled apart, hesitated, clustered together again. In places, the insects fell to the ground, then began to fly again, heavily, drunk on their own noise. Abel's cheeks and hands were covered in bloody weals, and he ran without pausing for breath, led on by the movement of his sling. Each time the strap struck the living cloud, he let out a shout, and Gaspar called back to him.

But the flight of the locusts did not stop. It gradually moved away above the swamp, still swaying, hesitating, fleeing toward the hills of stone. The last insects were already climbing into the air again, and the sky was emptying. The buzzing sound grew fainter, faded. When the light of the sun reappeared, the children went back to the house, exhausted. They lay down on the ground, their throats dry, their faces swollen.

Then the youngest children went away shouting through the tall grass to pick up the stunned locusts. They came back carrying armfuls of insects. Sitting around the hot embers, the children ate the locusts until dark. And for the wild dogs, too, that day there was a great feast in the tall grasses.

5

HOW MANY DAYS HAD GONE BY? THE MOON HAD WAXED, THEN
again became a thin crescent lying above the hills. It had disappeared
for some time from the black sky, and when it returned, the children
greeted it in their way, shouting and bowing. Now it was round and
smooth again in the night sky, and it bathed the valley of Genna in its
gentle, faintly blue light. There was something strange about its light,
however. There was something like a chill, like silence. The children
went to bed early in the house, but Gaspar stayed for a long time sitting on the threshold, looking at the moon floating in the sky. Abel,
too, was worried. During the day, he went off by himself, very far
away, and no one knew where he went. He set off, swinging his grass
sling along his thigh, and he only returned as night was falling. He no
longer brought back any meat, only from time to time some little birds
with dirty feathers that did not assuage their hunger. At night, he lay
down with the other children inside the house, but Gaspar knew that
he wasn't sleeping; he was listening to the sounds of the insects and
the songs of the toads around the house.

The nights were cold. The moon shone brightly, its light like a frost.
The cold wind burned Gaspar's face while he gazed out at the moonlit valley. Every time he exhaled, vapor formed as it left his nostrils.
Everything was dry and cold, hard, without shadow. Gaspar could see
clearly all the drawings on the face of the moon, the dark patches, the
cracks, the craters.

The wild dogs weren't sleeping. They prowled all the time on the
illuminated plain, growling and yapping. Hunger gnawed at their stom-
achs, and they looked in vain for scraps of food. When they came too
near the house, Gaspar threw stones at them. They leapt backward,
growling, then they came forward again.

That night, Abel decided to go hunting for Nach the snake. In the
middle of the night, he got up and came over to Gaspar. Standing next

to him, he looked at the moonlit valley. It was intensely cold, the stones glittered with mica, and the tall grasses glowed like blades. There was no wind. The moon seemed to be very near, as if there were nothing between earth and sky and you could touch the void. Around the moon, the stars did not glow.

Abel took a few steps, then he turned around and looked at Gaspar to ask him to go with him. The light of the moon painted his face white, and his eyes gleamed against the shadow of his face. Gaspar took his grass sling and walked with him. But they did not cross the grassy field. They went along the swamp, in the direction of the hills of stone.

When they came to the shrubs, Abel tied his strap around his neck. With his little knife, he cut two long branches that he then pruned carefully. He gave one stick to Gaspar and kept the other in his right hand.

And now he was walking quickly over the pebbly ground. He walked leaning forward, soundlessly, his face alert. Gaspar followed him, imitating his gestures. In the beginning, he did not know that they had started to hunt for Nach. Perhaps Abel had seen the tracks of a desert hare, and he would soon begin to whirl his sling. But that night, everything was different. The light was gentle and cold, and the child walked silently, the long stick in his right hand. Only Nach the snake, who glided slowly in the dust, rolling his rings like the roots of the trees, lived in this part of Genna.

Gaspar had never seen Nach. He had only heard him, at night, sometimes, when he went near the goats. It was the same sound he had heard the first time, when he had climbed over the stone wall on the way to Genna. Little Khaf had shown him how the snake dances, swaying its head, and how it slithers slowly across the ground. At the same time, she said, "Nach! Nach! Nach! Nach! Nach!" and with her mouth she imitated the rattling sound he made with the tip of his tail against the stones and the dead branches.

That night was truly Nach's night. Everything was like him, cold and dry, shining with scales. Somewhere at the foot of the hills of stone, on the cold slabs, Nach was slithering his long body, tasting the dust with the tip of his double tongue. He was looking for prey. Slowly, he went down to the herd of goats and sheep, pausing from time to time, motionless as a root, then setting off again.

Gaspar had been walking separately from Abel. Now they were walking side by side, a few yards apart. Leaning forward, they bent their knees and made slow movements with their arms and torsos, as if they were swimming. Their eyes had grown accustomed to the light of the moon, they were just as cold and pale, they saw every detail on the ground, every stone, every crack.

It was a bit like on the surface of the moon. They moved forward slowly over the naked ground, between the broken rocks and the black cracks. In the distance, hills as ragged as a volcano's edge glowed against the black sky. All around them they saw the sparks of mica, gypsum, rock salt. The two children walked as if in slow motion, in the middle of the land of stone and dust. Their faces and hands were very white, and their clothes were phosphorescent, tinged with blue.

This was the land of Nach.

The children looked for him, examining the terrain foot by foot, listening to all the sounds. Abel went ahead of Gaspar, making a large circle around the limestone plateau. Even when he was very far away, Gaspar could see the vapor that shone before his face, and he heard the sound of his breathing; everything was clear and precise, because of the cold.

Now Gaspar walked ahead through the undergrowth, along a ravine. Suddenly, just as he was passing by a leafless tree, an acacia burned by drought and cold, the young boy shivered. He stopped, his heart pounding, because he had heard the same rustling noise, the "Frrtt-frrtt" that had echoed the day he had climbed over the old wall of dry stones. Just above his head, he saw Nach the snake unwinding his body along a branch. Nach slowly slid down the acacia tree, every scale on his skin shining like metal.

Gaspar could not move. He stared at the snake that seemed to be endlessly sliding along the branch, and it wound itself around the trunk and began its descent. Every pattern on the serpent's skin shone clearly.

His body slid toward the ground, hardly touching the tree trunk, and at the end of his body was his triangular head with his eyes like metal. Nach took a long time going down the tree, soundlessly. Gaspar heard nothing but the beating of his own heart, loud in the silence. The moonlight shimmered on Nach's scales, on his hard pupils.

Gaspar must have moved, because Nach stopped and raised his head. He looked at the young boy, and Gaspar felt his body turn to ice. He would have liked to cry out, or call to Abel, but he could not get a sound past his throat. He had stopped breathing. After a moment, Nach began to move again. When he reached the ground, it was like water flowing through dust, a very long stream of pale water slowly seeping from the tree trunk. Gaspar heard the sound of the snake's skin rubbing on the earth, a light electric rustling, like the wind over dead leaves.

Gaspar stood perfectly still until Nach had disappeared. And then he began to tremble, so violently that he had to sit on the ground not to fall over. On his face he could still feel Nach's hard gaze, he could still see the cold water movement of the body sliding down the tree. Gaspar stayed there for a long time, still as a stone, listening to the beating of his heart in his chest. Above the earth, the round moon illuminated the deserted ravine.

Gaspar heard Abel calling him. He was whistling faintly through his teeth, but the sonorous air made the sound seem very close. Then Gaspar heard his footsteps. The young boy was coming so quickly that his feet hardly seemed to touch the ground. Gaspar stood up and went to join Abel. Together they followed the ravine, on Nach's trail.

Abel began to whistle again, and Gaspar understood that it was for Nach; that was the way he called him, softly, making a continuous, monotonous sound. In his hiding places among the roots of the acacia trees, Nach could hear the whistling, and he stretched out his neck, swaying his triangular head. His body slid and rolled on itself. Uneasy, Nach tried to determine where the whistling sound was coming from, but the shrill vibration surrounded him, seemed to be coming from all sides at once. It was a strange wave that prevented him from fleeing, that obliged him to roll his body in a knot.

When the two children appeared, tall white figures in the light of the moon, Nach struck his tail angrily against the pebbles, and there was a crackling of sparks. Nach's skin seemed phosphorescent. It hardly moved, like a shiver on the dusty ground. He unrolled his body, sliding across the gravel, stretching, unwinding, and Gaspar looked again at his triangular head and his eyes without eyelids. He felt the same chill as before, paralyzing his limbs, blocking his mind. Abel leaned forward and began to whistle more loudly, and Gaspar did the same. Both of them began to dance Nach's dance, with the slow gestures of swimmers. Their feet slid over the ground, forward, backward, and they struck their heels. Their outstretched arms drew circles, and their sticks whistled in the air. Nach continued to move toward the children, rolling his rings from side to side, and his head swayed high on his long, straight neck to follow the dance.

When Nach was only a few feet away from the children, they accelerated the movement of their dance. Now Abel was speaking. That is, he was speaking at the same time as he was whistling through his teeth, and it made strange, rhythmic noises, with violent explosions and creaking sounds, like the music of the wind echoing across the rocky plateau to the faraway hills, to the dunes. They were words like the cracking of stones in the cold, like the chirring of insects, like the light of the moon—strong, hard words that seemed to cover the entire earth.

Nach followed the words and the sound of their bare feet striking the ground, and his body swayed incessantly. At the top of his neck, his triangular head trembled. Slowly, Nach curled backward, swaying slightly to the side. The children were dancing less than six feet away from him. He stayed like that for a long time, tense and vibrant. Then suddenly, like a whip, he straightened and struck. Abel had seen his movement and jumped to the side. At the same time, his stick whistled and hit the serpent on his neck. Nach recoiled, hissing, while the children danced around him. Gaspar was no longer afraid. When Nach struck in his direction, he merely took a step to the side, and he in turn tried to strike the snake on the head. But Nach had recoiled at once, and the stick only raised a bit of dust.

They had to keep on whistling and talking, even as they breathed; the night must continue to echo. It was music like a gaze, music without weakness that kept Nach on the ground and prevented him from leaving. The music entered him through the skin on his body and gave him orders, a cold, deadly music that slowed his heart and confused his movements. In his mouth the poison was ready, swelling his glands; but the children's music and their undulating dance were more powerful still and kept them out of harm's way.

Nach rolled his body around a rock, the better to whip the air with his head. Before him, the white figures of the children moved incessantly, and he began to feel tired. Several times he dashed his head forward to bite, but his body, held back by the rock, was too short, and all he struck was the impalpable dust. And the sticks whistled, cracking against the vertebrae on his neck.

In the end, Nach left his stone support. His long body uncoiled on the ground, stretched out in all its beauty, glistening like armor, glittering like zinc. The regular patterns on his back looked like eyes. His tiny tailbones vibrated, making a shrill, dry music that mingled with the whistling and the rhythmic beating of the children's feet. Gradually he raised his head, drawing himself up straight. Abel stopped whistling and walked toward him, raising his thin stick high in the air, but Nach did not move. His head was at a right angle to his neck, and he continued to watch as the white image approached him, ever nearer. With a single clean blow, Abel struck the serpent and broke his neck.

After that there was not a sound on the limestone plateau. Only, from time to time, the passage of the cold wind through the shrubbery, through the acacia branches. The moon was high in the black sky, and the stars did not glitter. Abel and Gaspar stood for a moment looking at the body of the serpent stretched out on the ground, then they tossed down their sticks and went back to Genna.

6

Everything changed in Genna, very quickly. It was the sun burning brighter in the cloudless sky, the heat becoming unbearable in the afternoon. Everything was electric. There were sparks on the stones, and you could hear the crunching of the sand, the blades of grass, the thorns. The lake water had changed, too. Opaque and heavy, the color of metal, it reflected the light of the sky. There were no more animals in the valley, only ants and the scorpions that lived under the stones. The dust had come; it rose in the air when you walked, an acrid, hard dust that hurt.

During the day the children slept, tired by the light and the dry air. Sometimes they awoke to a new anxiety. They could feel the electricity in their bodies, in their hair. They ran like the wild dogs, aimlessly, looking perhaps for prey. But there were no more hares, no more birds. The animals had left Genna, and the children had not realized. To appease their hunger, they picked the grasses with big bitter leaves, and they dug up roots. Little Khaf was again making a stock of peppery grains for the departure. The only food they had was the goats' milk, and they shared it with Mim the fox. But the herd had become nervous. They went into the hills, and you had to go farther and farther to milk the goats. Augustin could no longer get anywhere near the big black billy goat. Hatrous scraped the ground angrily, digging up clouds of dust. Every day he drove the herd a bit farther, toward the top of the valley, where the hills began, as if he were about to give the signal for departure.

The nights were so cold that the children had no more strength. They had to stay huddled close together, neither moving nor sleeping. You could no longer hear the cries of the insects. All you could hear was the wind whistling and the sound of the stones contracting.

Gaspar thought that something was about to happen, but he did not understand what it might be. All night long he lay stretched out on his back, near Little Khaf, who was wrapped in his canvas jacket. The little girl did not sleep either; she was waiting, holding the fox close to her.

They were all waiting. Even Abel no longer went hunting. His grass sling around his neck, he lay by the door of the house, his eyes turned toward the moonlit hills. The children were alone in Genna, alone with the herd and the wild dogs whimpering quietly in their holes in the sand.

During the day, the sun burned the earth. The lake water had a taste of sand and ash. When the goats had drunk, they could feel a fatigue in their limbs, and their dark eyes were full of sleep. Their thirst had not been quenched.

One day, at around noon, Abel left the house with his grass sling in his fist. His face was tense, and his eyes burned with fever. Even though he hadn't asked him to, Gaspar walked behind him, armed with his own sling. They went in the direction of the swamp where the papyrus grew. Gaspar saw that the level of the water in the swamp had fallen and that it was the color of mud. Mosquitoes danced around the children's faces, and that was the only sound of life in that place. Abel went into the water, moving quickly. Gaspar lost sight of him. He went on alone, sinking into the mud of the swamp. Between the reeds, he saw the surface of the water, opaque and hard. There were flashes of dazzling light, and the heat was so intense that he had trouble breathing. Sweat was flowing down his face and his back, and his heart pounded loudly in his chest. Gaspar hurried, because he had just understood what Abel was looking for.

Suddenly, among the reeds, he saw the white bird that was king of Genna. His wings spread, he was immobile on the surface of the water, so white you would have thought he was a spot of foam. Gaspar stopped and looked at the bird, full of a joy that filled his entire body. The white bird was just as he had seen him the first time, inaccessible, surrounded by light, like an apparition. Gaspar thought that from the center of the swamp he silently governed the valley, the grass, the hills, and the dunes, all the way to the horizon. Perhaps he would know how to banish the fatigue and the drought that reigned everywhere; perhaps he would give his orders and everything would go back to the way it was.

When Abel reappeared, only a few feet away, the bird turned his head and looked at him in surprise. But he did not move, his large white wings spread above the shining water. He was not afraid. Gaspar was no longer looking at the bird. He saw the young boy raising his arm above his head, and in his fist the long green strap began to whirl, making its deadly chant.

"He's going to kill him!" thought Gaspar. Suddenly he rushed toward him. With all his strength, he ran through the swamp toward Abel, shoving aside the stalks of papyrus. He reached Abel at the very moment when the stone was about to fly out, and the two children fell into the mud. The white ibis beat the air with his wings and flew away.

Gaspar squeezed Abel's neck to keep him in the mud. The young shepherd was thinner than he was but more agile and stronger. He broke free in an instant from Gaspar's hold and took a few steps backward in the swamp. He stopped and looked at Gaspar, without saying a word. His dark face and eyes were full of anger. He whirled his slingshot above his head and let the strap fly. Gaspar ducked, but the pebble hit his left shoulder and threw him into the water like the blow of a fist. A second pebble whistled by his head. Gaspar had lost his sling while struggling in the swamp and he had to flee. He ran through the reeds. Anger, fear, and pain were like a great noise in his head. He ran as fast as he could, zigzagging to get away from Abel.

When he was back on solid ground, breathless, he saw that Abel had not followed him. Gaspar sat on the ground, hidden by clumps of reeds, and he stayed there for a long time, until his heart and lungs were calm again. He felt sad and tired, because he knew that now he would not be able to go back to the children. So, when the sun was very near the horizon, he took the path for the hills, and he left Genna behind.

He only turned around once, when he reached the top of the first hill. He looked at the valley for a long time—the grassy plain, the smooth patch of the lake. Near the water, he saw the little mud house and a column of blue smoke rising straight into the sky. He tried to see little Khaf's figure sitting by the fire, but he was too far away, and he saw no one. From there, on the top of the hill, the swamp seemed tiny, a dull mirror reflecting the black stalks of the reeds and the papyrus. Gaspar heard the yapping of the wild dogs, and a cloud of gray dust rose somewhere at the end of the valley, where the big billy goat Hatrous was leading his herd.

That night, Gaspar slept for three hours, curled in a hollow in the rocks. The intense cold numbed the pain of his wound, and fatigue made his body heavy and senseless like a stone.

It was the wind that woke Gaspar, just before dawn. It was not the same wind as usual. It was a warm breath, charged, coming from beyond the hills of stone. It came following the curve of the valleys and the ravines, hurtling through the caves, over the eolian rocks, a violent, threatening wind. Gaspar got up quickly, but the wind kept him from walking. Struggling, straining forward, Gaspar followed a narrow ravine blocked by walls of dry, crumbled stones. The wind pushed him along the ravine, until he reached the road. Gaspar began to run along the road, not looking where he was going. Now the day had risen, but there was a strange red and gray light rising from everywhere at once, as if there were a fire somewhere. The earth was little more than a layer of dust gliding in the horizontal wind. It was unreal, dissolving like a gas. The hard dust with its stinging grit struck the rocks, the trees, the grasses, it gnawed away with its millions of mandibles, it scraped and burned the skin. Gaspar ran without stopping for breath, and from time to time he waved his arms, shouting, the way the children had done to chase away the cloud of locusts. He ran barefoot along the road, his eyes half closed, and the red dust ran more quickly than he did. Like serpents, whirlwinds of sand slithered between his legs, enveloped him, spun around, sped along the road in long cascades. Gaspar could no longer see the hills or the sky. All he could see was this blurry glow in space, this strange red light surrounding the earth. The wind whistled and screamed along the road, pushing Gaspar and making him stumble, striking his back and shoulders. The dust got into his mouth and his nostrils, suffocating him. Several times Gaspar fell down on the road, scraping his hands and knees. But he felt no pain. He kept running, his arms folded in front of him, hunting for a place where he could shelter.

He ran like that for several hours, lost in the sandstorm. Then, on the side of the road, he saw the uncertain shape of a hut. Gaspar pushed the door and went in. The hut was empty. He closed the door, crouched against the wall, and put his head inside his shirt.

The wind lasted for a long time. The red glow lit the inside of the hut. Heat rose from the ground, the ceiling, the walls, like the inside of an oven. Gaspar stayed there without moving, scarcely breathing, his heart beating very slowly as if he were going to die.

When the wind stopped, there was a great silence, and the dust began to fall slowly back to earth. Gradually the red light faded.

Gaspar went out of the hut. He looked around him, not understanding. Outside, everything had changed. There were sand dunes in the road, like motionless waves. The earth, the stones, the trees were covered in red dust. Far away on the horizon, there was a strange smudge in the sky, like drifting smoke. Gaspar looked all around him, and he saw that the valley of Genna had disappeared. It was lost now, somewhere on the other side of the hills, inaccessible, as if it had never existed.

The sun came out. It shone with a gentle heat that penetrated Gaspar's body. He took a few steps along the road, shaking the dust from his hair and clothes. At the end of the road, a red-brick village was lit by the sun.

Then a truck arrived, with its headlights on. The rumbling of its engine grew louder, and Gaspar stood to one side. The truck drove by without stopping, in a cloud of red dust, and went on toward the village. Gaspar walked on the hot sand, along the road. He thought of the children following the billy goat Hatrous through the hills and the pebbly plains. The big black billy goat must have been angry because of the wind and the dust, because the children had waited too long to leave. Abel stood in front of his herd, his long green strap swinging from his arm. From time to time he shouted, "Ya! Yah!" and the other children called back to him. The wild dogs, all yellow with dust, ran in large circles, and they cried out, too.

They went through the red dunes; they went to the north, or the east, looking for fresh water. Perhaps farther away, when they had climbed over a wall of dry stones, they would find another valley like Genna, with an eye of water shining in the middle of a grassy plain. The tall palm trees swayed in the wind, and there they could build a house with branches and mud. There would be plateaus and ravines where desert hares lived, and clearings in the grass where the birds would go to sit before dawn. Above the swamp, there might even be a great white bird that would take flight, banking over the land like an airplane turning.

Gaspar did not look at the town that he was entering now. He did not see the brick walls or the windows closed with metal shutters. He was still in Genna, still with the children, with little Khaf and Abel and Antoine and Augustin, with the big billy goat Hatrous and the dog Noun. He really was with them, and he didn't need any words, even as he went into the office of the gendarmerie to answer the questions of a man sitting at an old typewriter:

"My name is Gaspar . . . I got lost . . ."